DIVING INTO THE WRECK

KRISTINE KATHRYN RUSCH

DIVING INTO THE WRECK

an imprint of Prometheus Books
Amherst, NY

Portions of the sections "Diving into the Wreck" and "Room of Lost Souls" first appeared in *Asimov's Science Fiction Magazine* in different form.

Published 2009 by Pyr®, an imprint of Prometheus Books

Inquiries should be addressed to
Pyr
59 John Glenn Drive
Amherst, New York 14228–2119
VOICE: 716–691–0133, ext. 210
FAX: 716–691–0137
WWW.PYRSF.COM

13 12 11 10 09   5 4 3 2 1

Library of Congress Cataloging-in-Publication Data

Rusch, Kristine Kathryn.
Diving into the wreck / by Kristine Kathryn Rusch.
p. cm.
ISBN 978–1–59102–786–7 (pbk. : alk. paper)
1. Historians—Fiction. I. Title.

PS3568.U7D58 2009
813'.54—dc22

2009026455

Printed in the United States on acid-free paper

For Sheila Williams

#21 06-01-2014 3:16PM
Item(s) checked out to Haas, Robert J.

TITLE: The new world : book three of the
BARCODE: 1973494477
DUE DATE: 06-30-14

TITLE: Diving into the wreck
BARCODE: 1974835850
DUE DATE: 06-30-14

614.882.7277 or westervillelibrary.org
Like Us! facebook.com/westervillelibrary

#21 06-01-2014 3:16PM

Item(s) checked out to Haas, Robert J.

TITLE: Cobra alliance
BARCODE: 1975119254
DUE DATE: 06-30-14

TITLE: The Elder Gods
BARCODE: 1974482430
DUE DATE: 06-30-14

614.882.7277 or westervillelibrary.org
Like Us! facebook.com/westervillelibrary

ACKNOWLEDGMENTS

Thanks on this one go to Sheila Williams, who supported this idea from the beginning (with two cover stories!); to Lou Anders, who shares my vision on what the book can be; to Dean Wesley Smith for talking me through my worries (and for all the diving details); and to the readers of *Asimov's* for all the support and encouragement.

I tell people I sleep alone because I prefer to be alone. I do prefer to be alone. I like my own company. But the reason I sleep alone is that I dream.

Or, more accurately, I nightmare.

I thrash and moan and frighten anyone within hearing distance. The cabins on my ship, Nobody's Business, *have soundproof walls, as does my berth on Longbow Station. I put my bed in the center room of my apartment on Hector Prime, and hope no one can hear me through the floor.*

So far no one has. Or, at least, no one has tried to come to my rescue.

Even though I was rescued before.

For almost forty years, I have had the dream every night—unless I'm traveling in the Business *or in my single ship. Movement—movement through space—somehow negates the dream.*

Or maybe it echoes the rescue.

For the dream is based on fact. The nightmare actually happened.

My mother and I suited up and walked, hand in hand, into a room on an abandoned space station. Mother wanted to explore, and I didn't want her to go alone. I was maybe four, maybe five. I don't remember exactly, and no one has ever talked of it.

What I do remember is a jumble—colored lights, beautiful voices singing in six-part harmony. Mother's face turned upward toward the lights.

"Beautiful," she said, her voice blending into the chorus. "Oh, so beautiful."

And then she left me and floated toward that light.

I called for her, but she never came back. I huddled on the floor of that room, surrounded by light and voices, and wrapped my spacesuited arms around my spacesuited knees, waiting.

Alone.

I didn't scream then, and I don't scream now. I never scream. But I gasp myself awake as the oxygen in my suit fails. My visor cracks, and even though I am four, maybe five, I know I am going to die.

Obviously, I didn't die. My father found me and brought me back to our ship. But he never did find my mother.

And he never spoke of her again.

PART ONE

DIVING INTO THE WRECK

ONE

I hurtle through the darkness of space, snug and secure in my single ship. I've just come back from a salvage operation run by a friend, a salvage operation that held no real interest for me except as a way to pick up some extra cash.

That, and my friend promised me I could have the tourist dive site if the wreck was one I could use. By use, we meant that I could bring inexperienced divers to the wreck and give them the pretend adventure their money has paid for. Since this wreck is suited for tourist dives, I'm planning to file a postsalvage claim when I get back to Hector Prime.

My single ship is small, little more than a cockpit (which fits only one) with a bedroom/galley behind. I never sleep on the single ship. It has automatic controls, but I shut them off as I travel.

If I can't take the ship from a port to a station or a station to a hub in thirty hours (which is the longest I can go safely without sleep), then I travel in my full-sized ship, *Nobody's Business*.

But the salvage is an easy week from Hector Prime and there are a lot of space stations along the way, so I take the single ship. It's inconspicuous, and I like that—not just as a woman alone in the vastness of space, but also as a wreck diver.

Too often, the *Business* has attracted thieves and claim jumpers, people who would just as soon kill you as give up the ship you've discovered.

No one has ever followed my single ship. To my knowledge, no one has ever tried.

On the way back, in the only stretch of space that made me nervous as I planned the trip, my sensors blip.

Most pilots ignore a blip like that. Most ships' automatic circuits actually filter such blips out. That's why I fly the single ship manually.

Small sensor blips mean that a faint energy signature is somewhere nearby—although "nearby" is relative in space—and faint energy signatures often point to abandoned and distressed ships.

I specialize in abandoned ships. I dive them, sometimes for salvage, sometimes for curiosity, sometimes to locate a good tourist wreck.

The work pays well enough that I can indulge my true love—diving ancient wrecks for the history value. I collect ship types the way some people collect glassware. I want to be able to say I dove a previously undiscovered Generation C-Class or an abandoned first-issue space yacht or a commandeered merchant ship from the Colonnade Wars.

After I dive the ships and map them, I often turn them over to museums or historical societies. Sometimes I leave them in place for tourist dives, and sometimes I don't report them at all, leaving them in their floating grave for some other enterprising diver to discover.

I've explored more than a thousand ships, and still a blip on my sensors sends my heart pounding.

As quick as I can, I drop out of faster-than-light. Then I press the screen in front of me, replaying the readout to make sure I haven't misread the blip.

I haven't. It existed for only a fraction of a second, but it existed.

I memorize the coordinates—which are a long way from me now—and I work my way back.

It takes two jumps and a half day of searching before I find the blip again and match its speed and direction.

I'm already fifteen hours alone in the single ship. I should find a place to get a meal and a good night's sleep, but I'm too far from anything. An energy signature this far out belongs to a ship that's lost.

My stomach clenches. I never know what I'm going to encounter when I find a lost ship.

Five separate times, I've found ships in distress. One still had its beacon going decades after everyone on board had died. Two other ships had dying crew members on board, crew members I was too late to save.

I had to help the last two ships jury-rig some kind of fail-safe, and then leave, promising that I would send help—which I always did. Leaving is the hardest part. The people on board, no matter how professional they are, have panicked. They're near the end, and they always believe that a single pilot will never send anyone back for them.

They're convinced I'll never tell anyone about them when they hear that I'm a professional wreck diver. They think I'm going to wait until they die so I can come back and loot the ship.

I'm sure some of my colleagues might do that, but I never would. I do business as ethically as a wreck diver can. I file the proper documentation (after I've dived, however), and I try to keep my group dives injury free. Every wreck diver has lost a team member at one point or another, and I'm no exception, but as dive companies go, mine is pretty accident free.

I pride myself on that, just like I pride myself on helping people who need it.

But I don't like helping. It's fraught with emotion of all kinds, and I do my best to stay out of emotional situations. I'm as pure a loner as someone can be. Space suits me. I can go weeks without speaking to anyone, and I don't miss the company.

So going from my single ship to a situation potentially filled with needy, dying people always makes me nervous.

I ease the single ship forward quietly, lights and communications array off. Once I happened upon a group of marauders who used a distress signal to lure in unsuspecting do-gooders. I managed to get away before they could harm me, but I've heard of several other pilots who've suffered the loss of their ships and worse.

I'm being as cautious as I can.

My sensors are on full, but I'm not recording with them. Instead, I'm using a link I've built into the single ship that attaches to a small computer I wear on my wrist.

The additional link was simple enough to build: single ships are designed to monitor the pilot's eyes, heart rate, and respiration rate. Should my heart slow, my breathing even, or my eyes close for longer than a minute, the automatic controls take over the entire ship. Unconsciousness isn't as much of a danger as it would be if the ship were completely manual, but consciousness isn't a danger either. No one can monitor my movements simply by tapping the ship's computer.

The additional link that I've set up only feeds information in one direction—into my personal computer. The coordinates of the blip, the readings I've taken as I've approached, and everything about the blip itself are stored on my system, not the single ship's.

All someone probing my ship from a distance will learn is that I've come to an unusual region of space for a reason they can't entirely determine.

But I know. The faint energy signature has led me to a black lump against the blackness of space.

A ship, just like I'd hoped and feared.

My breath catches. I scan for distress signals, for signs of life. But my sensors tell me that the ship has no environment and no active power systems. The energy signature I've found remains weak—one final system that refuses to turn off or, perhaps, a sort of stardrive that I don't entirely recognize. One that's built on some form of energy with a half-life that'll give off readings for generations.

The wreck is huge—five times the size of the *Business*—and it has a configuration I don't recognize. My single ship's computer hypothesizes that the ship is Old Earth make, at least five thousand years old, but I ignore that hypothesis since it has to be wrong.

Ships that old could never have made it this far from Earth, not in five thousand years. Maybe not even in ten.

This ship is something else, something my not-so-sophisticated single ship computer system doesn't recognize. The system doesn't guess per se—computers still lack the ability to do that—but it sends me information with confidence, picking the closest ship from the array it has in its database.

What I can tell for certain is this: The wreck has been alone and abandoned for a long time. The giant hull is pitted and space-scored, with some kind of corrosion on the outside.

As I circle the thing, moving slowly and keeping my distance, I notice some holes as well, where debris has hit the hull over time.

The holes mean there are no working shields and no way for someone to still be alive on that thing. I suspect, with something as old as this ship appears to be, that scavengers have already looted its interior.

The ship is derelict, abandoned and worthless.

To everyone but me.

I leave the ship as I've found it, drifting. I make no mention of it in the mandatory reports that I have to send to the next space base. I tell no one what I've seen.

I just make note, and I keep my own computer files on my personal system. I never let that system out of my sight.

It takes me three full travel days (with stops along the way) to get to Hector Prime. I keep an apartment there, although I don't call that home.

Home, to me, is *Nobody's Business*, which I have modified for my every need. But I keep two "real" residences—the apartment on Hector Prime and a berth at Longbow Station.

The berth at Longbow gives me privileges at the station. The apartment on Hector Prime allows me to store my stuff somewhere relatively safe.

I like Hector Prime. It's at the very edge of the Enterran Empire, so far away from the Empire's center that the government actually seems lax here. I'm not antigovernment; I just don't think about it much. Because if I do, I worry.

The Empire started the Colonnade Wars all those years ago. It wanted more territory, and it succeeded in getting that territory. If things had gone differently, Hector Prime would have been part of what the Empire calls Rebel Space. The rest of us call it the Nine Planets Alliance, and we travel back and forth between the Alliance and the Empire.

Technically, the Empire holds my citizenship, but in reality, the Alliance touches my heart. That's probably because the Alliance doesn't want my heart—and the Empire does.

Or maybe I just like misfits, since I consider myself one.

Still, my official address is on Hector Prime. I keep an apartment in one of the more expensive sections of the city. I like the area's security—the way it'll notify the *Business* if someone is breaking into apartments in the area, not to mention if someone were to break into mine.

Most of my possessions, while valuable, mean little to me. But the computer system that I store there is almost as valuable as the one I have hardwired into my quarters on the *Business*. On my apartment system, I keep coded records, logs, and other information.

I doubt anyone can break the codes, but I want to be informed if someone tries.

For buried within all that information—a lot of flotsam and jetsam of galaxy history, favorite reading materials, downloaded holoplays, and fake genealogy charts for the family I've long ago abandoned—are the locations of my favorite wrecks. Not the ones the tourists dive, but the ones that hold a special place in my heart.

The ones filled with history. The ones that matter more to me than anything.

I don't record the new ship's presence in any of those logs. I won't record it until after I've dived it. But I do make a hand-scrawled note and paste it to my kitchen wall. All the note has are numbers: the date I discovered the wreck followed by the identification number of my single ship intermingled with the wreck's coordinates. The code is simple, and a determined someone could break it, I suppose, but no one has yet.

And it's a nice security feature in case someone steals my systems—all of them.

Right now, I don't care about much of the information on them.

All I care about is the new wreck.

My apartment is almost as spare as the single ship. I have a kitchen, a bedroom, and a living room. I sleep in the living room and use the bedroom as a workspace. It's littered with computer parts, old and new. It would take a burglar a while to figure out which system is the current one.

Sometimes I change from a modern machine to an old one. Sometimes I add components that don't really fit just to throw people off.

While I have been robbed on the *Business*—by a former colleague, no less—I haven't been robbed in the apartment.

But a diver can't be too careful.

It's a competitive business, and what a diver has, besides her diving skills, are the locations of her favorite and upcoming wrecks. No matter how much money a diver has, no matter how much loot she finds, she learns that those things don't matter.

All that matters are the wrecks.

I switch the systems around again before I begin research on the new wreck. First I download the ship's shape and the specs I could gather by flying around it.

Then I let the database work, seeing if my extensive collection of historical ships has any record of something of this shape.

I'm loath to work on the public networks. Sometimes an inquiry is enough to notify a claim jumper. I prefer to use the databases I've developed.

Even using mine, it takes a full day of nonstop work before it locates a match.

The system shows me the match holographically, creating models of the ship I saw and the ship in the database. The holographic ships cover the carpeted floor. I can walk around them. I can put one image on top of the other. I can enlarge or reduce them.

I do all of these things. My computer believes these ships are the same, and my eyes tell me that they are as well.

But I don't like what I'm seeing.

Because that means my single ship computer was right: this wreck is five thousand years old.

Worse, it's Earthmade.

And even worse than that, it's a Dignity Vessel.

Dignity Vessels, while legendary, have never traveled more than fifty light-years from Earth.

Dignity Vessels weren't designed to travel huge distances, at least by current standards, and they weren't manufactured outside of Earth's solar system. Even drifting at the speed it's currently moving, it couldn't have arrived at its present location in five thousand years, or even fifty thousand.

Yet it's there.
Drifting. Filled with mystery.
Filled with time.
Waiting for someone like me to figure it out.

TWO

I need a team. I can't dive a ship the size of a Dignity Vessel alone even if I want to. First of all, it won't be safe. Second, I would spend the rest of my life mapping the damn thing. And third, no one would believe me if I decide that my information is right.

I take the *Business* to Longbow Station. Longbow sits at the very edges of Empire Space. When the Colonnade Wars began, Longbow belonged to the group the Empire now calls the rebels. Some maps place Longbow in the Nine Planets Alliance; others place it in the Enterran Empire.

Both the Empire and the Alliance long ago learned to leave Longbow alone. Longbow is such an important trading hub that both sides decided it was better—and safer—to let the station be just a little bit lawless, and to govern itself, than it was to attempt to take over the place.

As a result, a lot of people with iffy allegiances live on Longbow. You quickly learn that it's better not to ask people's politics or their past history.

Longbow started as a docking berth five hundred years ago. You can still see the original station, tucked inside one of the modular units that was new a hundred years before.

Over time, Longbow became a major hub. Instead of replacing sections, the owners simply built onto the existing parts. So the station looks like a child's toy, held together by spit and static. Depending on how you approach it, you can't even see where the ships dock.

The station looks like a creature with a thousand tentacles and no center core.

But there is a center core. It's buried underneath all the rebuilding. Very few people make it to that core. Only longtime spacers even know where the core is, which is fortunate, since the old spacers' bar on Longbow doesn't let tourists and first-timers through the door.

The old spacers' bar is the only bar on Longbow that doesn't have a name. No name, no advertising across the door or the back wall, no cute little logos on the magnetized drinking cups. The door is recessed into a grungy wall that looks like it's temporary due to construction.

To get in, you need one of two special chips. The first is handheld—given by the station's manager after careful consideration. The second is built into your ID. You get that one only if you're a legitimate spacer, operating or working for a business that requires a pilot's license.

I have had the second chip since I was eighteen years old.

And I know that the people I will find in that bar will be as experienced as I am. As experienced, as space-worn, and as skeptical.

They'll also be on break or looking for work.

In essence, any divers I see inside will be exactly what I need.

In the end, I settle on five divers.

The least experienced are a father-and-son team, Jypé and Junior. I tourist-dived with them a few times, years ago, when they were starting to get their space legs. I'm the one who encouraged them to go beyond the safe dives and move to wreck diving, salvage, and historical diving.

They both have natural diving talent, an ability to float through zero-g even though both are land-born. They understand history and they love new places, new things.

They're also one of the best teams I've ever worked with. They move in synch, think in synch, and work in synch. They even look alike. Junior is a younger version of Jypé, same black hair, dark skin, and strong bone structure—stronger than that of most divers. The fact that they're land-born shows in their build. But their background doesn't harm their diving.

Besides, they have the money to pursue this new career. Jypé made a fortune in some land-based business and now invests it in preserving historical wrecks—wrecks he's helped discover.

I trust Jypé's knowledge of historical ships almost as much as I trust my own.

Deep down, I was hoping I'd find Jypé and Junior when I came to Longbow. The fact that I have makes me feel like this mission is destined.

The next two people I hire are also a longtime team. I first met Squishy and Turtle when I started wreck diving, decades ago.

Squishy and Turtle have been a couple as long as I've known them. They're both thin, active women who can run their own team if they have to. Squishy's a bit secretive—she doesn't like to talk about her past—and Turtle respects that. But every dive we've gone on together has been successful. They have a level of expertise that no other divers I know have achieved.

Turtle has an uncanny sense of corners and danger spots. She's also a good pilot. She's saved my life more than once.

And somewhere along the way, Squishy learned field medicine. I discovered long ago that it's best to have a medic on each mission.

It's even better to have a medic who dives.

It takes me nearly a week to find the last member of the team. Many of the more established divers say no to me when I refuse to tell them what kind of ship we're diving.

All I will tell anyone is that we have a mystery vessel, one that will tax their knowledge, their beliefs, and their wreck-recovery skills.

I don't want anyone who goes to the coordinates to know we have a Dignity Vessel before we arrive. I don't want to prejudice them, don't want to force them along one line of thinking.

I also don't want to be wrong.

Besides, while I'm hunting for the last member of the team, I don't want to tip my hand. If we do have a Dignity Vessel, it'll be worth a fortune in curiosity value alone. The wrong word to the wrong person and my little discovery will disappear as if it hasn't existed at all.

But a lot of divers won't go into a wreck blind. They believe it's better to know what they're facing, even if they later discover that they're wrong about the type of ship.

Because of that, a lot of experienced divers turn me down.

That's how I end up with Karl.

Even though I've known him for more than ten years, we've rarely worked together. He has always intimidated me. He's big for a diver, blond, muscular, and very pale. Yet he is one of the best divers in the sector. He has incredible rankings from almost every certifying body that exists. He's gone on more dives than I have and has dived more kinds of ships than I ever will.

But he is also cautious, and caution isn't always compatible with historical wreck diving. Some of his dive partners have made fun of the redundant equipment he carries and the large knife he sticks into his belt.

I think the knife is dangerous—he could poke a hole in his environmental suit—but I also know I can't convince him to give the knife up. It's saved his life more than once—the last time when he was solo diving a wreck he discovered and got ambushed by three claim jumpers.

He killed them, finished the dive, and then reported his actions. I was on Longbow when he went up on charges and ably defended himself with holocordings, audio, and not a little bit of personal outrage.

Karl is the only member of the team who worries me. If I can't keep him under control, he might take over the dive.

And there's nothing I hate more than losing control of a mission. Except losing a member of my team.

THREE

We approach the wreck in stealth mode: lights and communications array off, sensors on alert for any other working ship in the vicinity. I'm the only one in the cockpit of the *Nobody's Business*. I'm the only one with the exact coordinates.

The rest of the team sits in the lounge, their gear in cargo. I personally searched each one of them before sticking them to their chairs. No one, but no one, knows where the wreck is except me. That is our agreement.

They hold to it or else.

We're six days from Longbow Station, but it took us ten to get here. Misdirection again, although I'd only planned on two days working my way through an asteroid belt around Beta Six. I ended up taking three, trying to get rid of a bottom-feeder that tracked us, hoping to learn where we're diving.

Hoping for loot.

After I'm sure I have lost every chance of being tracked, I let the *Business* slide into a position far enough from the wreck that we're out of normal scanner range. We can't eyeball the wreck either. We match the wreck's speed, but do little else.

I use this precaution on all of my valuable wreck dives. If my ship's energy signals are caught on someone else's scans, they won't pick up the faint energy signal of the wreck. I have a half dozen cover stories ready, depending on who might spot us. I'll tell them lies about why we're in this area of space. I'll tell them anything I can to get rid of them.

But most of all, I hope no one will stumble upon us while we dive the wreck.

Taking this precaution means we need transport to and from the wreck. That's the only drawback of this kind of secrecy.

First mission out, I'm ferry captain—a role I hate, but one I have to play. We're using the skip instead of the *Business*. The skip is designed for short trips. It has a main room that melds into the pilot's area, a cargo bay, a galley kitchen, and a bathroom. It also has two escape pods in case something goes wrong. The pods only fit one person each—a design flaw, since the skip itself holds four.

The skip is also designed to travel anonymously. I had the name and logo removed right after I bought it. Not even the pods have any identifying features. I don't want to be easily identified, particularly when I'm diving an unknown wreck.

On this trip, there's only three of us—me, Turtle, and Karl. Usually we team-dive wrecks, but this deep and this early, I need two different kinds of players. Turtle can dive anything, and Karl can kill anything. I can fly anything.

We're set.

The process we're about to embark on gets its name from the dangers: in olden days, wreck diving was called space diving to differentiate it from the planetside practice of diving into the oceans.

We don't face water here—we don't have its weight or its unusual properties, particularly at huge depths. We have other elements to concern us: no gravity, no oxygen, extreme cold.

And greed.

My biggest problem is that I'm land-born, something I don't confess to often. I spent the last forty years of my life trying to forget that my feet were once stuck to a planet's surface by real gravity. I even came to prolonged zero-g late: fifteen years old, already landlocked. My first instructors told me I'd never unlearn the thinking real atmosphere ingrains into the body.

They were mostly right; land pollutes me, takes out an edge that the space-raised come to naturally. I have to consciously choose to go into the deep and dark; the space-raised glide in like it's mother's milk. But if I compare myself to the landlocked, I'm a spacer of the first order, someone who understands vacuum like most understand air.

But because I'm the least able diver on the skip, I'll stay on board, even though I'm the one who discovered the Dignity Vessel. I trust Karl and Turtle; besides, they'll record everything they see.

It will almost be as if I've dived with them.

Almost.

I fly the skip with the portals unshielded. It looks like we're inside a piece of black glass moving through open space. Turtle paces most of the way, walking back to front to back again, peering through the portals, hoping to be the first to see the wreck.

She's even thinner than she was when I first met her decades ago. Her bones look fragile enough to snap. Her skin is rough from the chemicals some suits are contaminated with and from weird exposures from bad dives. Her fingers are long, birdlike.

She no longer looks like the woman we nicknamed Turtle. Then her head had been the smallest thing about her. When she put on an environmental suit, it seemed like she put on a protective shell.

In those days, I was convinced she could slide her helmeted head inside her suit and pretend to be a rock, just like a real turtle.

Now her head seems large against her skeletal frame. Middle age has not treated her well, although she is as strong and healthy as ever.

Karl monitors the instruments as if he's flying the skip instead of me. If I hadn't worked with him before, I'd be freaked. I'm not; I know he's watching for unusuals, whatever comes our way.

Karl is the opposite of Turtle. He looks as sturdy as she seems fragile. He has a broad open face and close-cut blond hair.

Everything about him seems efficient and strong, as powerful as that knife he carries everywhere he goes.

The wreck looms ahead of us—a megaship, from the days when size equaled power. Still, it seems small in the vastness, barely a blip on the front of my sensors.

Turtle bounces past. She's fighting the grav that I left on for me—that landlocked thing again—and she's so nervous, someone who doesn't know her would think she's on something.

"What the hell is it?" she asks. "Old Empire?"

"Older." Karl is bent at the waist, looking courtly as he studies the instruments. He prefers readouts to eyeballing things; he trusts equipment more than he trusts himself.

"There can't be anything older out here," Turtle says.

"'Can't' is relative," Karl says.

I let them tough it out. I'm not telling them what I know. The skip slows, and shuts down. I'm easing in, leaving no trail.

"It's gonna take more than six of us to dive that puppy," Turtle says. "Either that, or we'll spend the rest of our lives here."

"As old as that thing is," Karl says, "it's probably been plundered and replundered."

"We're not here for the loot." I speak softly, reminding them it's a historical mission.

Karl turns his angular face toward me. In the dim light of the instrument panel, his gray eyes look silver. "You know what this is?"

I don't answer. I'm not going to lie about something as important as this, so I can't make a denial. But I'm not going to confirm either. Confirming will only lead to more questions, which is something I don't want just yet. I need them to make their own minds up about this find.

"Huge, old." Turtle shakes her head. "Dangerous. You know what's inside?"

"Nothing, for all I know."

"Didn't check it out first?"

Some dive team leaders head into a wreck the moment they find one. Anyone working salvage knows it's not worth your time to come back to a place that's been plundered before.

"No." I pick a spot not far from the main doors and set the skip to hold position with the monster wreck. With no trail, I hoped no one was gonna notice the tiny energy emanation the skip gives off.

"Too dangerous?" Turtle asks. "That why you didn't go in?"

"I have no idea if it's dangerous." I'm referring to the skip, not diving alone.

Diving alone is always dangerous.

"There's a reason you brought us here." She sounds annoyed. "You gonna share it?"

I shake my head. "Not yet. I just want to see what you find."

She glares, but the look has no teeth. She knows my methods and even approves of them sometimes. And she should know that I'm not good enough to dive alone.

She peels off her clothes—no modesty in this woman—and slides on her suit. The suit adheres to her like it's a part of her. She wraps five extra breathers around her hips—just-in-case emergency stuff, barely enough to get her out if her suit's internal oxygen system fails. Her suit is minimal—it has no backup for environmental protection. If her primary and secondary units fail, she's a little block of ice in a matter of seconds.

She likes the risk; Karl doesn't. His suit is bulkier, not as form-fitting, but it has external environmental backups. He has had environmental failures and has barely survived them. I've heard that lecture half a dozen times. So has Turtle, even though she always ignores it.

He doesn't go naked under the suit either, leaving some clothes in case he has to peel quickly. Different divers, different situations. He only carries two extra breathers, both so small that they fit on his hips without expanding his width. He uses the extra loops for weapons, mostly lasers, although he's got that knife stashed somewhere in all that preparedness.

They don't put on the headpieces until I give them the plan. One hour only: twenty minutes to get in, twenty minutes to explore, twenty minutes to return. Work the buddy system. We just want an idea of what's in there.

One hour gives them enough time on their breathers for some margin of error. One hour also prevents them from getting too involved in the dive and forgetting the time.

They have to stay on schedule.

They get the drill. They've done it before, with me anyway. I have no idea how other team leaders run their ships. I have strict rules about everything, and expect my teams to follow.

Headpieces on—Turtle's is as thin as her face, tight enough to make her look like some kind of cybernetic human. Karl goes for the full protection—seven layers, each with a different function; double night vision, extra cameras on all sides; computerized monitors layered throughout the external cover. He gives me the handheld, which records everything he sees. It's not as good as the camera eye view they'll bring back, but at least it'll let me know my team is still alive.

Not that I can do anything if they're in trouble. My job is to stay in the skip. Theirs is to come back to it in one piece.

They move through the airlock—Turtle bouncing around like she always does, Karl moving with caution—and then wait the required two minutes. The suits adjust, then Turtle presses the hatch, and Karl sends the lead to the other ship.

We don't tether exactly, but we run a line from one point of entry to the other. It's cautionary. A lot of divers get wreck blindness—hit the wrong button, expose themselves to too much light, look directly into a laser, or the suit malfunctions in ways I don't even want to discuss—and they need the tactical hold to get back to safety.

I don't deal with wreck blindness either, but Squishy does. She knows eyes, and can replace a lens in less than fifteen minutes. She's saved more than one of my crew in the intervening years. And after overseeing the first repair—the one in which she got her nickname—I don't watch.

Turtle heads out first, followed by Karl. They look vulnerable out there, small shapes against the blackness. They follow the guideline, one hand resting lightly on it as they propel themselves toward the wreck.

This is the easy part: should they let go or miss by a few meters, they use tiny air chips in the hands and feet of their suits to push them in the right direction. The suits have even more chips than that. Should the diver get too far away from the wreck, they can use little propellants installed throughout their suits.

I haven't lost a diver going or coming from a wreck.

It's inside that matters.

My hands are slick with sweat. I nearly drop the handheld. It's not providing much at the moment—just the echo of Karl's breathing, punctuated by an occasional "fuck" as he bumps something or moves slightly off-line.

I don't look at the images he's sending back either. I know what they are—the gloved hand on the lead, the vastness beyond, the bits of the wreck in the distance.

Instead, I walk back to the cockpit, sink into my chair, and turn all monitors on full. I have cameras on both of them and readouts running on another monitor watching their heart and breathing patterns. I plug the handheld into one small screen, but I don't watch it until Karl approaches the wreck.

The main door is scored and dented. Actual rivets still remain on one side. I haven't worked a ship old enough for rivets; I've only seen them in museums and histories. I stare at the bad image Karl's sending back, entranced. How have those tiny metal pieces remained after centuries? For the first time, I wish I'm out there myself. I want to run the thin edge of my glove against the metal surface.

Karl does just that, but he doesn't seem interested in the rivets. His fingers search for a door release, something that will open the thing easily.

After centuries, I doubt there is any easy here. Finally, Turtle pings him.

"Got something over here," she says.

She's on the far side of the wreck from me, working a section I hadn't examined that closely. Karl keeps his hands on the wreck itself, sidewalking toward her.

My breath catches. This is the part I hate: the beginning of the actual dive, the place where the trouble starts.

Most wrecks are filled with space, inside and out, but a few still maintain their original environments, and then it gets really dicey—extreme heat or a gaseous atmosphere that interacts badly with the suits.

Sometimes the hazards are even simpler: a jagged metal edge that punctures even the strongest suits; a tiny corridor that seems big enough until it narrows, trapping the diver inside.

Every wreck has its surprises, and surprise is the thing that leads to the most damage—a diver shoving backward to avoid a floating object, a diver slamming his head into a wall that jars the suit's delicate internal mechanisms, and a host of other problems, all of them documented by survivors and none of them the same.

The handheld shows a rip in the exterior of the wreck, not like any other caused by debris. Turtle puts a fisted hand in the center, then activates her knuckle lights. From my vantage, the hole looks large enough for two humans to go through side by side.

"Send a probe before you even think of going in there," I say into her headset.

"Think it's deep enough?" Turtle asks, her voice tinny as it comes through the speakers.

"Let's try the door first," Karl says. "I don't want surprises if we can at all avoid them."

Good man. His small form appears like a spider attached to the ship's side. He returns to the exit hatch, still scanning it.

I look at the timer, running at the bottom of my main screen.

17:32

Not a lot of time to get in.

I know Karl's headpiece has a digital readout at the base. He's conscious of the time, too, and is as cautious about that as he is about following procedure.

Turtle scuttles across the ship's side to reach him, slips a hand under a metal awning, and grunts.

"How come I didn't see that?" Karl asks.

"Looking in the wrong place," she says. "This is real old. I'll wager the metal's so brittle we could punch through the thing ourselves."

"We're not here to destroy it." There's disapproval in Karl's voice.

"I *know*."

19:01. I'll come on the line and demand they return if they go much over twenty minutes.

Turtle grabs something that I can't see, braces her feet on the side of the ship, and tugs. I wince. If she loses her grip, she propels, spinning, far and fast into space.

"Crap," she says. "Stuck."

"I could've told you that. These things are designed to remain closed."

"We have to go in the hole."

"Not without a probe," Karl says.

"We're running out of time."

21:22

They are out of time.

I'm about to come on and remind them when Karl says, "We have a choice. We either try to blast this door open or we probe that hole."

Turtle doesn't answer him. She tugs. Her frame looks small on my main screen, all bunched up as she uses her muscles to pry open something that may have been closed for centuries.

On the handheld screen, enlarged versions of her hands disappear under that awning, but the exquisite detail of her suit shows the ripple of her flesh as she struggles.

"Let go, Turtle," Karl says.

"I don't want to damage it," Turtle says. "God knows what's just inside there."

"Let go."

She does. The hands reappear, one still braced on the ship's side.

"We're probing," he says. "Then we're leaving."

"Who put you in charge?" she grumbles, but she follows him to that hidden side of the ship. I see only their limbs as they move along the exterior—the human limbs against the pits and the dents and the small holes punched by space debris. Shards of protruding metal near rounded gashes beside pristine swatches that still shine in the thin light from Turtle's headgear.

I want to be with them, clinging to the wreck, looking at each mark, trying to figure out when it came, how it happened, what it means.

But all I can do is watch.

The probe makes it through sixteen meters of stuff before it doesn't move any farther. Karl tries to tug it out, but the probe is stuck, just like my team would've been if they'd gone in without it.

They return, forty-two minutes into the mission, feeling defeated.

I'm elated. They've gotten farther than I ever expected.

FOUR

We take the probe readouts back to the *Business*, over the protests of the team. They want to recharge and clean out the breathers and dive again, but I won't let them. That's another rule I have to remind them of—only one dive per twenty-four-hour period. There are too many unknowns in our work; it's essential that we have time to rest.

We all get too enthusiastic about our dives—we take chances we shouldn't. Sleep, relaxation, downtime all prevent the kind of haste that gets divers killed.

Once we're in the *Business*, I download the probe readouts, along with the readings from the suits, the gloves, and the handheld. Everyone gathers in the lounge. I have three-D holotech in there that'll allow us all to get a sense of the wreck.

As I'm sorting through the material, thinking of how to present it (handheld first? overview? a short lecture?), the entire group arrives. Turtle's taken a shower. Her hair's wet, and she looks tired. She swore to me she wasn't stressed out there, but her eyes tell me otherwise. She's exhausted.

Squishy follows, looking somber. She looks solid next to Turtle's thinness. But Squishy is thin too, just not as brittle. She has muscles like Karl does and a squat square face. Her hair is cut like his as well, shorn against her skull, which makes it easier for her to dive.

Jypé and Junior are already there, in the best seats. They've been watching me set up. They look like father and son. When Junior grows into his bone structure, he'll be a handsome man like his father.

Right now, he looks like a partially completed sketch.

The completed sketch sits next to him. Jypé has a land-born's way of moving—heavy and solid—but he looks too light to be land-born. He's adapted to space better than I have.

Junior was born in space and raised in it, alternating between zero-g and Earth normal. He has the grace that his father lacks.

Leaning on the built-in couch, they both look strong and rested, ready for anything.

I hope that they are.

Karl is late. When he arrives—also looking tired—Squishy stops him at the door.

"Turtle says it's old."

Turtle shoots Squishy an angry look.

"She won't say anything else." Squishy glances at me as if it's my fault. Only I didn't swear the first team to secrecy about the run. That was their choice.

"It's old," Karl says, and squeezes by her.

"She's says it's weird-old."

Karl looks at me now. His angular face seems even bonier. He seems to be asking me silently if he can talk.

I continue setting up.

Karl sighs, then says, "I've never seen anything like it."

No one else asks a question. They wait for me. I start with the images the skip's computer downloaded, then add the handheld material. I've finally decided to save the suit readouts for last. I might be the only one who cares about the metal composition, the exterior hull temperature, and the number of rivets lining the hatch.

The group watches in silence as the wreck appears, watches intently as the skip's images show a tiny Turtle and Karl slide across the guideline.

The group listens to the arguments, and Jypé nods when Karl makes his unilateral decision to use the probe. The nod reassures me. Jypé is as practical as I remembered.

I move to the probe footage next. I haven't previewed it. We've all seen probe footage before, so we ignore the grainy picture, the thin light, and the darkness beyond.

The probe doesn't examine so much as explore: its job is to go as far inside as possible, to see if that hole provides an easy entrance into the wreck.

It looks so easy for ten meters—nothing along the edges, just light and darkness and weird particles getting disturbed by the probe's movements.

Then the hole narrows and we can see the walls as large shapes all around. The hole narrows more, and the walls become visible in the light—a shinier metal, one less damaged by space debris. The particles thin out too.

Finally a wall looms ahead. The hole continues, so small that it seems like the probe can't continue. The probe actually sends a laser pulse and gets back a measurement: the hole is six centimeters in diameter, more than enough for the equipment to go through.

But when the probe reaches that narrow point, it slams into a barrier. The barrier isn't visible. The probe runs several more readouts, all of them denying that the barrier is there.

Then there's a registered tug on the line: Karl trying to get the probe out. Several more tugs later, Karl and Turtle decide the probe's stuck. They take even more readouts, and then shut it down, planning to use it later.

The readouts tell us nothing except that the hole continues, six centimeters in diameter, for another two meters.

"What the hell do you think that is?" Junior asks. His voice hasn't finished its change yet, even though both Jypé and Junior swear he's over eighteen.

"Could be some kind of force field," Squishy says.

"In a vessel that old?" Turtle asks. "Not likely."

"How old is that?" Squishy's entire body is tense. It's clear now that she and Turtle have been fighting.

"How old is that, Boss?" Turtle asks me.

They all look at me. They know I have an idea. They know age is one of the reasons they're here.

I shrug. "That's one of the things we're going to confirm."

"Confirm." Karl catches the word. "Confirm what? What do you know that we don't?"

"Let's run the readouts before I answer that," I say.

"No." Squishy crosses her arms. "Tell us."

Turtle gets up. She pushes two icons on the console beside me, and the suits' technical readouts come up. She flashes forward, through numbers and diagrams and chemical symbols, to the conclusions.

"Over five thousand years old." Turtle doesn't look at Squishy. "That's what the boss isn't telling us. This wreck is human-made, and it's been here longer than humans have been in this section of space."

Karl stares at it, then he shakes his head. "Not possible. Nothing human-made would've survived to make it this far out. Too many gravity wells, too much debris."

"Five thousand years," Jypé says.

I let them talk. In their voices, in their argument, I hear the same argument that went through my head when I got my first readouts about the wreck.

It's Junior who stops the discussion. In his half-tenor, half-baritone way, he says, "C'mon, gang, think a little. That's why the boss brought us out here. To confirm her suspicions."

"Or not," I say.

Everyone looks at me as if they've just remembered I'm there.

"Wouldn't it be better if we knew your suspicions?" Squishy asks.

Karl is watching me, eyes slitted. It's as if he's seeing me for the first time.

"No, it wouldn't be better." I speak softly. I make sure to have eye contact with each of them before I continue. "I don't want you to use my scholarship—or lack thereof—as the basis for your assumptions."

"So should we even bother to discuss this with each other?" Squishy's using that snide tone with me now. I don't know what has her so upset, but I'm going to have to find out. If she doesn't calm down soon, she's not going near the wreck.

"Sure," I say.

"All right." She leans back, staring at the readouts still floating before us. "If this thing is five thousand years old, human-made, and somehow it came to this spot at this time, then it can't have a force field, at least not as we understand it."

"Or fake readouts like the probe found," Jypé says.

"Hell," Turtle says. "It shouldn't be here at all. Space debris should've pulverized it. That's too much time. Too much distance."

"So what's it doing here?" Karl asked.

I shrug for the third and last time. "Let's see if we can find out."

They don't rest. They're as obsessed with the readouts as I've been. They study time and distance and drift, forgetting the weirdness inside the hole. I'm the one who focuses on that.

I don't learn much. We need to know more, so we revisit the probe twice while looking for another way into the ship. Even then, we don't get a lot of new information.

Either the barrier is new technology or it is very old technology—technology that has been lost. So much technology has been lost in the thousands of years since this ship was built. It seems like humans constantly have to reinvent everything.

We know some of what our ancestors knew. We know a little of what they did.

Some of it sounds like magic to me, and some of it sounds like incredible science, the kind that should be beyond human beings. Actually, now, much of it is beyond us. We have forgotten so much—or lost it—or never truly learned it in the first place.

Some old spacers stay away from wrecks. These old-timers believe the wrecks are haunted—not by the dead crew, but by old science, the kind that could kill us because we don't understand it.

I think we should always strive for understanding, and I believe in rediscovery.

I believe in never letting anything important get lost.

Six dives later and we still haven't found a way inside the ship. Six dives, and no new information. Six dives, and my biggest problem is Squishy.

She has become angrier and angrier as the dives continue. I've brought her along on the seventh dive to man the skip with me, so that we can talk.

Junior and Jypé are the divers. They're exploring what I consider to be the top of the ship, even though I'm only guessing. They're going over the surface centimeter by centimeter, exploring each part of it, looking for a weakness that we can exploit.

I monitor their equipment using the skip's computer, and I monitor them with my eyes, watching the tiny figures move along the narrow blackness of the skip itself.

Squishy stands beside me at military attention, her hands folded behind her back.

She knows she's been brought for conversation only; she's punishing me by refusing to speak until I broach the subject first.

Finally, when J&J are past the dangerous links between two sections of the ship, I mimic Squishy's posture—hands behind my back, shoulders straight, legs slightly spread.

"What's making you so angry?" I ask.

She stares at the team on top of the wreck. Her face is a smooth reproach to my lack of attention; the monitor on board the skip should always pay attention to the divers.

I taught her that. I believe that. Yet here I am, reproaching another person while the divers work the wreck.

"Squishy?" I ask.

She isn't answering me. Just watching, with that implacable expression.

"You've had as many dives as everyone else," I say. "I've never questioned your work, yet your mood has been foul, and it seems to be directed at me. Do we have an issue I don't know about?"

Finally she turns, and the move is as military as the stance. Her eyes narrow.

"You could've told us this was a Dignity Vessel," she says.

My breath catches. She agrees with my research. I don't understand why that makes her angry.

"I could've," I say. "But I feel better that you came to your own conclusion."

"I've known it since the first dive," she says. "I wanted you to tell them. You didn't. They're still wasting time trying to figure out what they have here."

"What they have here is an anomaly," I say, "something that makes no sense and can't be here."

"Something dangerous." She crosses her arms. "Dignity Vessels were used in wartime."

"I know the legends." I glance at the wreck, then at the handheld readout. J&J are working something that might be a hatch.

"A lot of wartimes," she says, "over many centuries, from what historians have found out."

"But never out here," I say.

And she concedes. "Never out here."

"So what are you so concerned about?"

"By not telling us what it is, we can't prepare," she says. "What if there're weapons or explosives or something else—"

"Like that barrier?" I ask.

Her lips thin.

"We've worked unknown wrecks before, you and me."

She shrugs. "But they're of a type. We know the history, we know the vessels, we know the capabilities. We don't know this at all. No one really knows what these ancient ships were capable of. It's something that shouldn't be here."

"A mystery," I say.

"A dangerous one."

"Hey!" Junior's voice is tinny and small. "We got it open! We're going in."

Squishy and I turn toward the sound. I can't see either man on the wreck itself. The handheld's imagery is shaky.

I press the comm, hoping they can still hear me. "Probe first. Remember that barrier."

But they don't answer, and I know why not. I wouldn't either in their situation. They're pretending they don't hear. They want to be the first inside, the first to learn the secrets of the wreck.

The handheld moves inside the darkness. I see four tiny lights—Jypé's glove lights—and I see the same particles I saw before, on the first images from the earliest probe.

Then the handheld goes dark. We were going to have to adjust it to transmit through the metal of the wreck.

"I don't like this," Squishy says.

I've never liked any time I was out of sight and communication with the team.

We stare at the wreck as if it can give us answers. It's big and dark, a blob against our screen. Squishy actually goes to the portals and looks as if she can see more through them than she can through the miracle of science.

But she doesn't. And the handheld doesn't wink on.

On my screen, the counter ticks away the minutes.

Our argument isn't forgotten, but it's on hold as the first members of our little unit vanish inside.

After thirty-five minutes—fifteen of them inside (Jypé has rigorously stuck to the schedule on each of his dives, something that has impressed me)—I start to get nervous.

I hate the last five minutes of waiting. I hate it even more when the waiting goes on too long, when someone doesn't follow the timetable I've devised.

Squishy, who's never been in the skip with me, is pacing. She doesn't say any more—not about danger, not about the way I'm running this little trip, not about the wreck itself.

I watch her as she moves, all grace and form, just like she's always been. She's never been on a real mystery run. She's done dangerous ones—maybe two hundred deep-space dives into wrecks that a lot of divers, even the most greedy, would never touch.

But she's always known what she's diving into, and why it's where it is.

Not only are we uncertain as to whether or not this is an authentic Dignity Vessel (and really, how can it be?), we also don't know why it's here, how it came here, or what its cargo was. We have no idea what its mission was, either—if, indeed, it had a mission at all.

J&J have a little over two minutes left inside.

Squishy's stopped pacing. She looks out the portals again, as if the view has changed. It hasn't.

"You're afraid, aren't you?" I ask. "That's the bottom line, isn't it? This is the first time in years that you've been afraid."

She stops, stares at me as if I'm a creature she's never seen before, and then frowns.

"Aren't you?" she asks.

I shake my head.

The handheld springs to life, images bouncy and grainy on the corner of my screen. My stomach unclenches. I've been breathing shallowly and not even realizing it.

Maybe I am afraid, just a little.

But not of the wreck. The wreck is a curiosity, a project, a conundrum no one else has faced before.

I'm afraid of deep space itself, of the vastness of it. It's inexplicable to me, filled with not just one mystery, but millions, and all of them waiting to be solved.

A crackle, then a voice—Jypé's.

"We got a lot of shit." He sounds gleeful. He sounds almost giddy with relief.

Squishy lets out the breath she's obviously been holding.

"We're coming in," Junior says.

It's 40:29.

FIVE

The wreck's a Dignity Vessel, all right. It's got a DV number etched inside the hatch, just like the materials say it should. We mark the number down to research later.

Instead, we're gathered in the lounge, watching the images J&J have brought back.

They have the best equipment. Their suits don't just have sensors and readouts, but they have chips that store a lot of imagery woven into the suits' surfaces. Most suits can't handle the extra weight, light as it is, or the protections to ensure that the chips don't get damaged by the environmental changes—the costs are too high, and if the prices stay in line, then either the suits' human protections are compromised or the imagery is.

Two suits, two vids, so much information.

The computer cobbles it together into two different information streams—one from Jypé's suit's perspective, the other from Junior's. The computer cleans and enhances the images, clarifies edges if it can read them and leaves them fuzzy if it can't.

Not much is fuzzy here. Most of it is firm, black-and-white only because of the purity of the glove lights and the darkness that surrounds them.

Here's what we see:

From Junior's point-of-view, Jypé going into the hatch. The edge is up, rounded, like it's been opened a thousand times a day instead of once in thousands of years. Then the image switches to Jypé's leg cams and at that moment, I stop keeping track of which images belong to which diver.

The hatch itself is round, and so is the tunnel it leads down. Metal rungs are built into the wall. I've seen these before: they're an ancient form of ladder, ineffective and dangerous. Jypé clings to one rung, then turns and pushes off gently, drifting slowly deep into a darkness that seems profound.

Numbers are etched on the walls, all of them following the letters DV, done in ancient script. The numbers are repeated over and over again—the same ones—and it's Karl who figures out why: each piece of the vessel has the numbers etched into it, in case the vessel was destroyed. Its parts could always be identified then.

Other scratches marked the metal, but we can't read them in the darkness. Some of them aren't that visible, even in the glove lights. It takes Jypé a while to remember he has lights on the soles of his feet as well—a sign, to me, of his inexperience with this kind of dive.

Ten meters down, another hatch. It opens easily, and ten meters beneath it is another.

That one reveals a nest of corridors leading in a dozen different directions. A beep resounds in the silence, and we all glance at our watches before we realize it's on the recording.

The reminder that half the dive time is up.

Junior argues that a few more meters won't hurt. Maybe see if there are items off those corridors, something they can remove, take back to the *Business*, and examine.

But Jypé keeps to the schedule. He merely shakes his head, and his son listens.

Together they ascend, floating easily along the tunnel as they entered it, leaving the interior hatches open and only closing the exterior one, as we'd all learned in dive training.

The imagery ends, and the screen fills with numbers, facts, figures, and readouts that I momentarily ignore. The people in the room are more important. We can sift through the numbers later.

There's energy here—a palpable excitement—dampened only by Squishy's fear. She stands with her arms wrapped around herself, as far from Turtle as she can get.

"A Dignity Vessel," Karl says, his cheeks flushed. "Who'd've thought?"

"You knew," Turtle says to me.

I shrug. "I hoped."

"It's impossible," Jypé says, "and yet I was inside it."

"That's the neat part," Junior says. "It's impossible and it's here."

Squishy is the only one who doesn't speak. She stares at the readouts as if she can see more in them than I ever will.

"We have so much work to do," says Karl. "I think we should go back home, research as much as we can, and then come back to the wreck."

"And let others dive her?" Turtle says. "People are going to ghost us, track our research, look at what we're doing. They'll find the wreck and claim it as their own."

"You can't claim this deep," Junior says, then looks at me. "Can you?"

"Sure you can," I say. "But a claim's an announcement that the wreck's here. Something like this, we'll get jumpers for sure."

"Karl's right." Squishy's voice is the only one not tinged with excitement. "We should go back."

"What's wrong with you?" Turtle says. "You used to love wreck diving."

"Have you read about early period stealth technology?" Squishy asks. "Do you have any idea what damage it can do?"

Everyone is looking at her now. She still has her back to us, her arms wrapped around herself so tightly her shirt pulls. The screen's readout lights her face, but all we can see are parts of it, illuminating her skull, making her seem half dead.

"Why would you have studied stealth tech?" Karl asks.

"She was military," Turtle says. "Long, long ago, before she realized she hates rules. Where'd you think she learned field medicine?"

"Still," Karl says, "I was military too—"

Which explained a lot.

"—and no one ever taught me about stealth tech. It's the stuff of legends and kids' tales."

"It was banned." Squishy's voice is soft, but has power. "It was banned five hundred years ago, and every few generations, we try to revive it or modify it or improve it. Doesn't work."

"What doesn't work?" Junior asks.

The tension is rising. I can't let it get too far out of control, but I want to hear what Squishy has to say.

"The tech shadows the ships, makes them impossible to see, even with the naked eye," Squishy says.

"Bullshit," Turtle says. "Stealth just masks instruments, makes it impossible to read the ships on equipment. That's all."

Squishy turns, lets her arms drop. "You know all about this how? Did you spend three years studying stealth? Did you spend two years of postdoc trying to re-create it?"

Turtle is staring at her like she's never seen her before. "Of course not."

"You have?" Karl asks.

Squishy nods. "Why do you think I find things? Why do you think I *like* finding things that are lost?"

Junior shakes his head. I'm not following the connection either.

"Why?" Jypé asks. Apparently he's not following it as well.

"Because," Squishy says, "I've accidentally lost so many things."

"Things?" Karl's voice is low. His face seems pale in the lounge's dim lighting.

"Ships, people, materiel. You name it, I lost it trying to make it invisible to sensors. Trying to re-create the tech you just found on that ship."

My breath catches. "How do you know it's there?"

"We've been looking at it from the beginning," Squishy says. "That damn probe is stuck between one dimension and another. There's only one way in and no way out. And the last thing you want—the very last thing—is for one of us to get stuck like that."

"I don't believe it," Turtle says with such force that I know she and Squishy have been having this argument from the moment we first saw the wreck.

"Believe it." Squishy says that to me, not Turtle. "Believe it with all that you are. Get us out of here, and if you're truly humane, blow that wreck up, so no one else can find it."

"Blow it up?" Junior whispers.

The action is so opposite anything I know that I feel a surge of anger. We don't blow up the past. We may search it, loot it, and try to understand it, but we don't destroy it.

"Get rid of it." Squishy's eyes are filled with tears. She's looking at me, speaking only to me. "Boss, please. It's the only sane thing to do."

SIX

Sane or not, I'm torn.

If Squishy's right, then I have a dual dilemma: the technology is lost, new research on it banned, even though the military keeps conducting research anyway, trying, if I'm understanding Squishy right, to rediscover something we knew thousands of years before.

Which makes this wreck so very valuable that I could more than retire with the money we'd get for selling it. I would—we would—be rich for the rest of our very long lives.

Is the tech dangerous because the experiments to rediscover it are dangerous? Or is it dangerous because there's something about it that makes it unfeasible now and forever?

Karl is right: to do this properly, we have to go back and research Dignity Vessels, stealth tech, and the last few thousand years.

But Turtle's also right: we'll take a huge chance of losing the wreck if we do that. We'll be like countless other divers who sit around bars throughout this sector and bemoan the treasures they lost because they didn't guard them well enough.

We can't leave. We can't even let Squishy leave. We have to stay until we make a decision.

Until I make a decision.

On my own.

First, I look up Squishy's records. Not her dive histories, not her arrest records, not her disease manifolds—the stuff any dive captain would examine—but her personal history, who she is, what she's done, who she's become.

I haven't done that on any of my crew before. I've always thought it an invasion of privacy. All we need to know, I'd say to other dive captains, is whether the crew can handle the equipment, whether they'll steal from their team members, and if their health is good enough to handle the rigors.

And I believed it until now, until I found myself digging through layers of personal history that are threaded into the databases filling the *Business*'s onboard computer.

Fortunately for me and my nervous stomach, the more sensitive databases are linked only to me—no one else even knows they exist (although anyone with brains would guess that they do)—and even if someone finds the databases, no one can access them without my codes, my retinal scan, and in many cases, a sample of my DNA.

Still, I'm skittish as I work this—sound off, screen on dim. I'm in the cockpit, which is my domain, and I have the doors to the main cabin locked. I feel like everyone on the *Business* knows I'm betraying Squishy. And I feel like they all hate me for it.

Squishy's real name is Rosealma Quintinia. She was born forty years ago in a multinational cargo vessel called *The Bounty*. Her parents insisted she spend half her day in artificial gravity so she wouldn't develop spacer's limbs—truncated, fragile—and she didn't. But she gained a grace that enabled her to go from zero-g to Earth normal and back again without much transition at all, a skill few ever gain.

Her family wanted her to cargo, maybe even pirate, but she rebelled. She had a scientific mind, and without asking anyone's permission, took the boards—scoring a perfect 100, something no cargo monkey had ever done before.

A hundred schools all over the known systems wanted her. They offered her room, board, and tuition, but only one offered her all expenses paid both coming and going from the school, covering the only cost that really mattered to a spacer's kid—the cost of travel.

She went, of course, and vanished into the system, only to emerge twelve years later—too thin, too poor, and too bitter to ever be considered a success. She signed on with a cargo vessel as a medic and soon became one of its best and most fearless divers.

She met Turtle in a bar, and they became lovers. Turtle showed her that private divers make more money and brought her to me.

I sigh, rub my eyes with my thumb and forefinger, and lean my head against the screen.

Much as I regret it, it's time for questions now.

Of course, she's waiting for me.

She's brought down the privacy wall in the room she initially shared with Turtle, making their rift permanent. Her bed is covered with folded clothes. Her personal trunk is open at the foot. She's already packed her nightclothes and underwear inside.

"You're leaving?" I ask.

"I can't stay. I don't believe in the mission. You've preached forever the importance of unity, and I believe you, Boss. I'm going to jeopardize everything."

"You're acting like I've already made a decision about the future of this mission."

"Haven't you?" She sits on the edge of the bed, hands folded primly in her lap, her back straight. Her bearing *is* military—something I've always seen, but never really understood until now.

"Tell me about stealth tech," I say.

She raises her chin slightly. "It's classified."

"That's fucking obvious."

She glances at me, clearly startled. "You tried to research it?"

I nod. I tried to research it when I was researching Dignity Vessels. I tried again from the *Business*. I couldn't find much, but I didn't have to tell her that.

That was fucking obvious too.

"You've broken rules before," I say. "You can break them again."

She looks away, staring at that opaque privacy wall—so representative of what she'd become. The solid backbone of my crew suddenly doesn't support any of us anymore. She's opaque and difficult, setting up a divider between herself and the rest of us.

"I swore an oath."

"Well, let me help you break it," I snap. "If I try to enter that barrier, what'll happen to me?"

"Don't." She whispers the word. "Just leave, Boss."

"Convince me."

"If I tell you, you gotta swear you'll say nothing about this."

"I swear." I'm not sure I believe me. My voice is shaky, my tone something that sounds strange even to me.

But the oath—however weak it is—is what Squishy wants.

Squishy takes a deep breath, but she doesn't change her posture. In fact, she speaks directly to the wall, not turning toward me at all.

"I became a medic after my time in Stealth," she says. "I decided I had to save lives after taking so many of them. It was the only way to balance the score. . . ."

Experts believe stealth tech was deliberately lost. Too dangerous, too risky. The original stealth scientists all died under mysterious circumstances, all much too young and without recording any part of their most important discoveries.

Through the ages, their names were even lost, only to be rediscovered by a major researcher, visiting Old Earth in the latter part of the past century.

Squishy tells me all this in a flat voice. She sounds like she's reciting a lecture from very long ago. Still, I listen, word for word, not asking any questions, afraid to break her train of thought.

Afraid she'll never return to any of it.

Earth-owned Dignity Vessels had all been stripped centuries before, used as cargo ships, used as junk. An attempt to reassemble one about five hundred years ago failed because the Dignity Vessels' main components and their guidance systems were never, ever found, either in junk or in blueprint form.

A few documents, smuggled to the colonies on Earth's moon, suggested that stealth tech was based on interdimensional science: The ships didn't vanish off radar because of a "cloak" but because they traveled, briefly, into another world—a parallel universe that's similar to our own.

I recognized the theory—it's the one on which time travel is based, even though we've never discovered time travel, at least not in any useful way, and researchers all over the universe discourage experimentation in it. They prefer the other theory of time travel, the one that says time is not linear, that we only perceive it as linear, and to actually time travel would be to alter the human brain.

But what Squishy is telling me is that it's possible to time travel, it's possible to open small windows in other dimensions and bend them to our will.

Only, she says, those windows don't bend as nicely as we like, and for every successful trip, there are two that don't function as well.

I ask for explanation, but she shakes her head.

"You can get stuck," she says, "like that probe. Forever and ever."

"You think this is what the Dignity Vessels did?"

She shakes her head. "I think their stealth tech is based on some form of this multidimensional travel, but not in any way we've been able to reproduce."

"And this ship we have here? Why are you so afraid of it?" I ask.

"Because you're right." She finally looks at me. There are shadows under her eyes. Her face is haunted, the lower lip trembling. "The ship shouldn't be here. No Dignity Vessel ever left the sector of space around Earth. They weren't designed to travel vast distances, let alone halfway across the known universe."

I nod. She's not telling me something I don't already know. "So?"

"So," she says. "Dozens and dozens of those ships never returned to port."

"Shot down, destroyed." This is what the databases say, and the news doesn't surprise me. Dignity Vessels were battleships, after all.

"Shot down, destroyed, or lost," she says. "I vote for lost. Or used for something, some mission now forgotten in time."

I shrug. "So?"

"So you wondered why no one's seen this before, why no one's found it, why the ship itself has drifted so very far from home."

I nod.

"Maybe it didn't drift."

"You think it was purposely sent here?"

She shakes her head. "What if it stealthed on a mission to the outer regions of Old Earth's area of space?"

My stomach clenches.

"What if," she says, "the crew tried to destealth—and ended up here?"

"Five thousand years ago?"

She shakes her head. "A few generations ago. Maybe more, maybe less. But not very long. And you were just the lucky one who found it."

SEVEN

I spend the entire night listening to Squishy's theories.

I hear about the experiments, the forty-five deaths, the losses she suffered in a program that started the research from scratch.

After she left R&D and went into medicine, she used her high security clearance to explore older files. She found pockets of research dating back nearly five centuries, the pertinent stuff gutted, all but the assumptions gone.

Stealth tech. Lost, just like I assumed. And no one'd been able to recreate it.

I listen and evaluate, and realize, somewhere in the dead of night, that I'm not a scientist.

But I am a pragmatist, and I know, from my own research, that Dignity Vessels, with their stealth tech, existed for more than two hundred years. Certainly not something that would have happened had the stealth technology been as flawed as Squishy said.

So many variables, so much for me to weigh.

And beneath it all, a greed pulses, one that—until tonight—I thought I didn't have.

For the last five centuries, our military has researched stealth tech and failed.

Failed.

I might have all the answers only a short distance away, in a wreck no one else has noticed, a wreck that is—for the moment anyway—completely my own.

I leave Squishy to sleep. I tell her to clear her bed, that she has to remain with the group, no matter what I decide.

She nods as if she's expecting that, and maybe she is. She grabs her nightclothes as I let myself out of the room and into the much cooler, more dimly lit corridor.

As I walk to my own quarters, Jypé finds me.

"She tell you anything worthwhile?" His eyes are a little too bright. Is greed eating at him like it's eating at me? I'm almost afraid to ask.

"No," I say. "She didn't. The work she did doesn't seem all that relevant to me."

I'm lying. I really do want to sleep on this. I make better decisions when I'm rested.

"There isn't much history on the Dignity Vessels—at least that's specific," he says. "And your database has nothing on this one, no serial number listing, nothing. I wish you'd let us link up with an outside system."

"You want someone else to know where we are and what we're doing?" I ask.

He grins. "It'd be easier."

"And dumber."

He nods. I take a step forward and he catches my arm.

"I did check one other thing," he says.

I am tired. I want sleep more than I can say. "What?"

"I learned long ago that if you can't find something in history, you look in legends. There're truths there. You just have to dig more for them."

I wait. The sparkle in his eyes grows.

"There's an old spacers' story that has gotten repeated through various cultures for centuries as governments have come and gone. A spacers' story about a fleet of Dignity Vessels."

"Of course there was a fleet of them," I say. "Hundreds, if the old records are right."

He waves me off. "More than that. Some say the fleet's a thousand strong, some say it's a hundred strong. Some don't give a number. But all the legends talk about the vessels being on a mission to save the worlds beyond the stars, and how the ships moved from port to port, with parts cobbled together so that they could move beyond their design structures."

I'm awake again, just like he knew I would be. "There are a lot of these stories?"

"And they follow a trajectory—one that would work if you were, say, leading a fleet of ships out of your area of space."

"We're far away from the Old Earth area of space. We're so far away, humans from that period couldn't even imagine getting to where we are now."

"So we say. But think how many years this would take, how much work it would take."

"Dignity Vessels didn't have faster-than-light engines," I say.

"Maybe not at first." He's fairly bouncing from his discovery. I'm feeling a little more hopeful as well. "But consider this. They've traveled for a long time. What if one of the places they stopped had developed FTL? What if the engineers there helped them cobble that FTL into a Dignity Vessel?"

"You mean gave it to them?" I ask. No one in the worlds I know gives anyone anything.

"Or sold it to them. Can you imagine? One legend calls them a fleet of ships for hire, out to save worlds they've never seen."

"Sounds like a complete myth."

"Yeah," he says, "it's only a legend. But I think sometimes these legends become a little more concrete."

"Why?"

"We have an actual Dignity Vessel out there that got here somehow."

"Did you see evidence of cobbling?" I ask.

"How would I know?" he asks. "Have you checked the readouts? Do they give different dates for different parts of the ship?"

I haven't looked at the dating. I have no idea if it is different. But I don't say that.

"Download the exact specs for a Dignity Vessel," I say. "The materials, where everything should be, all of that."

"Didn't you do that before you came here?" he asks.

"Yes, but not in the detail of the ship's composition. Most people rebuild ships exactly as they were before they got damaged, so the shape would remain the same. Only the components would differ. I meant to check our readouts against what I'd brought, but I haven't yet. I've been diverted by the stealth tech thing, and now I'm going to get a little sleep. So you do it."

He grins. "Aye, aye, Captain."

"Boss," I mutter as I stagger down the corridor to my bed. "I can't tell you how much I prefer 'boss.'"

I sleep, but not long. My brain's too busy. I'm sure those specs are different, which confirms nothing. It just means that someone repaired the vessel at one point or another. But what if the materials are the kind that weren't available in the area of space around Earth when Dignity Vessels were built? That disproves Squishy's worry about the tech.

Doesn't it?

I'm at my hardwired terminal when Squishy comes to my door. I've gone through five or six layers of security to get to some very old data, data that isn't accessible from any other part of my ship's networked computer system.

Squishy waits. I'm hoping she'll leave, but of course she doesn't. After a few minutes, she coughs.

I sigh audibly. "We talked last night."

"I have one more thing to ask."

She steps inside, unbidden, and closes the door. My quarters feel claustrophobic with another person inside them. I'd always been alone here—always—even when I had a liaison with one of the crew. I'd go to his quarters, never bring him into my own.

The habits of privacy are long ingrained, and the habits of secrecy even longer. It's how I've protected my turf for so many years, and how I've managed to first-dive so many wrecks.

I dim the screen and turn to her. "Ask."

Her eyes are sunken into her face. She looks like she's gotten even less sleep than I have.

"I'm going to try one last time," she says. "Please blow the wreck up. Make it go away. Don't let anyone else inside. Forget it was here."

I fold my hands on my lap. Yesterday I hadn't had an answer for that request. Today I do. I'd thought about it off and on all night, just like I'd thought about the differing stories I'd heard from her and from Jypé, and how, I realized fifteen minutes before my alarm, neither of them had to be true.

"Please," she says.

"I'm not a scientist," I say, which should warn her right off, but of course it doesn't. Her gaze doesn't change. Nothing about her posture changes. "I've been thinking about this. If this stealth tech is as powerful as you claim, then we might be making things even worse. What if the explosion triggers the tech? What if we blow a hole between dimensions? Or maybe destroy something else, something we can't see?"

Her cheeks flush slightly.

"Or maybe the explosion'll double-back on us. I recall something about Dignity Vessels being unfightable, that anything that hit them rebounded to the other ship. What if that's part of the stealth tech?"

"It was a feature of the shields," she says with a bit of sarcasm. "They were unknown in that era."

"Still," I say. "You understand stealth tech more than I do, but you don't really *understand* it or you'd be able to replicate it, right?"

"I think there's a flaw in that argument—"

"But you don't really grasp it, right? So you don't know if blowing up the wreck will create a situation here, something worse than anything we've seen."

"I'm willing to risk it." Her voice is flat. So are her eyes. It's as if she's a person I don't know, a person I've never met before. And something in those eyes, something cold and terrified, tells me that if I had met her just this morning, I wouldn't want to know her.

"I like risks," I say. "I just don't like that one. It seems to me that the odds are against us."

"You and me, maybe," she says. "But there's a lot more to 'us' than just this little band of people. You let that wreck remain and you bring something dangerous back into our lives, our culture."

"I could leave it for someone else," I say. "But I really don't want to."

"You think I'm making this up. You think I'm worrying over nothing." She sounds bitter.

"No," I say. "But you already told me that the military is trying to recreate this thing, over and over again. You tell me that people die doing it. My research tells me these ships worked for hundreds of years, and I think maybe your methodology was flawed. Maybe getting the real stealth tech into the hands of people who can do something with it will *save* lives."

She stares at me, and I recognize the expression. It must have been the one I'd had when I looked at her just a few moments ago.

I'd always known that greed and morals and beliefs destroyed friendships. I also knew they influenced more dives than I cared to think about.

But I'd always tried to keep them out of my ship and out of my dives. That's why I pick my crews so carefully; why I call the ship *Nobody's Business*.

Somehow, I never expected Squishy to start the conflict.

Somehow, I never expected the conflict to be with me.

"No matter what I say, you're going to dive that wreck, aren't you?" she asks.

I nod.

Her sigh is as audible as mine was, and just as staged. She wants me to understand that her disapproval is deep, that she will hold me accountable if all the terrible things she imagines somehow come to pass.

We stare at each other in silence. It feels like we're having some kind of argument, an argument without words. I'm loath to break eye contact.

Finally, she's the one who looks away.

"You want me to stay," she says. "Fine. I'll stay. But I have some conditions of my own."

I expected that. In fact, I'd expected that earlier, when she'd first come to my quarters, not this prolonged discussion about destroying the wreck.

"Name them."

"I'm done diving," she says. "I'm not going near that thing, not even to save lives."

"All right."

"But I'll man the skip, if you let me bring some of my medical supplies."

So far, I see no problems. "All right."

"And if something goes wrong—and it will—I reserve the right to give my notes, both audio and digital, to any necessary authorities. I reserve the right to tell them what we found and how I warned you. I reserve the right to tell them that you're the one responsible for everything that happens."

"I *am* the one responsible," I say. "But the entire group has signed off on the hazards of wreck diving. Death is one of the risks."

A lopsided smile fills her face, but doesn't reach her eyes. The smile itself seems like sarcasm.

"Yeah," she says as if she's never heard me make that speech before. "I suppose it is."

EIGHT

I tell the others that Squishy has some concerns about the stealth tech and wants to operate as our medic instead of as a main diver. No one questions that. Such things happen on long dives—someone gets squeamish about the wreck; or terrified of the dark; or nearly dies and decides to give up wreck diving then and there.

We're a superstitious bunch when it gets down to it. We put on our gear in the same order each and every time; we all have one piece of equipment we shouldn't but we feel we need just to survive; and we like to think there's something watching over us, even if it's just a pile of luck and an ancient diving belt.

The upside of Squishy's decision is that I get to dive the wreck. I have a good pilot, although not a great one, manning the skip, and I know that she'll make sensible decisions. She'll never impulsively come in to save a team member. She's said so, and I know she means it.

The downside is that she's a better diver than I am. She'd find things I never would; she'd see things I'll never see; she'd avoid things I don't even know are dangerous.

Which is why, on my first dive to that wreck, I set myself up with Turtle, the most experienced member of the dive team after Squishy.

The skip ride over is tense: those two have gone beyond not talking, into painful and outspoken silence. I spend most of my time going over and over my equipment looking for flaws. Much as I want to dive this wreck—and I have since the first moment I saw her—I'm scared of the deep and the dark and the unknown. Those first few instances of weightlessness always catch me by surprise, always remind me that what I do is somehow unnatural.

Still, we get to our normal spot, I suit up, and somehow I make it through those first few minutes, zip along the tether with Turtle just a few meters ahead of me, and make my way to the hatch.

Turtle's gonna take care of the recording and the tracking for this trip. She knows the wreck is new to me. She's been inside once now, and so has Karl. Junior and Jypé had the dive before this one.

The one thing I don't like about this wreck is the effect it has on our communications. The skip doesn't have the power to send into the wreck, for reasons I don't entirely understand. We've tried boosting power through the skip's diagnostic, and even with the *Business*'s diagnostic, and we don't get anything.

If there's trouble when we're inside, the skip can't notify us. That didn't bother me as much when I piloted the skip, but the very idea bothers me now that I'm about to go inside.

It's clearly an issue of control for me. If I'm diving, I'm no longer in charge. But I tell no one about my personal worries, even though they know the communications problem. I simply try to set the worries aside.

I've assigned three corridors: one to Karl, one to J&J, and one to Turtle. Once we discover what's at the end of those babies, we'll take a few more. I'm a floater; I'll take the corridor of the person I dive with.

Descending into the hatch is trickier than it looks on the recordings. The edges are sharper; I have to be careful about where I put my hands.

Gravity isn't there to pull at me. I can hear my own breathing, harsh and insistent, and I wonder if I shouldn't have taken Squishy's advice: a ten/ten/ten split on my first dive instead of a twenty/twenty/twenty. It takes less time to reach the wreck now; we get inside in nine minutes flat. I would've had time to do a bit of acclimatizing and to have a productive dive the next time.

But I hadn't been thinking that clearly, obviously. I'd been more interested in our corridor, hoping it led to the control room, wherever that was.

Squishy had been thinking, though. Before I left, she tanked me up with one more emergency bottle. She remembered how on my first dives after a long layoff, I used too much oxygen.

She remembered that I sometimes panic.

I'm not panicked now, just excited. I have all my exterior suit lights on, trying to catch the various nooks and crannies of the hatch tube that leads into the ship.

Turtle's not far behind. Because I'm lit up like a tourist station, she's not using her boot lights. She's letting me set the pace, and I'm probably setting it a little too fast.

We reach the corridors in at 11:59. Turtle shows me our corridor at 12:03. We take off down the notched hallway at 12:06, and I'm giddy as a child on her first space walk.

Giddy we have to watch. Giddy can be the first sign of oxygen deprivation, followed by a healthy disregard for safety.

But I don't mention this giddy. I've had it since Squishy bowed off the teams, and the giddy's grown worse as my dive day got closer. I'm a little concerned—extreme emotion adds to the heavy breathing—but I'm going to trust my suit. I'm hoping it'll tell me if the oxygen's too low, the pressure's off, or the environmental controls are about to fail.

The corridor is human-sized and built for full gravity. But it seems bare. There are no obvious safety devices.

To me, that shows an astonishing trust in technology, one I've always read about but have never seen. No ship lacks emergency oxygen supplies spaced every ten meters or so, although this one does. No ship lacks communications equipment near each door, although this one does.

The past feels even farther away than I thought it would. I thought once I stepped inside the wreck—even though I couldn't smell the environment or hear what's going on around me—I'd get a sense of what it would be like to spend part of my career in this place.

But I have no sense. I'm in a dark, dreary hallway that lacks the emergency supplies I'm used to. Turtle's moving slower than my giddy self wants, although my cautious, experienced boss self knows that slow is best.

She's finding handholds, and signaling them for me, like we're climbing the outside of an alien vessel. We're working on an ancient system—the lead person touches a place, deems it safe, uses it to push off, and the rest of the team follows.

There aren't as many doors as I would have expected. A corridor, it seems to me, needs doors funneling off it, with the occasional side corridor bisecting it.

But there are no bisections, and every time I think we're in a tunnel not a corridor, a door does appear. The doors are regulation height, even now, but recessed farther than I'm used to.

Turtle tries each door. They're all jammed or locked. At the moment, we're just trying to map the wreck. We'll pry open the difficult places once the map is finished.

But I'd love to go inside one of those closed-off spaces, probably as much as she would.

Finally, she makes a small scratch on the side of the wall and nods at me.

The giddy fades. We're done. We go back now—my rule—and if you get back early so be it. I check my readout: 29:01. We have ten minutes to make it back to the hatch.

I almost argue for a few more minutes, even though I know better. Sure, it didn't take us as long to get here as it had in the past, but that doesn't mean the return trip is going to be easy. I've lost four divers over the years because they made the mistake I want to make now.

I let Turtle pass me. She goes back, using the same push-off points as before. As she does that, I realize she's marked them somehow, probably with something her suit can pick up. My equipment's not that sophisticated, but I'm glad hers is. We need that kind of expertise inside this wreck. It might take us weeks just to map the space, and we can expect each other to remember each and every safe touch spot because of it.

When we get back to the skip and I drop my helmet, Squishy glares at me.

"You had the gids," she says.

"Normal excitement," I say.

She shakes her head. "I see this coming back the next time, and you're grounded."

I nod, but know she can't ground me without my permission. It's my ship, my wreck, my job. I'll do what I want.

I take off the suit and indulge in some relaxation while Squishy pilots. We didn't get much, Turtle and I, just a few more meters of corridor mapped, but it feels like we discovered a whole new world.

Maybe that is the gids, I don't know. But I don't think so. I think it's just the reaction of an addict who returns to her addiction—an elation so great that she needs to do something with it besides acknowledge it.

And this wreck. This wreck has so many possibilities.

Only I can't discuss them on the skip, not with Squishy at the helm and Turtle across from me. Squishy hates this project, and Turtle's starting to. Her enthusiasm is waning, and I don't know if it's because of her personal war with Squishy or because Squishy has convinced her the wreck is even more dangerous than usual.

I stare out a portal, watching the wreck grow tinier and tinier in the distance. It's ironic. Even though I'm surrounded by tension, I finally feel content.

NINE

Half a dozen more dives, maybe sixty more meters, mostly corridor. One potential storage compartment, which we'd initially hoped was a stateroom or quarters, and a mechanic's corridor, filled with equipment we haven't even begun to catalogue.

I spend my off-hours analyzing the materials. So far, nothing conclusive. Lots of evidence of cobbling, but that's pretty common for any ship—with FTL or not—that's made it on a long journey.

What there's no evidence of are bodies. We haven't found one, and that's even more unusual. Sometimes there are skeletons floating—or pieces of them at least—and sometimes we get the full-blown corpse, suited and intact. A handful aren't suited. Those are the worst. They always make me grateful we can't smell the ship around us.

The lack of bodies is beginning to creep out Karl. He's even talked to me in private about skipping the next few dives.

I'm not sure what's best. If he skips them, his attitudes might become ingrained, and he might not dive again. If he goes, the fears might grow worse and paralyze him in the worst possible place.

I move him to the end of the rotation and warn Squishy she might have to suit up after all.

She just looks at me and grins. "Too many of the team quit on you, you'll just have to go home."

"I'll dive it myself, and you all can wait," I say, but it's bravado and we both know it.

That wreck isn't going to defeat me, not with the perfect treasure hidden in its bulk.

That's what's fueling my greed. The perfect treasure: *my* perfect treasure. Something that answers previously unasked historical questions—previously unknown historical questions; something that will reveal facts about our history, our humanity, that no one has suspected before; and something that, even though it does all that, is worth a small fortune.

I shake every time I think about it, and before each dive, I do feel the gids. Only now I report them to Squishy. I tell her that I'm a tad too excited, and she offers me a tranq that I always refuse. Never go into the unknown with senses dulled, that's my motto, even though I know countless people who do it.

We're on a long diving mission, longer than some of these folks have ever been on, and we're not even halfway through. We'll have gids and jitters and too many superstitions. We'll have fears and near emergencies, and God forbid, real emergencies as well.

We'll get through it, and we'll have our prize, and no one, not any one person, will be able to take that away from us.

Only I'm not sure we will get through it. Not after what happened this afternoon.

I'm captaining the skip. Squishy's back at the *Business*, taking a boss-ordered rest. I'm tired of her complaints and her constant negative attitude. At first, I thought she'd bring Turtle to her point of view, but Turtle finally got pissed and decided she'd enjoy this run.

I caught Squishy ragging on J&J, my strong links, asking them if they really want to be mining a death ship. They didn't listen to her, not really—although Jypé argued with her just a little—but that kind of talk can depress an entire mission, sabotage it in subtle little ways, ways that I don't even want to contemplate.

So I'm manning the skip alone, while J&J are running their dive, and I'm listening to the commentary, not looking at the grainy, nearly worthless images from the handheld. Mostly I'm thinking about Squishy and how to send her back without sending information too, and I can't come to any conclusions at all when I hear:

". . . yeah, it opens." Junior.

"Wow." Jypé.

"Jackpot, eh?" Junior again.

And then a long silence. Much too long for my tastes, not because I'm afraid for J&J, but because a long silence doesn't tell me one goddamn thing.

I punch up the digital readout, see we're at 25:33—plenty of time. They got to the new section faster than they ever have before.

The silence runs from 25:33 to 28:46, and I'm about to chew my fist off, wondering what they're doing. The handheld shows me grainy walls and more grainy walls. Or maybe it's just grainy nothing. I can't tell.

For the first time in weeks, I want another person in the skip with me just so that I have someone to talk to.

"Almost time," Jypé says.

"Dad, you gotta see this." Junior has a touch of breathlessness in his voice. Excitement—at least that's what I'm hoping.

And then there's more silence . . . thirty-five seconds of it, followed by a loud and emphatic "Fuck!"

I can't tell if that's an angry "fuck," a scared "fuck," or an awed "fuck." I can't tell much about it at all.

Now I'm literally chewing on my thumbnail, something I haven't done in years, and I'm watching the digital, which has crept past thirty-one minutes.

"Move your arm," Jypé says, and I know then that wasn't a good fuck at all.

Something happened.

Something bad.

"Just a little to the left," Jypé says again, his voice oddly calm. I'm wondering why Junior isn't answering him, hoping that the only reason is he's in a section where the communications relay isn't reaching the skip.

I can think of a thousand other reasons, none of them good, that Junior's communication equipment isn't working.

"We're five minutes past departure," Jypé says, and in that, I'm hearing the beginning of panic.

More silence.

I'm actually holding my breath. I look out a portal, see nothing except the wreck, looking like it always does. The handheld has been showing the same grainy image for a while now.

37:24

If they're not careful, they'll run out of air. Or worse.

I try to remember how much extra they took. I didn't really watch them suit up this time. I've seen their ritual so many times that I'm not sure what I think I saw is what I actually saw. I'm not sure what they have with them, and what they don't.

"Great," Jypé says, and I finally recognize his tone. It's controlled parental panic. Sound calm so that the kid doesn't know the situation is bad. "Keep going."

I'm holding my breath, even though I don't have to. I'm holding my breath and looking back and forth between the portal and the handheld image. All I see is the damn wreck and that same grainy image.

"We got it," Jypé says. "Now careful. Careful—son of a bitch! Move, move, move—ah, hell."

I stare at the wreck, even though I can't see inside it. My own breath sounds as ragged as it did inside the wreck. I glance at the digital:

44:11

They'll never get out in time. They'll never make it, and I can't go in for them. I'm not even sure where they are.

"C'mon." Jypé is whispering now. "C'mon, Son, just one more, c'mon, help me, c'mon."

The "help me" wasn't a request to a hearing person. It was a comment. And I suddenly know.

Junior's trapped. He's unconscious. His suit might even be ripped. It's over for Junior.

Jypé has to know it on some deep level.

Only he also has to know it on the surface, in order to get out.

I reach for my own communicator before I remember there's no talking to them inside the wreck.

"C'mon, Son." Jypé grunts. I don't like that sound.

The silence that follows lasts thirty seconds, but it seems like forever. I move away from the portal, stare at the digital, and watch the numbers change. They seem to change in slow motion:

45:24 to

. . . 25 to

. . . 2 . . . 6 . . .

to

. . . 2 . . . . 7 . . .

until I can't even see them change anymore.

Another grunt, and then a sob, half muffled, and another, followed by—

"Is there any way to send for help? Boss?"

I snap to when I hear my name. It's Jypé and I can't answer him.

I can't answer him, dammit.

I can call for help, and I do. Squishy tells me that the best thing I can do is get the survivor—her word, not mine, even though I know it's obvious too—back to the *Business* as quickly as possible.

"No sense passing midway, is there?" she asks, and I suppose she's right.

But I'm cursing her—after I get off the line—for not being here, for failing us, even though there's not much she can do, even if she's here, in the skip. We don't have a lot of equipment, medical equipment, back at the *Business*, and we have even less here, not that it matters, because most of the things that happen are survivable if you make it back to the skip.

Still, I suit up. I promise myself I'm not going to the wreck, I'm not going to help with Junior, but I can get Jypé along the guideline if he needs me too.

"Boss. Call for help. We need Squishy and some divers and oh, shit, I don't know."

His voice sounds too breathy. I glance at the digital.

56:24.

Where has the time gone? I thought he was moving quicker than that. I thought I was too.

But it takes me a while to suit up, and I talked to Squishy, and everything is fucked up.

What'll they say when we get back? The mission's already filled with superstitions and fears of weird technology that none of us really understand.

And only me and Jypé are obsessed with this thing.

Me and Jypé.

Probably just me now.

"I left him some oxygen. I dunno if it's enough. . . ."

So breathy. Has Jypé left all his extra? What's happening to Junior? If he's unconscious, he won't use as much, and if his suit is fucked, then he won't need any.

"Coming through the hatch . . ."

I see Jypé, a tiny shape on top of the wreck. And he's moving slowly, much too slowly for a man trying to save his own life.

My rules are clear: let him make his own way back.

But I've never been able to watch someone else die.

I send to the *Business*: "Jypé's out. I'm heading down the line."

I don't use the word help on purpose, but anyone listening knows what I'm doing. They'll probably never listen to me again, but what the hell.

I don't want to lose two on my watch.

When I reach him six minutes later, he's pulling himself along the guideline, hand over hand, so slowly that he barely seems human. A red light flashes at the base of his helmet—the out-of-oxygen light, dammit. He did use all of his extra for his son.

I grab one small container, hook it to the side of his suit, and press the "on" only halfway, knowing too much is as bad as too little.

His look isn't grateful: it's startled. He's so far gone, he hasn't even realized that I'm here.

I brought a grappler as well, a technology I always said was more dangerous than helpful, and here's the first test of my theory. I wrap Jypé against me, tell him to relax, I got him, and we'll be just fine.

He doesn't. Even though I pry him from the line, his hands still move, one over the other, trying to pull himself forward.

Instead, I yank us toward the skip, moving as fast as I've ever moved. According to my suit, I'm burning oxygen at three times my usual rate and I don't really care. I want him inside, I want him safe, I want him *alive*, goddammit.

I pull open the door to the skip. I unhook him in the airlock, and he falls to the floor like an empty suit. I make sure the back door is sealed, open the main door, and drag Jypé inside.

His skin is a grayish blue. Capillaries have burst in his eyes. I wonder what else has burst, what else has gone wrong.

There's blood around his mouth.

I yank off the helmet, his suit protesting my every move.

"I gotta tell you," he says. "I gotta tell you."

I nod. I'm doing triage, just like I've been taught, just like I've done half a dozen times before.

"Set up something," he says. "Record."

So I do, mostly to shut him up. I don't want him wasting more energy. I'm wasting enough for both of us, trying to save him, and cursing Squishy for not getting here, cursing everyone for leaving me on the skip, alone, with a man who can't live, and somehow has to.

"He's in the cockpit," Jypé says.

I nod. He's talking about Junior, but I really don't want to hear it. Junior is the least of my worries.

"Wedged under some cabinet. Looks like—battlefield in there."

That catches me. Battlefield how? Because there are bodies? Or because it's a mess?

I don't ask. I want him to wait, to save his strength, to *survive*.

"You gotta get him out. He's only got an hour's worth, maybe less. Get him out."

Wedged beneath something, stuck against a wall, trapped in the belly of the wreck. Yeah, like I'll get him out. Like it's worth it.

All those sharp edges.

If his suit's not punctured now, it will be by the time I'm done getting the stuff off him. Things have to be piled pretty high to get them stuck in zero-g.

I'll wager the *Business* that Junior's not stuck, not in the literal, gravitational sense. His suit's hung up on an edge. He's losing—he's lost—environment and oxygen, and he's probably been dead longer than his father's been on the skip.

"Get him out." Jypé's voice is so hoarse it sounds like a whisper.

I look at his face. More blood.

"I'll get him," I say just to calm him.

Jypé smiles. Or tries to. And then he closes his eyes, and I fight the urge to slam my fist against his chest.

"I'll get him," I say again, and this time, it's a promise, not a lie.

A promise to a man who can no longer hear me.

A man who is already dead.

TEN

Squishy declared him dead the moment she arrived on the skip. Not that it was hard. He'd already sunken in on himself, and the blood—it isn't something I want to think about.

She flew us back. Turtle was in the other skip, and she never came in, just flew back on her own.

I stayed on the floor, expecting Jypé to rise up and curse me for not going back to the wreck, for not trying, even though we all knew—even he probably had known—that Junior was dead.

When we got back to the *Business*, Squishy took Jypé's body to her little medical suite. She's going to make sure he died from suit failure or lack of oxygen or something that keeps the regulators away from us.

Who knows what the hell he actually died of. Panic? Fear? Stupidity? Maybe that's what I'm doomed for. Hell, I let a man dive with his son, even though I'd ordered all of my teams to abandon a downed man.

Who can abandon his own kid anyway?

And who listens to me?

Not even me.

My quarters seem too small, the *Business* seems too big, and I don't want to go anywhere because everyone'll look at me with an I-told-you-so followed by a let's-hang-it-up.

And I don't really blame them. Death's the hardest part. It's what we flirt with in deep dives.

We claim that flirting is partly love.

I close my eyes and lean back on my bunk, but all I see are digital readouts. Seconds moving so slowly they seem like days. The spaces between time. If only we can capture that—the space between moments.

If only.

I shake my head, wondering how I can pretend I have no regrets.

When I come out of my quarters, Turtle and Karl are already watching the vids from Jypé's suit. They're sitting in the lounge, their faces serious.

As I step inside, Turtle says, "They found the heart."

It takes me a minute to understand her, then I remember what Jypé said. They were in the cockpit, the heart, the place we might find the stealth tech.

He was stuck there. Like the probe?

I shudder in spite of myself.

"Is the event on the vid?" I ask.

"Haven't got that far." Turtle shuts off the screens. "Squishy's gone."

"Gone?" I shake my head just a little. Words aren't processing well. I'm having a reaction. I recognize it: I've had it before when I've lost crew.

"She took the second skip, and left. We didn't even notice until I went to find her." Turtle sighs. "She's gone."

"Jypé too?" I ask.

She nods.

I close my eyes. The mission ends, then. Squishy'll go to the authorities and report us. She's going to tell them about the wreck and the accident and Junior's death. She's going to show them Jypé, whom I haven't reported yet because I didn't want anyone to find our position, and the authorities'll come here—whatever authorities have jurisdiction over this area—and confiscate the wreck.

At best, we'll get a slap, and I'll have a citation on my record.

At worst, I—maybe we—will face charges for some form of reckless homicide.

"We can leave," Karl says.

I shake my head. "She'll report the *Business*. They'll know who to look for."

"If you sell the ship—"

"And what?" I ask. "Not buy another? That'll keep us ahead of them for a while, but not long enough. And when we get caught, we get nailed for the full count, whatever it is, because we acted guilty and ran."

"So maybe she won't say anything," Karl says, but he doesn't sound hopeful.

"If she was going do that, she would have left Jypé," I say.

Turtle closes her eyes and rests her head on the seat back. "I don't know her anymore."

"I think maybe we never did," I say.

"I never used to think she got scared," Turtle says. "I yelled at her—I told her to get over it, that diving's the thing. And she said it's not the thing. Surviving's the thing. She never used to be like that."

I think of the woman sitting on her bunk staring at her opaque wall—a wall you think you can see through, but you really can't—and wonder. Maybe she always used to be like that. Maybe surviving was always her thing. Maybe diving was how she proved she was alive, until the past caught up with her all over again.

The stealth tech.

She thinks it killed Junior.

I nod toward the screen. "Let's see it," I say to Karl.

He gives me a tight glance, almost—but not quite—expressionless. He's trying to rein himself in, but his fears are getting the best of him.

I'm amazed mine haven't gotten the best of me.

He starts it up. The voices of men so recently dead, just passing information—"Push off here." "Watch the edge there."—makes Turtle open her eyes.

I lean against the wall, arms crossed. The conversation is familiar to me. I heard it just a few hours ago, and I'd been too preoccupied to give it much attention, thinking of my own problems, thinking of the future of this mission, which I thought was going to go on for months.

Amazing how much your perspective changes in the space of a few minutes.

The corridors look the same. It takes a lot so that I don't lose focus—I've been in that wreck, watched similar vids, and in those I haven't learned much. But I resist the urge to tell Karl to speed it up—there can be something, some wrong movement, some piece of the wreck that attaches to one of my guys—my former guys—before they even get to the heart.

But I don't see anything like that, and since Turtle and Karl are quiet, I assume they don't see anything like that either.

Then J&J find the heart. They say something, real casual—which I'd missed the first time—a simple "shit, man" in a tone of such awe that if I'd been paying attention, I would've known.

I bite back the emotion. If I took responsibility for each lost life, I would never dive again. Of course, I might not after this anyway. One of the many options the authorities have is to take my pilot's license away.

The vids don't show the cockpit ahead. They show the same old grainy walls, the same old dark and shadowed corridor. It's not until Jypé turns his suit vid toward the front that the pit's even visible, and then it's a black mass filled with lighter squares, covering the screen.

"What the hell's that?" Karl asks. I'm not even sure he knows he's spoken.

Turtle leans forward and shakes her head. "Never seen anything like it."

Me either. As Jypé gets closer, the images become clearer. It looks like every piece of furniture in the place has become dislodged, and has shifted to one part of the cockpit.

Were the designers so confident of their artificial gravity that they didn't bolt down the permanent pieces? Could any ship's designers be that stupid?

Jypé's vid doesn't show me the floor, so I can't see if these pieces have been ripped free. If they have, then that place is a minefield for a diver, more sharp edges than smooth ones.

My arms tighten in their cross, my fingers forming fists. I feel a tension I don't want—as if I can save both men by speaking out now.

"You got this before Squishy took off, right?" I ask Turtle.

She understands what I'm asking. She gives me a disapproving sideways look. "I took the vids before she even had the suit off."

Technically, that's what I want to hear, and yet it's not what I want to hear. I want something to be tampered with, something to be slightly off, because then, maybe then, Jypé might still be alive.

"Look," Karl says, nodding toward the screen.

I have to force myself to see it. The eyes don't want to focus. I know what happens next—or at least, how it ends up. I don't need the visual confirmation.

Yet I do. The vid can save us, if the authorities come back. Turtle, Karl, even Squishy can testify to my rules. And my rules state that an obviously dangerous site should be avoided. Probes get to map places like this first.

Only I know J&J didn't send in a probe. They might not have because we lost the other probe so easily, but most likely, it was that greed, the same one that has been affecting me. The tantalizing idea that somehow, this wreck, with its ancient secrets, is the dive of a lifetime.

And the hell of it is, beneath the fear and the panic and the anger—more at myself than at Squishy for breaking our pact—this wreck is the discovery of a lifetime.

I'm thinking, if we can just get the stealth tech before the authorities arrive, it'll all be worth it. We'll have a chip, something to bargain with.

Something to sell to save our own skins.

Junior goes in. His father doesn't tell him not to. Junior's blurry on the vid—a human form in an environmental suit, darker than the pile of things in the center of the room, but grayer than the black around them.

And it's Junior who says, "It's open," and Junior who mutters, "Wow," and Junior who says, "Jackpot, huh?" when I thought all of that had been a dialogue between them.

He points at a hole in the pile, then heads toward it, but his father moves forward quickly, grabbing his arm. They don't talk—apparently that was the way they worked, such an understanding they didn't need to say much, which makes my heart twist—and together they head around the pile.

The cockpit shifts. It has large screens that appear to be unretractable. They're off, big blank canvases against dark walls. No windows in the cockpit at all, which is another one of those technologically arrogant things—what happens if the screen technology fails?

The pile is truly in the middle of the room, a big lump of things. Why Jypé called it a battlefield, I don't know. Because of the pile? Because everything is ripped up and moved around?

My arms get even tighter, my fists clenched so hard my knuckles hurt.

On the vid, Junior breaks away from his father and moves toward the front (if you can call it that) of the pile. He's looking at what the pile's attached to.

He mimes removing pieces, and the cameras shake. Apparently Jypé is shaking his head.

Yet Junior reaches in there anyway. He examines each piece before he touches it, then pushes at it, which seems to move the entire pile. He moves in closer, the pile beside him, something I can't see on his other side. He's floating, headfirst, exactly like we're not supposed to go into one of these spaces—he'd have trouble backing out if there's a problem—

And of course there is.

Was.

"Ah, hell," I whisper.

Karl nods. Turtle puts her head in her hands.

On screen nothing moves.

Nothing at all.

Seconds go by, maybe a minute—I forgot to look at the digital readout from earlier, so I don't exactly know—and then, finally, Jypé moves forward.

He reaches Junior's side, but doesn't touch him. Instead the cameras peer in, so I'm thinking maybe Jypé does too.

And then the dialogue begins.

I've only heard it once, but I have it memorized.

Almost time.

Dad, you've gotta see this.

Jypé's suit shows us something—a wave? a blackness? a table?—something barely visible just beyond Junior. Junior reaches for it, and then—

Fuck!

The word sounds distorted here. I don't remember it being distorted, but I do remember being unable to understand the emotion behind it. Was that from the distortion? Or my lack of attention?

Jypé has forgotten to use his cameras. He's moved so close to the objects in the pile that all we can see now are rounded corners and broken metal (apparently these did break off then) and sharp, sharp edges.

Move your arm.

But I see no corresponding movement. The visuals remain the same, just like they did when I was watching from the skip.

Just a little to the left.

And then:

We're five minutes past departure.

That was panic. I had missed it the first time, but the panic began right there. Right at that moment.

Karl covers his mouth.

On screen, Jypé turns slightly. His hands grasp boots, and I'm assuming he's tugging.

Great. But I see nothing to feel great about. Nothing has moved. *Keep going.*

Going where? Nothing is changing. Jypé can see that, can't he?

The hands seem to tighten their grip on the boots, or maybe I'm imagining that because that's what my hands would do.

We got it.

Is that a slight movement? I step away from the wall, move closer to the vid, as if I can actually help.

Now careful.

This is almost worse because I know what's coming, I know Junior doesn't get out, Jypé doesn't survive. I know—

Careful—son of a bitch!

The hands slid off the boot, only to grasp back on. And there's desperation in that movement, and lack of caution, no checking for edges nearby, no standard rescue procedures.

Move, move, move—ah, hell.

This time, the hands stay. And tug—clearly tug—sliding off.

C'mon.

Sliding again.

C'mon, Son.

Again.

Just one more.

And again.

C'mon, help me, c'mon.

Until, finally, in despair, the hands fall off. The feet are motionless, and, to my untrained eye, appear to be in the same position they were in before.

Now Jypé's breathing dominates the sound—which I don't remember at all—maybe that kind of hiss doesn't make it through our patchwork system—and then vid whirls. He's reaching, grabbing, trying to pull things off the pile, and there's no pulling, everything goes back like it's magnetized.

He staggers backward—all except his hand, which seems attached—sharp edges? No, his suit wasn't compromised—and then, at the last moment, eases away.

Away, backing away, the visuals are still of those boots sticking out of that pile, and I squint, and I wonder—am I seeing other boots? Ones that are less familiar?—and finally he's bumping against walls, losing track of himself.

He turns, moves away, coming for help even though he has to know I won't help (although I did) and panicked—so clearly panicked. He gets to the end of the corridor, and I wave my hand.

"Turn it off." I know how this plays out. I don't need any more.

None of us do. Besides, I'm the only one watching. Turtle still has her face in her hands, and Karl's eyes are squinched shut, as if he can keep out the horrible experience just by blocking the images.

I grab the controls and shut the damn thing off myself.

Then I slide onto the floor and bow my head. Squishy was right, dammit. She was so right. This ship has stealth tech. It's the only thing still working, that one faint energy signature that attracted me in the first place, and it has killed Junior.

And Jypé.

And if I'd gone in, it would've killed me.

No wonder she left. No wonder she ran. This is some kind of flashback for her, something she feels we can never ever win.

And I'm beginning to think she's right, when a thought flits across my brain.

I frown, flick the screen back on, and search for Jypé's map. He had the system on automatic, so the map goes clear to the cockpit.

I superimpose that map on the exterior, accounting for movement, accounting for change—

And there it is, clear as anything.

The probe, our stuck probe, is pressing against whatever's near Junior's faceplate.

I'm worried about what'll happen if the stealth tech is open to space, and it always has been—at least since I stumbled on the wreck.

Open to space and open for the taking.

Karl's watching me. "What're you gonna do?"

Only that doesn't sound like his voice. It's the greed. It's the greed talking, that emotion I so blithely assumed I didn't have.

Everyone can be snared, just in different ways.

"I don't know what to do," I say. "I have no idea at all."

I go back to my room, sit on the bed, stare at the portal, which mercifully doesn't show the distant wreck.

I'm out of ideas, out of energy, and out of time.

Squishy and the calvary'll be here soon to take the wreck from me, confiscate it, and send it into governmental oblivion.

And then my career is over. No more dives, no more space travel.

No more nothing.

I think I doze once because suddenly I'm staring at Junior's face inside his helmet. His eyes move, ever so slowly, and I realize—in the space of a heartbeat—that he's alive in there: his body's in our dimension, his head on the way to another.

And I know, as plainly as I know that he's alive, that he'll suffer a long and hideous death if I don't help him, so I grab one of the sharp edges—with my bare hands (such an obvious dream)—and slice the side of his suit.

Saving him.

Damning him.

Condemning him to an even uglier slow death than the one he would otherwise experience.

I jerk awake, nearly hitting my head on the wall. My breath is coming in short gasps. What if the dream is true? What if he is still alive? No one understands interdimensional travel, so he could be, but even if he is, I can do nothing.

Absolutely nothing, without condemning myself.

If I go in and try to free him, I will get caught as surely as he is. So will anyone else.

I close my eyes, but don't lean back to my pillow. I don't want to fall asleep again. I don't want to dream again, not with these thoughts on my mind. The nightmares I'd have, all because stealth tech exists, are terrifying, worse than any I'd had—

And then my breath catches. I open my eyes, rub the sleep from them, think:

This is a Dignity Vessel. Dignity Vessels have stealth tech, unless they've been stripped of them. Squishy described stealth tech to me—and this vessel, this *wreck*, has an original version.

Stealth tech has value.

Real value, unlike any wreck I've found before.

I can stake a claim. The time to worry about pirates and privacy is long gone, now.

I get out of bed, pace around the small room. Staking a claim is so foreign to wreck divers. We keep our favorite wrecks hidden, our best dives secret from pirates and wreck divers and the Empire.

But I'm not going to dive this wreck. I'm not going in again—none of my people are—and so it doesn't matter that the entire universe knows what I have here.

Except that other divers will come, gold diggers will try to rob me of my claim—and I can collect fees from anyone willing to mine this, anyone willing to risk losing their life in a long and hideous way.

Or I can salvage the wreck and sell it. The Empire buys salvage.

If I file a claim, I'm not vulnerable to citations, not even to reckless homicide charges, because everyone knows that mining exacts a price. It doesn't matter what kind of claim you mine, you could still lose some, or all, of your crew.

But best of all, if I stake a claim on that wreck, I can quarantine it—and prosecute anyone who violates the quarantine. I can stop people from getting near the stealth tech if I so choose.

Or I can demand that whoever tries to retrieve it, retrieve Junior's body.

His face rises, unbidden, not the boy I'd known, but the boy I'd dreamed of, half alive, waiting to die.

I know there are horrible deaths in space. I know that wreck divers suffer some of the worst.

I carry these images with me, and now, it seems, I'll carry Junior's.

Is that why Jypé made me promise to go in? Had he had the same vision of his son?

I sit down at the network and call up the claim form. It's so simple. The key is giving up accurate coordinates. The system'll do a quick double check to see if anyone else has filed a claim, and if so, an automatic arbitrator will ask if I care to withdraw. If I do not, then the entire thing will go to the nearest court.

My hands itch. This is so contrary to my training.

I start to file—and then stop.

I close my eyes—and he's there again, barely moving, but alive.

If I do this, Junior will haunt me until the end of my life. If I do this, I'll always wonder.

Wreck divers take silly, unnecessary risks, by definition.

The only thing that's stopping me from taking this one is Squishy and her urge for caution.

Wreck divers flirt with death.

I stand. It's time for a rendezvous.

ELEVEN

Turtle won't go into the Dignity Vessel. She wants to quit, even though she won't admit it. I've never seen her so agitated. She paces through the *Business* like we've caged her inside.

Even though she won't talk to us, it's clear that she's stressed, terrified, and blinded by Squishy's betrayal.

Turtle, my best diver, would be useless on a dive right now. She's not clearheaded enough, and I worry that her extreme emotional swings would make her reckless.

Fortunately, Karl has no qualms about diving the Dignity Vessel. His fears left with Jypé's body. Apparently Karl knew something awful would happen, and when it finally did, it calmed him.

I appreciate the calm. I'm stressed too and stunned by Squishy's departure. I guess I never knew her, which is odd, since I once thought I knew her very well.

Mostly, though, I'm worried, worried that I'm breaking my promise to Jypé, worried that I've left one of my divers to a slow death on an empty ship.

So it's Karl I go to, Karl I ask to partner with me on a dive in the Dignity Vessel. I tell him I want to see what happened in there for myself.

He actually smiles when he hears that.

"Thought you weren't going to come around," he says.

But I have.

Turtle doesn't protest this mission. In fact, she too thinks it's the right thing to do.

Some of her agitation fades. Apparently she thought that I agreed with Squishy and was afraid that I'd be abandoning Junior forever.

I almost did.

Turtle asks to man the skip. We need her, Karl and I, and we both think she's calm enough to handle any emergency that comes up.

Karl and I are going in, knowing we have good backup. Knowing that we're doing all we can.

We've decided on thirty/forty/thirty, because we're going to investigate that cockpit. Karl theorizes that there's some kind of off switch for the stealth tech, and of course he's right. But the off switch would have to be on the tech itself, wherever that is, since the wreck has no real power.

The designers had too much faith in their technology to build redundant safety systems—I'm assuming they had too much faith to design a secondary off switch for their most dangerous technology, a dead-man's switch that'll allow the stealth tech to go off even if the wreck has no power.

I mention that to Karl and he gives me a startled look.

"You ever wonder what's keeping the stealth tech on, then?" he asks.

I've wondered, but I have no answer. Maybe when Squishy comes back with the Empire ships, I'll be able to ask her. What my nonscientific mind is wondering is this: Can the stealth tech operate from both dimensions? Is something on the other side powering it?

Is part of the wreck—that hole we found in the hull on the first day, maybe—still in that other dimension?

Karl and I suit up, take extra oxygen, and double-check our suits' environmental controls. I'm not giddy this trip—I'm not sure I'll be giddy again—but I'm not scared either.

Just coldly determined.

I promised Jypé I was going back for Junior, and now I am.

No matter what the risk.

The trip across is simple, quick, and familiar. Going down the entrance no longer seems like an adventure. We hit the corridors with fifteen minutes to spare.

Jypé's map is accurate to the millimeter. His push-off points are marked on the map and with some corresponding glove grips. We make record time as we head toward that cockpit.

Record time, though, is still slow. I find myself wishing for all my senses: sound, smell, taste. I want to know if the effects of the stealth tech have made it out here, if something is off in the air—a bit of an acrid odor, something foreign that raises the small hairs on the back of my neck. I want to know if Junior is already decomposing, if he's part of a group (the crew?) pushed up against the stealth tech, never to go free again.

But the wreck doesn't cough up those kind of details. This corridor looks the same as the other corridor I pulled my way through.

Karl moves as quickly as I do, although his suit lights are on so full that looking at him almost blinds me. That's what I did to Turtle on our trip, and it's a sign of nervousness.

It doesn't surprise me that Karl, who claimed not to be afraid, is worried.

He's the one who had doubts about this trip once he'd been inside the wreck. He's the one I thought wouldn't make it through all of his scheduled dives.

The cockpit looms in front of us, the doors stuck open. It does look like a battlefield from this vantage: the broken furniture, the destruction all cobbled together on one side of the room, like a barricade.

The odd part about it is, though, that the barricade runs from floor to ceiling, and unlike most things in zero-g, seems stuck in place.

Neither Karl nor I give the barricade much time. We've vowed to explore the rest of the cockpit first, looking for the elusive dead-man switch. We have to be careful; the sharp edges are everywhere.

Before we left, we used the visuals from Jypé's suit, and his half-finished map, to assign each other areas of the cockpit to explore. I'm going deep, mostly because this is my idea, and deep—we both feel—is the most dangerous place. It's closest to the probe, closest to that corner of the cockpit where Junior still hangs, horizontal, his boots kicking out into the open.

As I float into the cockpit, I hear a faint hum. The sound is familiar, something I've heard before. It's tantalizing, like a song whose tune is just out of reach—a hint of a remembered melody.

A shiver runs down my spine. The triggered memory is just out of reach as well, and something tells me I don't want to think about it now.

I need all my concentration to focus on the search for the dead-man switch.

I go in the center, heading toward the back, not using handholds. I've pushed off the wall, so I have some momentum, a technique that isn't really my strong suit. But I volunteered for this, knowing the edges in the front would slow me down, knowing that the walls would raise my fears to an almost incalculable height.

Instead, I float over the middle of the room, see the uprooted metal of chairs and the ripped shreds of consoles. There are actual wires protruding from the middle of that mess, wires and stripped bolts—something I haven't seen in space before, only in old colonies—and my stomach churns as I move forward.

The back wall is dark, with its distended screen. The cockpit feels like a cave instead of the hub of the Dignity Vessel. I wonder how so many people could have trusted their lives to this place.

Just before I reach the wall, I spin so that I hit it with the soles of my boots. The soles have the toughest material on my suit. The wall is mostly smooth, but there are a few edges here, too—more stripped bolts, a few twisted metal pieces that I have no idea what they once were part of.

This entire place feels useless and dead.

It takes all of my strength not to look at the barricade, not to search for the bottoms of Junior's boots, not to go there first. But I force myself to shine a spot on the wall before me, then on the floor, and the ceiling, looking for something—anything—that might control part of this vessel.

But whatever they had, whatever machinery there'd been, whatever computerized equipment, is either gone or part of that barricade. My work in the back is over quickly, although I take an extra few minutes to record it all, just in case the camera sees something I don't.

It takes Karl a bit longer. He has to pick his way through a tiny debris field. He's closer to a possible site: there's still a console or two stuck to his near wall. He examines them, runs his suit-cam over them as well, but shakes his head.

Even before he tells me he's found nothing, I know.

I know.

I join him at a two-pronged handhold, where his wall and mine meet. The handhold was actually designed for this space, the first such design I've seen on the entire Dignity Vessel.

Maybe the engineers felt that only the cockpit crew had to survive uninjured should the artificial gravity go off. More likely, the lack of grab bars was simply an oversight in the other areas, or a cost-saving measure.

"You see a way into that barricade?" Karl asks.

"We're not going in," I say. "We're going to satisfy my curiosity first."

He knows about the dream; I told him when we were suiting up. I have no idea if Turtle heard—if she did, then she knows too. I don't know how she feels about the superstitious part of this mission, but I know that Karl understands.

"I think we should work off a tether," he says. "We can hook up to this handhold. That way, if one of us gets stuck—"

I shake my head. There might be other bodies in that barricade, and if there are, I would wager that some of them have tethers and bits of equipment attached.

If the stealth tech is as powerful as I think it is, then these people had no safeguard against it. A handhold won't defend us either, even though, I believe, the stealth tech is running at a small percentage of capacity.

"I'm going first," I say. "You wait. If I get pulled in, you go back. You and Turtle get out."

We've discussed this drill. They don't like it. They believe leaving me behind will give them two ghosts instead of one.

Maybe so, but at least they'll still be alive to experience those ghosts.

I push off the handhold, softer this time than I did from the corridor, and let the drift take me to the barricade. I turn the front suit-cams on high. I also use zoom on all but a few of them. I want to see as much as I can through that barricade.

My suit lights are also on full. I must look like a child's floaty toy heading in for a landing.

I stop near the spot where Junior went in. His boots are there, floating, like expected. I back as far from him as I can, hoping to catch a reflection in his visor, but I get nothing.

I have to move to the initial spot, that hole in the barricade that Junior initially wanted to go through.

I'm more afraid of that than I am of the rest of the wreck, but I do it. I grasp a spot marked on Jypé's map, and pull myself toward that hole.

Then I train the zoom inside, but I don't need it.

I see the side of Junior's face, illuminated by my lights. The helmet is what tells me that it's him. I recognize the modern design, the little logos he glued to its side.

His helmet has bumped against the only intact console in the entire place. His face is pointed downward, the helmet on clear. And through it, I see something I don't expect: the opposite of my fears.

He isn't alive. He hasn't been alive in a long, long time.

As I said, no one understands interdimensional travel, but we suspect it manipulates time. And what I see in front of me makes me realize my hypothesis is wrong.

Time sped up for him. Sped to such a rate that he isn't even recognizable. He's been mummified for so long that the skin looks petrified, and I bet, if we were to somehow free him and take him back to the *Business*, that none of our normal medical tools could cut through the surface of his face.

There are no currents and eddies here, nothing to pull me forward. Still, I scurry back to what I consider a safe spot, not wanting to experience the same fate as the youngest member of our team.

"What is it?" Karl asks me.

"He's gone," I say. "No sense cutting him loose."

Even though cutting isn't the right term. We'd have to free him from that stealth tech, and I'm not getting near it. No matter how rich it could make me, no matter how many questions it answers, I no longer want anything to do with it.

I'm done—with this dive, this wreck—and with my brief encounter with greed.

TWELVE

We do have answers, though, and visuals to present to the Empire's ships when they arrive. There are ten of them—a convoy—unwilling to trust something as precious as stealth tech to a single ship.

Squishy didn't come back with them. I don't know why I thought she would. She dropped off Jypé, reported us and the wreck, and vanished into Longbow Station, not even willing to collect a finder's fee that the Empire gives whenever it locates unusual technologies.

Squishy's gone, and I doubt she'll ever come back.

Turtle's not speaking to me now, except to say that she's relieved we're not being charged with anything. Our vids showed the Empire we cared enough to go back for our team member, and also that we had no idea about the stealth tech until we saw it function.

We hadn't gone into the site to raid it, just to explore it—as the earlier vids showed. Which confirmed my claim—I'm a wreck diver, not a pirate, not a scavenger—and that allowed me to pick up the reward that Squishy abandoned.

The reward is embarrassingly large. I've never seen that much money all at once.

Normally, though, I would have left it. I don't like making money that way.

But I couldn't leave it this time. I needed to fund the expedition, and I'm not going to be able to do it the way I'd initially planned—by taking tourists to the Dignity Vessel so far from home.

The Empire chased us away from the vessel. They're talking about moving it to some storehouse or warehouse or way station, but I'm not sure how they're going to do it.

I don't think they dare move it, not with the stealth tech still functioning. I think they'll lose some divers and some equipment, just like the rest of us have.

But I didn't tell them that. I didn't get a chance to tell them much of anything. All I could do was defend myself and my crew, accept the ticket for the lost claim and the hollow thanks of the agent in charge of that convoy.

As we left that group of ten ships, we couldn't even see the Dignity Vessel they surrounded. Turtle now agrees with Squishy; she thinks we should have blown the vessel up.

Karl is just glad that it's no longer part of our lives.

But it'll always be a part of mine.

I think about it constantly, speculating. Worrying.

Wishing I had more answers to all the questions the Vessel raised.

Like this one: That vessel had been in service a while—that much was clear from how it had been refitted. When someone activated the stealth, something went wrong. What happened to the crew then? Did they abandon the vessel or die in it? Did they try to shut the stealth tech off or did they run from it?

Were they running tests with minimal crew, or had the real crew looked at that carnage in the cockpit and decided, like we did, that it wasn't worth the risk to go in? Was this a repair mission gone wrong?

I never looked for escape pods, but such things existed on Dignity Vessels—at least they do in the specs. Maybe the rest of the crew bailed, got rescued, and blended into cultures somewhere far from home.

Maybe that's where Jypé's legends come from.

Or so I like to believe.

I'll never know.

Just like I'll never know how the vessel got to the place I found it. There's no way to tell if it traveled in stealth mode over those thousands of years, although that doesn't explain how the ship avoided gravity wells and other perils that lie in wait in a cold and difficult universe. Or maybe it had been installed with an updated FTL.

I was never able to examine it well enough to figure that out, and what images I got from the cockpit raised more questions than they answered.

The entire ship raises more questions than it answers.

And I can't shake it.

But I have to, and I pretend that I have as we pull into Longbow Station.

The station has never seemed so much like home. It'll be nice to shed the silent Karl, and Turtle, who claims her diving days are behind her.

My diving days are behind me too, only in not quite the same way. The *Business* and I'll still ferry tourists to various wrecks, promising scary dives and providing none.

But I've had enough of undiscovered wrecks and danger for no real reason. Curiosity sent me all over this part of space, looking for hidden pockets, places where no one has been in a long time.

Now that I've found the ultimate hidden pocket—and I've seen what it can do—I'm not looking anymore. I'm hanging up my suit and reclaiming my land legs.

Less danger there, on land, in normal gravity. Not that I'm afraid of wrecks now. I'm not, no more than the average spacer.

I'm more afraid of that feeling, the greed, which came on me hard and fast, and made me tone-deaf to my best diver's concerns, my old friend's fears, and my own giddy response to the deep.

I'm getting out before I turn pirate or scavenger, before my greed—which I thought I didn't have—draws me as inexorably as the stealth tech drew Junior, pulling me in and holding me in place, before I even realize I'm in trouble.

Before I even know how impossible it'll be to escape.

This isn't the life I imagined for myself, but as I look around the station, I realize none of us live the life we imagined. For some of us, life is better than anything our imaginations could conjure.

For others, it's worse.

I've lived an adventurous life.

I'm getting too old to continue on that path.

At least, that's what I'm telling myself right now.

And I suspect I'll tell myself that for a long, long time to come.

PART TWO

THE ROOM OF LOST SOULS

THIRTEEN

She's land-born. I don't need to see her thick body with its heavy bones to know that. Her walk says it all.

I am sitting in the old spacers' bar in Longbow Station. Sometimes I think I live here. Ever since the Dignity Vessel, I have made Longbow my permanent residence.

I sold my possessions and my apartment on Hector Prime. I have no more secrets to keep. I no longer wreck dive.

I take tourists to famous wrecks and pretend we're having an adventure.

Sometimes even that pretense is too much for me.

So I tilt my chair back and watch the woman weave her way through the tables. The other spacers watch too. They're wondering the same thing that I am: Who is she coming to see? What is she doing here, with her land-heavy legs and her know-it-all expression?

She so clearly does not belong.

The space-born have a grace—a lightness—to everything they do. This woman has a way of putting one foot in front of the other as if she expects the floor to take her weight. I used to walk like that.

We have the same build, she and I—that thickness that comes from strong bones, the fully formed female body that comes from the good nutrition usually found planetside.

She sits down at my table. The other spacers look away, as if they expected it all along.

But I didn't, and neither did they. They're watching out of the corners of their eyes, making sure she really came for me.

Making sure she does no harm.

She says my name as if she's entitled to. She has come for me, then, and somehow she knew where to find me.

"How'd you get in here?" I pull my drink across the scarred plastic table and lean my chair against the wall. Balancing chairs feels like that second after the gravity gets shut off but hasn't yet vanished—a half-and-half feeling of being both weighted and weightless.

"I have an invitation," she says and holds up the cheap St. Christopher's medal that houses this week's guest chip. Station management shifts the chip housing every week or two so the chips can't be scalped or manufactured. After five guest chips are given out, management changes housing. There is no predictable time, nor is there predictable housing.

"I didn't invite you," I say, picking up my drink and balancing its edge on my flat stomach. I can't quite get the balance right, and I catch the drink before it spills.

"I know," the woman says, "but I needed to see you."

"If you want to hire my ship to do some wreck diving, go through channels. Send a message, my system'll scan your background, and if you pass, you can see any one of a dozen wrecks that're open to amateurs."

"I'm not interested in diving," the woman says.

"Then you have no reason to talk to me." I take a drink. The liquid, which is a fake but tasty honey-and-butter ale, has warmed during the long afternoon. The warmth brings out the ale's flavor, which is why I nurse it—or at least why I say I nurse it. I don't like to get drunk—I hate the loss of control—but I like drinking and I like to sit in this dark, private, enclosed bar and watch people I know, people who won't give me any guff.

"But I do have a reason to talk to you." She leans toward me. She has pale green eyes surrounded by dark lashes. The eyes make her seem even more exotic than her land-born walk does. "You see, I hear you're the best—"

My snort interrupts her. "There is no best. There's a half a dozen companies that'll take you touring wrecks—and that's without diving. All of us are certified. All of us are bonded and licensed, and all of us guarantee the best touring experience in this sector. It just varies in degree—do you want the illusion of danger or do you want a little bit of history with your deep-space adventure? I don't know who sent you in here—"

She starts to answer, but I raise a finger, stopping her.

"—and I don't care. I do want you to contact someone else for a tour. This is my private time, and I hate having it interrupted."

"I'm sorry," she says, and the apology sounds sincere.

I expect her to get up and leave the bar or maybe move to another table, but she does neither.

Instead she leans closer and lowers her voice.

"I'm not a tourist," she says. "I have a mission, and I'm told you're the only one who can help me."

In the two years since the Dignity Vessel, no one has tried this old con on me. In the twenty years before, I'd get one or two of these approaches a year, mostly from rivals wanting coordinates to the wrecks I refused to salvage.

I've always believed that certain wrecks have historical value only when they're intact—not a popular belief among salvagers and scavengers and most wreck divers—but one that I've adhered to since I started in this business at the ripe old age of eighteen.

I point to Karl. He too has made Longbow his home. But we haven't spoken in two years. We nod at each other when we pass in the corridors, although mostly we avoid each other's eyes.

We try not think about that last dive, about Junior's legs sticking out of that barricade, about Jypé's body collapsing in on itself, about Squishy's betrayal.

Or maybe it's just me who tries not to think about it.

I do know that we've never discussed it, and we probably never will.

"Karl's good," I say to the woman. "In fact, if you want real adventure, not the touristy kind, he's the best. He'll take you to deep space, no questions asked."

"I want you," the woman says.

I sigh. Maybe she does. Maybe she's been led astray by some old-timer. Maybe she thinks I still have some valuable coordinates locked in my ship.

I don't. I dumped pretty much everything the day I decided I would only do tourist runs.

"Please," she says. "Just let me tell you what's going on."

I sigh. She's not going to leave without telling me. Unless I force her. And I'm not going to force her because it would take too much effort.

I take another swig of my ale.

She folds her hands together, but not before I see that her fingers are shaking.

"I'm Riya Trekov, the daughter of Commander Ewing Trekov. Have you heard of him?"

I shake my head. I haven't heard of most people. Among the living, I only care about divers, pilots, and scavengers. Among the dead, I know only the ones whose wrecks would have once made my diving worthwhile. I also knew the ones who had piloted the wrecks I found, as well as the people who sent them, and the politicians, leaders, or famous people of their time, their place, their past.

But modern commanders, people whose names I should recognize? I am always at a loss.

"He was the supreme commander for the Enterran Empire in the Colonnade Wars."

Her voice is soft, and it needs to be. The Colonnade Wars aren't popular out here. Most of the spacers sitting in this bar are the children or grandchildren of the losers.

"That was a hundred years ago," I say.

"So you do know the wars." Her shoulders rise up and down in a small sigh. She apparently expected to tell me about them.

"You're awfully young to be the daughter of a supreme commander from those days." I purposely don't say the wars' name. It's better not to rile up the other patrons.

She nods. "I'm a post-loss baby."

It takes me a minute to understand her. At first I thought she meant post-loss of the Colonnade Wars, but then I realize that anyone titled supreme commander in that war had been on the winning side. So she meant loss of something else.

"He's missing?" I ask before I can stop myself.

"He has been for my entire life," she says.

"Was he missing before you were born?"

She takes a deep breath, as if she's considering whether or not she should tell me. Her caution piques my curiosity. For the first time, I'm interested in what she's saying.

"For fifty years," she says quietly.

"Fifty *standard* years?" I ask.

She nods.

I decide not to be delicate. "So you're what? You can't be an afterthought, not after fifty years. You're bottle grown?"

"Implanted," she says. "My parents froze embryos. It was common in wartime."

"But fifty years," I say.

She shrugs, clearly not willing to tell me any more about her own creation.

So, if I'm guessing her age right, and if she's not lying, then her father went missing before the peace treaties were signed.

"Did your father go missing in action?" I ask.

She shakes her head.

"A prisoner of war?" Our side—well, the side that populates this part of space, which is only mine by default—didn't give the prisoners back even though that was one of the terms of the treaty.

"That's what we thought," she says.

The "we" is new. I wonder if it means she and her family or she and someone else.

"But?" I ask.

"But I put detectives on the trail years ago, and there's no evidence he was ever captured. No evidence that he met with anyone from the other side," she says with surprising diplomacy. "No evidence that his ship was captured. No evidence that he vanished during the last conflicts of the war, like the official biographies say."

"No real evidence?" I ask. "Or just no evidence that can be found after all this time?"

"No real evidence," she says. "We've looked in the official records and the unofficial ones. I've interviewed some of his crew."

"From the missing vessel," I say.

"That's just it," she says. "His ship isn't missing."

So I frown. She has no reason to approach me. Even in my old capacity, I didn't search for missing humans. I searched for famous ships.

"Then I don't understand," I say.

"We know where he is," she says. "I want to hire you to get him back."

"I don't find people," I say, mostly because I don't want to tell her that he's probably not still alive.

No human lives more than 120 years without enhancements. No human who has spent a lot of time in space can survive an implantation of those enhancements.

"I'm not asking you to," she says. "I'm hoping you'll recover him."

"Recover?" She's got my full attention now. "Where is he?"

The tip of her tongue touches her top lip. She's nervous. It's clear she isn't sure she should tell me, even though she wants to hire me.

Finally, she says, "He's in the Room of Lost Souls."

Ask anyone and they'll tell you: The Room of Lost Souls is a myth.

I've only heard it talked about in whispers. An abandoned space station, far from here, far from anything. Most crews avoid it. Those that do stay do so only in an emergency, and even then they don't go deep inside.

Because people who go into the room at the center of the station—what would be, in modern space stations, the control room but which clearly isn't—those people never come out.

Sometimes you can see them, floating around the station or pounding at the windows, crying for help.

Their companions always mount rescue attempts, always lose one or two more people before giving up, and hoping—praying—that what they're seeing isn't real.

Then they make repairs or do whatever it is they needed to do when they arrive, and fly off, filled with guilt, filled with remorse, filled with sadness, happy to be the ones who survived.

I've heard that story, told in whispers, since I got to Longbow Station decades ago, and I've never commented. I've never even rolled my eyes or shaken my head.

I understand the need for superstition.

Sometimes its rituals and talismans give us a necessary illusion of safety.

And sometimes it protects us from places that are truly dangerous.

Like the Room of Lost Souls.

"Why in the known universe would I go there to help you?" I ask, with a little too much edge in my voice.

She studies me. I think I have surprised her. She expected me to tell her that the Room of Lost Souls is a myth, that someone had lied to her, that she is staking her quest on something that has never existed.

"You know it, then." She doesn't sound surprised. Somehow she knows that I've been there. Somehow she knows that I am one of the only people to come out of the Room alive.

I don't answer her question. Instead, I drain my ale and stand. I'm sad to leave the old spacers' bar this early in the day, but I'm going to.

I'm going to leave and walk around the station until I find another bar as grimy as this one.

Then I'm going to go inside, and I am, mostly likely, going to get drunk. Because she mentioned the Room, I'll have my nightmare tonight. I'll have the nightmare for the next week, maybe more, and I'll curse her.

But mostly, I'll curse the Room of Lost Souls.

"You should help me," she says softly, "because I know what the Room is."

I start to get up, but she grabs my arm.

"And I know," she says, "how to get people out."

FOURTEEN

How to get people out.

The words echo in my head as I walk out of the bar. I stop in that barren corridor and place one hand against the wall, afraid I'm going to be sick.

Voices swirl in my head, and I will them away.

Then I take a deep breath and continue on, heading into the less habitable parts of the station, the parts slated for renovation or closure.

I want to be by myself.

I need to.

And I don't want to return to my berth, which suddenly seems too small, or my ship, which suddenly seems too risky.

Instead I walk across ruined floors and through half-gutted walls, past closed businesses and graffiti-covered doorways. It's colder down here—life support is on, but at the minimum provided by regulation—and I almost feel like I'm heading into a wreck, the way I used to head into a wreck when I was a beginner, without thought and without care.

What I remember of the Room and what I dream about it are different. If I actually try to remember the Room, I get only a few sensations. In the dream—the nightmare—I'm in the middle of it, feeling it, but not really seeing it.

What do I remember? Not much. I remember thinking it looked pretty. Colored lights—pale blues and reds and yellows—extended as far as the eye could see. They twinkled. Around them, only blackness.

My mother held my hand. Her grip was tight through the double layer of our spacesuit gloves. She muttered how beautiful the lights were.

Before the voices started.

Before they built, piling one on top of the other, until—it seemed—we got crushed by the weight.

I don't remember getting out.

I remember my father, cradling me, trying to stop my shaking. I remember him giving orders to someone else to steer the damn ship, get us out of this godforsaken place.

I remember my mother's eyes through her headpiece, reflecting the multicolored lights, as if she had swallowed a sea of stars.

And I remember her voice, blending with the others, like a soprano joining tenors in the middle of a cantata—a surprise, and yet completely expected.

For years, I heard her voice—strong at first and unusual in its power, then blending, and mixing, until I couldn't pick it out any longer.

I didn't know if that voice—mixing with other voices—was an aural hallucination, a dream, or a reality. Sometimes I thought it both.

But it sneaks up on me at the most unexpected moments, sometimes beginning with just a hum. The hum sends shivers down my back, and I do whatever I can to silence the voices.

Which is usually nothing.

Nothing except wait.

After three days, Riya Trekov finds me.

I'm having dinner in Longbow's most exclusive restaurant. The food is exquisite—fresh meat from nearby ports, vegetables grown on the station itself, sauces prepared by the best chef in the sector. There's fresh bread and creamy desserts and real fruit, a rarity no matter what spaceport you dock on.

The view is exquisite as well—windows everywhere except the floor. If you look up, you see the rest of the station towering above you, lights in some of the guest rooms, decoration in some of the berths. If you look out one set of side windows, you see the docks with the myriad of ships—from tiny single ships to armored yachts to passenger liners.

Another group of windows show the gardens with their own airlocks and bays, the grow lights sending soft rays across the entire middle of the station.

On this night, I'm having squid in dark chocolate sauce. The squid isn't what Earthers think of as squid, but an ocean-faring creature from one of the nearby planets. It has a salty nutlike taste that the chocolate accents.

I try to focus on the food as Riya sits down. She's carrying a plate and a full glass of wine.

Clearly she had been eating somewhere else in the restaurant, on one of the layers I can't see from my favorite table. But she had seen me come in, and somehow, she thinks that gives her permission to join me.

"Have you thought about it?" she asks, as if she made an offer and I said I would consider it.

I can lie and say I hadn't thought about any of it. I can be blunt and say that I want nothing to do with the Room of Lost Souls.

Or I can be truthful and say that her words have played through my head for the last three days. Tempting me. Frightening me.

Intriguing me.

At odd moments, I find myself wondering how I would view the place, after all my years of wreck diving, after all the times I've risked my life, after all the hazards I've survived.

"You have," she says with something like triumph.

Of course I thought of it. I dreamed of it. Only the dream has changed. I force myself awake as my mother's voice blends with the other voices.

I continue to eat, but I'm no longer savoring the taste. I almost push my plate away—it's a crime not to taste this squid—but I don't.

I don't want Riya Trekov to see any emotion from me at all.

"You have questions," she says as if I'm actually taking part in this conversation. "You want to know how I found you."

The hell of it is that I do want to know that. Hardly anyone knows I survived the Room of Lost Souls. I can't say that no one knows because the crew on my father's ship knew. And I have no idea what happened to all of them.

"I have people who can find almost anything," she says.

People. She has people. Which means she's rich.

"If you have people," I say with an emphasis on that phrase, "then have them go to the Room themselves and have them 'recover' your father."

Her cheeks flush. She looks away, but only for a minute. Then she takes a deep breath, as if she needs courage to dive back into this conversation.

"They don't believe that anyone can get out. They think that's as much a myth as the Room itself."

I don't know how I got out. My memory is fluid, and try as I might to recover that moment, I can't.

When it becomes clear that I am not going to confirm or deny what happened to me, she says, "Your father is still alive."

I jolt. I had no idea the old man had made it this long.

"Have you ever asked him about the Room?"

I haven't, mostly because I never had the chance. But I don't tell her that. Instead, I say, "You spoke to my father."

She nods. "He's happy to know you're still alive."

I'm not sure I'm happy to know that he is. I prefer to think of myself as a person without a family, a woman without a past.

"Quite honestly," she says, "he's the one who recommended you for this job. I first approached him, and he says he's too old."

I slide my plate to the edge of the table to hide my face as I do the calculations. He turns seventy this year, which is not old at all.

"He also said you have all the skills I need for this job." She hasn't touched her food. "He says he doesn't."

That much is true. He's never gone diving—at least that I know of. He captained a ship, but in the old-fashioned way—not as a hands-on pilot, but as a planet-bound owner who told others what to do.

We were on some kind of pleasure cruise, I think, when my mother and I wandered into the Room. Or maybe we were moving from one system to another.

I honestly don't know. I don't remember and I never asked him.

He wasn't around much anyway. After Mother vanished into that Room, he dumped me with my maternal grandparents and went in search of the very thing Riya claims she found: a way to recover people from the Room of Lost Souls.

"It makes no sense that he has refused to help you," I say as a bus tray arrives, sends out a small metal arm that sweeps my plate into its interior, and then floats away. "He's always wanted a way into the Room."

"He says the problem is not the way in, but the way out." She finally picks up her fork and picks at her now-cold food.

A chill runs through me. Does my father speak with that kind of authority because he has sent people in after my mother? Or because he's thinking of what happened to us all those years ago?

"And yet you claim you have that way out."

A serving tray appears with an ice cream glass filled with red and black berries separated by layers of cream. My coffee steams beside it. My standing order. I shouldn't take it, but I do.

"I do have a way out," she says.

"But you can't find anyone stupid enough to test it," I say.

She lets out a small laugh. "Is that what you think? You think I need a test subject?"

I take a sip of my coffee. It's slightly bitter, like all coffee on Longbow station. Somehow the beans grown here lack the richness I've found on other stations.

"The way out has been tested. Going in and returning is no longer an issue. What I need is someone with enough acumen to bring out my father."

Something in her tone reaches me. It's a hint of frustration, a bit of anger. Her people have failed her. Which is why she's coming to me.

"You've done this before," I say.

She nods. "Six times. Everyone survived. Everyone is healthy. There are no residual problems."

"Except they can't find your father."

"Oh," she says. "They have found him. They just can't recover him."

Now I am intrigued. "Why not?"

"Because," she says, "they can't convince him to leave."

I take a bite of the berries and cream. I need a few moments to think about this. I still feel as if she's conning me, but I'm not sure how. Or why she would do so.

"Why did he leave?" I ask.

She blinks at me in surprise. She clearly didn't expect curiosity from me. "Leave?"

"You said he didn't show up for the treaty signings. That he essentially missed the end of the war. Why?"

She frowns just enough so that I realize she's never considered this question. She's been looking at her father as someone—some*thing*—she lost, not as a person in his own right. Oh, he has history, but it's history without her, and therefore not relevant.

"No one knows," she says.

Someone always knows. And if that someone is no longer alive, the answer would probably be in the records. Something this modern is easy to trace; it's the old stuff whose history gets lost to time, like the Dignity Vessels, that can be difficult to figure out.

She's finally hooked me, and she probably doesn't even know how. I don't want to return to the Room for my mother—I barely remember her, and what I do remember is vague. I don't even want to return to face my own past.

I want to solve this mystery Riya Trekov has unwittingly presented me with. I want to know why a famous man, a man who won some of the most important battles of an important war, disappears before the war ends and winds up in a place he knew better than to approach.

For the first time in years, the historian in me, the *diver* in me, senses a challenge. Not like the old challenges, the ones that cost me so many friends and colleagues.

But a new challenge, one that will threaten me alone.

One that has the risk I miss combined with the historical mysteries that I love.

I try not to let my sudden enthusiasm show. I ask, as coldly as I can, "What are you paying?"

Her eyes light up. She seems surprised. Maybe she thought she'd never catch me. Maybe I am her last hope.

She names a figure. It's astoundingly high.

Still, I say, "Triple it and I'll consider the job."

"If you can get him out," she says, her voice breathless with excitement, "I'll give you one hundred times that much."

Now I'm feeling breathless. That's more money than I've earned in two decades.

But I don't have a use for the money I have. I can't imagine what I'd do with a sum that large.

Still, I negotiate because that too is in my blood. "I want it all up front."

"Half," she says. "And half when you recover him."

That's fair. Half would provide me a berth at Longbow and all of my expenses for the rest of my life. I'd never have to touch the rest of my money, the stuff I earned these past few years.

"Half up front," I say, agreeing, "and half when I recover him—only if you pay all expenses for the entire investigation and journey."

"Investigation?" She frowns, as if she doesn't like the word.

I nod. "Before I go after him, I need to know who he is."

"I told you—"

"I need to know *him*, not his reputation."

Her frown grows. "Why?"

"Because," I say, "in all the hundreds of theories about that Room, only one addresses the souls trapped inside."

"So?"

"So haven't you wondered how a man like your father got lost in there?"

I can tell from her expression that she hasn't considered that at all.

"Or why the name of the place—in all known languages—is the Room of Lost Souls? Are the souls lost because they entered? Or were they lost before they opened the door?"

She shifts slightly in her chair. She doesn't like what I'm saying.

"You've thought of this before," she says.

"Of course I have." I keep my voice down.

She nods. "You think he was lost before he went in?"

"I have no idea," I say, "but I plan to find out."

FIFTEEN

By the time I arrive at my berth, the money is in my accounts. That surprises me. I thought, after our conversation, that Riya would back out. She doesn't want to know her father as a human being. She wants only the image of him that she built up through her lonely childhood. The war hero who vanished. The strong man who got trapped.

Not a sad survivor who might have gotten lost long before he opened a door into a forbidden place.

Still, she has paid me and she has given me free rein.

I sit at the built-in desk and move the money to all of my accounts. I'm going to have to create some new ones before I leave so that my holdings are diversified. Before I do that, I pay for this berth for the next five years.

I warned Riya that the recovery could take a long time. She wants it done right. After I heard her tales of the previous attempts, I knew that part of the problem was that she hired thieves and ruffians and risk takers who specialized in cross-system possession recovery.

She hired disposable people who usually committed snatch-and-grabs. People who didn't care much for her mission or their own lives.

People who wouldn't be missed.

In that, they were a lot like me.

Riya and I finished the negotiations as I drank my coffee. She showed me the device her people had used to get out of the Room. I examined it. It looked unusual enough.

But she wouldn't give me its specs until I was ready to go to the Room.

I was fine with that. It gave both of us an illusion of control: me, the ability to say I was done before I went into the Room; and her, the belief that I had no idea how to use what she had shown me.

We made a verbal record of our negotiations. Both of our attorneys would work together to make a formal agreement that we would sign within the month.

She seemed nervous and uncertain, while I was nervous and happy. If someone had asked me before we started the negotiations who would feel what, I would have said that I'd be the uncertain one while she would be happy with all that we'd done.

I fully expected her to terminate before I arrived in my berth.

Instead she paid me.

I finish transferring the money. I contact and pay my attorney, notifying her of her obligations in drafting this agreement.

Then I lean back in my chair.

For the first time since I've come to Longbow Station, balancing my chair on two legs does not satisfy me. The berth—with its built-in desk, view of the grow pods, and slide-out soft bed—no longer feels like home.

I need to move. I need to get out of here.

I need to spend the night on my ship.

By modern standards, *Nobody's Business* is a small ship, but by mine, it's huge. The *Business* can fly with a single pilot, but it's designed for twenty to fifty people.

When I was wreck diving, I'd fly with ten or fewer, and to me, that felt crowded. I'd close off the lower levels and lock up the cargo bays.

Sometimes I forget all the space I'm not using. The main level has the bridge and auxiliary controls. It also has the lounge, where I've put most of my viewing technology so that I can review dives. There are six cabins on this level as well, including mine.

The captain's cabin is two levels up. I never use it. My cabin is the same size as all the others. It looks the same, as well, except for the hardwired terminal that I use when I don't want anyone hacking into my work.

Most (but not all) of the other systems on the *Business* are networked, and I'm up-front with any crew that I hire that I watch the systems diligently. If they put something on the system, from a virus to a piece of information, it's mine. I've learned a lot that way.

The *Business* is docked in the permanent section of the station. I pay extra to keep her systems disconnected from the station's systems. I also bribe the officials to keep an eye on her, to make sure no one enters illegally.

Even so, I still run several security programs—all of them redundant. No one, not even the best hacker, can shut off all of them and still have time to case my ship.

As I enter the *Business*, I stand in the airlock and check the first layer of security, seeing who—if anyone—has crossed this threshold since I last went through.

According to the programs, no one has.

I let myself in, breathing the stale air. I keep the environmental systems on low when I'm station bound—no sense wasting the energy. I power up, check more redundant security systems, and run a full diagnostic that I network to my own internal computer.

Long ago, I set up the *Business* and my single ship to communicate with me—mostly to make sure I remain awake and alert when I'm piloting either ship. But I also use the links to communicate with the *Business* about internal matters, mostly so that I'm not tied to the bridge.

The air has become cool as the environmental systems kick in. My cabin still smells faintly of incense from an abortive and mistaken attempt at relaxation on the last trip full of tourists. I make a mental note to have this room cleaned top to bottom, and then I sit at the hardwired terminal.

It's covered with a faint layer of dust. I haven't touched it in more than a year. I'm not even sure it'll power up.

But it does. Then it runs its own diagnostics and shows me all the security video from the cabin itself. I let the video play in a corner of the touch screen while I access my financials.

I move 90 percent of the money that Riya paid me from my public accounts to my private ones. In a day or so, I'd create some new accounts, and divide the money up even more.

Then I settle into my chair and order lunch from my personal store.

I'm going to be here for a while. I have a lot of research to do, and I don't want it traced.

I start with the Colonnade Wars.

I learned long ago to research everything, especially something you're certain of, because the memory plays tricks. And something you're certain of is most likely to be the thing you'll get wrong.

The Colonnade Wars lasted nearly one hundred years. The wars began as a series of skirmishes on the far end of this sector. Then actual war broke out toward the other end, on a small planet that had been colonized for so long that some believed the humans on that planet actually evolved there.

Other battles—with different participants—started throughout the sector.

At first, the weapons brokers and the mercenaries seemed to be the only ones who knew about the various skirmishes, but then it became clear that powerbrokers from several nation-states were financing their favorites in each conflict. And sometimes those powerbrokers backed both factions at the same time.

The battle turned away from the petty internal squabbles—over land, over entitlements, over religious shrines—and turned against those who funded the fights.

Suddenly the powerful found themselves fighting on several fronts. Their massive armies and huge weapon systems were no match to the smaller, more creative warfare of their enemies.

And it looked, for a long time, as if the massive armies would break.

Enter Commander Ewing Trekov and his cohorts. All of them had been injured on one front or another. Most of them had come within a heartbeat of dying.

They ended up at the same treatment facility in the very center of the sector, and there they realized they had the same philosophy about the wars.

First, they believed that the Colonnade Wars were not wars at all, but a single war—a large, scattered battlefield that spread across several systems. These men and women, brilliant all, realized that fighting each front as if it were a separate war was what was destroying the army. A military could have no coherent strategy when it believed it was fighting a dozen wars at once.

So these people, as they healed, began studying the history of warfare—not just in this sector, but throughout human history, as far back as they could go. They discussed superweapons and super troops. They discussed a unified front and a robotized military. They explored remote fighting versus hands-on.

And they realized that nothing—no discovery, no miracle weapon, no well-equipped soldier—had ever taken the place of living commanders with a broad and unified vision.

And sometimes that vision was as simple as this: *Annihilate the enemy wherever you find him; whoever he might be.*

According to the histories, the man who first articulated that simple vision in the Colonnade Wars was Commander Ewing Trekov. Whether or not that's true is another matter.

What is true—and verifiable—is that Commander Trekov was the most effective leader of the war. He destroyed more enemy strongholds, captured more ships, and killed more soldiers—from all sides—than any other commander in the war.

He was supposed to be at the victory celebration. More important, he was supposed to be at the treaty-signing ceremony. There wasn't just one treaty to be signed, but dozens—all with various governments (or, as one observer more accurately called them, various survivors). Trekov's presence wasn't just symbolic. He had negotiated several of the treaties himself.

Slowly I realize that I could spend the rest of my life reading about the Colonnade Wars and not get to all the details.

But those details don't concern me. All that concerns me is Commander Trekov.

And he's there but not there. Mentioned but not quoted. Observed but not really seen.

So I look up Trekov himself—when he was born, where he went to school, where he got his training. I look for family information—both on his family of origin and on the family he left behind.

I find Riya Trekov. She's significantly younger than I thought—born to Trekov's childless fifth wife nearly two decades after his disappearance. The other children want nothing to do with Riya—they believe her to be illegitimate, even though her DNA, her provenance (so to speak), is probably surer than theirs.

She has an easily accessible history—with degrees in accounting and business, a long career in high finance, and a personal wealth that's almost legendary. She accumulated those funds on her own and is known around the sector as one of the most intuitive investors around.

Now she's invested in me—the first whim I could find in her entire history—and I wonder if this investment will pay off.

It's certainly turning into a research nightmare on my end.

Because the backstory on Ewing Trekov is confusing. His origins seem lost in time. His education is classified, as is most of his military experience. His battles are well documented, but that's about the only part of his life that is.

In the official histories, Trekov's personal history is deliberately vague. Which makes me wonder what's hidden there, and why no one is supposed to know.

For a while, I pace around the main level, trying to figure out how to discover the man and not the myth. And then I realize I'm researching him wrong.

I need to approach him as if he were a ship, a wreck I'm trying to discover.

I need to go backward—from the last known sighting—and then I need to dig in the unofficial records, the half-hidden reports, and the highlights of his personal past.

Within forty-eight hours, my ship is stocked, my meager belongings on board, and I am heading to a little-known military outpost at what once was the edge of the sector.

The last recorded place anyone saw Ewing Trekov alive.

SIXTEEN

By all rights, this little outpost should be famous. It is not only the last place Ewing Trekov was seen alive, but it is also the place where he and the other commanders planned their strategy.

Military outposts are security minded. They make places like Longbow Station seem lawless. So I've come with letters of introduction from a general whom I supervised on tourist dives, a colonel who has known me since I began my career, and an imperial official who testified to the fact that my research is never for public purposes, only to find important "historical information."

I also have a letter of explanation from Riya Trekov, giving me permission to look into her family's confidential files. I have no idea if such a letter will open doors for me—I have never researched a human subject before—but I figure such a letter can't hurt.

This outpost is top-of-the-line. The materials in the public areas are new and smell faintly of recently assembled metal. The lighting is set brighter than any I've seen in a commercial outpost, and the environmental systems are running at maximum comfort.

My tax dollars keep these soldiers in relative luxury, at least for spacefarers. Most off-duty personnel walk around in shirtsleeves and thin pants. Anyone on Longbow wearing such flimsy clothing would freeze.

I am given a bracelet that opens doors to the sections of the outpost that I'm allowed in. I've been given a guest suite—they don't call civilian quarters "berths" here—and with the suite comes the suggestion that I use it instead of staying shipside.

The suite is larger than the captain's cabins on most luxury yachts. It doesn't take me long to find out that I'm in one of the VIP rooms, courtesy, it seems, of my ties with the general. His letter, which I scan after I look at my quarters, asks that the military treat me like one of their own.

Apparently they take that to mean they should treat me like they would treat him.

My rooms—and I have five of them—all have a view of the concentric rings, as well as a private kitchen (along with a personal chef should I not want cafeteria food), a valet should I require it, and a daily cleaning service. I don't require a valet or room cleaning service (although I know they won't waive that entirely), and I stress to everyone how much I value my privacy.

My in-room computer system can access the public library of the base, and I start there, sitting on one of the most comfortable chairs I've ever used in my life and scrolling through list upon list of recorded information pertaining to Commander Trekov himself.

It takes me nearly three days, but I finally find visual and audio files of his arrival on the base. No holographic files, at least not yet. But the visual and audio ones are the first I've found of the commander at all.

He's imposing, nearly six-seven, which is tall for someone who spent his life in ships. His walk marks him as planet-raised as well, as do his thick bones and well-defined muscles.

He's not a handsome man, although he might have been once. His face is care-lined and his eyes are sad. His hair is cut short—regulation then as now—and he has a fastidiousness that seems extreme even in this military environment.

I freeze one of the images of his face and frame it. Then I set it, as a holopicture, on the tabletop near my workstation. I used to do this with ships that I was searching for. Ships that had disappeared or whose wrecks existed somewhere in a grid that no one had bothered searching for decades.

The images of the ships were always of them new. I used to compare that image with the wreck when I found it, not to find my way around it but so that I could get a sense of what hopes were lost in the ship's ultimate destruction.

But the image I keep of Ewing Trekov isn't of his youth, but of what he looked like toward the end. It's an acknowledgement that I'm searching for the part of him that's left over, the skeleton, the frame, the bits and pieces that survived.

I am no closer to getting him out of that Room by staring at his image than I got close to a wreck by staring at the original image of a ship. But I feel closer. I feel like this image holds something important, something I'm missing.

Or maybe, something I'm not yet allowed to see.

There are actually people on the outpost who remember Ewing Trekov. They're old now, but most of them still work in their respective departments.

All of them are willing to talk with me, and after days of interviews, only one seems to have a story that I can't find in the records.

Her name is Nola Batinet. She wants to meet in the officers' mess.

The mess isn't a dining hall, like the mess for regular soldiers. The officers' mess is divided into six different restaurants, each with its own entrance off the central bar. People in uniform fill that bar. They all have an air of authority.

A tiny woman stands near a real potted plant. The plant is taller than I am, probably taller than Trekov was. It's bright green, has broad leaves, and smells strongly of mint.

The woman is so small she could hide among the leaves. She seems too tiny to have worked as a doctor, particularly one with as many accolades as she has.

As I approach, she holds out a hand, which I take gently in greeting. The bones are as fragile as I feared. I'm careful not to squeeze at all, afraid I'll break her.

"We have a reservation in Number Four," she says.

Apparently the six restaurants here have no names. They go by number.

Number Four is dark and smells of garlic. There are no tables, just built-in booths with backs so high you can't see the other diners.

A serving unit—a simple holographic menu with audio capabilities—whisks us to the nearest seat. At first, I figure that the unit does so with each customer. Then I realize it's addressing Nola Batinet by name and has reassured her that they never let her favorite booth go when there's the possibility that she will come into the mess.

She thanks it as if it were human, nods when it asks if she wants the usual, and then she turns to me. I haven't even looked over the menu yet, but I'm not really here for the food. I take whatever it is she's having, order some coffee and some water, and wait until the server unit floats away.

"So," she says, "Ewing Trekov. I knew him well."

A faint smile crosses her face as she thinks of him. Her memories—at least the one she's lost in—are clearly pleasant.

A tray floats over with our beverages and with a large plate of cheeses and meats. I've never seen so many different kinds. The meats are clearly manufactured and are composed of so many different colors that I'm hesitant at first.

But Nola has been eating here for decades and seems no worse for it. After she eats a few pieces, I try one. The meat is peppery and filled with the garlic that I've been smelling. It's remarkably good.

"You're working for his daughter, right?" Nola asks. "The created one."

"She wants me to recover her father," I say, even though I'd told Nola this when I first contacted her through the outpost networks. "She thinks he's in the Room of Lost Souls."

Nola nods just enough to confuse me. That tiny movement could mean she knows he's in the Room or that she has heard of this daughter's whim before. Or it could simply be an acknowledgment of what I have to say.

"Why does she want him?" Nola asks. "She never knew him."

And I had neglected to ask that question. Or maybe it wasn't neglect at all. If I knew, I wouldn't have taken the job, and the job had—in the end—intrigued me.

"It's not my concern," I say. "I'm just supposed to find him."

"You won't find him," Nola says. "He's long gone."

"How did you know him?" I ask, trying to get the conversation away from my job and back to her.

That small smile has returned. "The way most women knew him."

"You were lovers."

She nods. For a moment, her gaze rests somewhere to the left of me, and I know she's not seeing me or the booth or any part of Number Four. She's lost in the past with Ewing Trekov.

"You make it sound like he had a lot of lovers," I say.

Her eyes focus and move toward me. When they rest on me, they hold a bit of contempt. She knows what I'm doing, and she doesn't like it. She wants to control this conversation.

"A lot of lovers," she says, "a lot of wives, and more children than he could keep track of."

Maybe that's where the disapproval comes from. Riya Trekov isn't special in Nola's eyes.

"He didn't care about family?" I ask.

Nola shrugs. "The man I knew didn't have time for relationships. Not long ones, anyway. His entire life was about the wars and the entire sector. He saw lives the way we see stars—something far away and yet precious. Individual lives meant something to him only for a few weeks. Then he moved on."

There's pain in her voice.

"He moved on from you," I say as I take some yellow cheese. It's slimy against my fingers, but I don't dare put it back.

"Of course he did. Anyone who believed he would do otherwise was a fool."

But the bitter twist on the word "fool" makes it clear to me who "anyone" was.

"You said that you know things no one else does." I make myself eat the slimy cheese. It's remarkably good. Rich and sharp, a taste that goes well with the pepper and garlic of the meat.

"Of course I do," she says. "And some of it will go with me to my own death."

It's my turn to nod. I understand that kind of privacy.

She sets the plate near the edge of the table. Something moving so fast that I can barely see it whisks the plate away.

"But the story I'm going to tell you," she says, "isn't one of those. And it's not something you'll find in the histories either."

I wait.

"It's about his plans," she says with that secret smile. "He never planned to go to any of the ceremonies, and he wasn't going to sign any treaties."

"He told you this?" I ask, mostly because she's surprised me. Everything I've seen says he fully intended to go to the ceremonies. He sent notice as to when his ship would arrive. He had a contingent of honor guards waiting for him on another outpost nearer to the ceremony. He even had a dress uniform ordered special for the occasion.

"No, he didn't tell me anything," she says. "At least, not in so many words. He wasn't that kind of man. I figured it out, years later."

She figured it out when she remembered what happened that last day. How he'd been, how sad he seemed.

They met in his VIP cabin. It was large and lovely, with a bed the size of her quarters. But he wasn't interested in sex, although they had some.

He ordered food for them—an astonishing meal for a place this remote. Yet he didn't enjoy the food. He picked at it, letting much of it go to waste. She couldn't—she hadn't had a meal this good since she was stationed here.

But he waited until she was finished before he spoke.

"How do you do it?" he asked. "How do you save lives when you know they'll just go to waste?"

She didn't understand what he meant. "Go to waste?"

"Most of your patients here, they'll get sent back out and they'll die out there. Or they'll go home and they won't be the same. Their families will no longer know them. Their lives will be different."

"But not wasted," she said.

He kept picking at the food. He wouldn't look at her. "How do you know?"

"How do you?" she asked.

He shrugged.

"Most of these soldiers I see, they're children," she said. "They'll go home and remake their lives."

He shrugged again. "What about career military?"

She set her own fork down and pushed her plate away. She realized then she had to pay attention to this conversation, that it seemed to be about one thing and was really about another.

"Are you worried about what'll happen to you after the ceremonies?" she asked.

He shook his head, but he still didn't look up. He was developing a bald spot near his crown, and he hadn't paid for enhancements. The small circle of skin made him seem vulnerable in a way she'd never noticed before.

"This isn't about me," he said, but she didn't believe him.

"You can stay in the military," she said. "They need planners. Even in peacetime, they'll need a standing army. Governments always do."

"Seriously, Nola," he said with some irritation. "It's not about me."

"What is it about then?" she asked.

He shook his head again. The movement was small, almost involuntary, as if he were speaking to himself instead of her.

"Your units? The people under your command?"

He kept shaking his head.

"Your injured?"

"The dead," he said softly.

She was silent for a long time, hoping he would elaborate. But he didn't. So she struggled to understand.

"We can't help them," she said. "Even now with the technology that we have, the knowledge that we have, we can't help them. We just try to prevent death."

"And how do you do that?" he asked, raising his head. "How do you know who's worthy?"

She frowned. She was a doctor. She had been all her adult life. "I don't choose the worthy ones. That's not my decision."

"I've seen triage," he said. "You pick. You always pick."

Her breath caught.

"I don't choose by worthiness," she said softly. "I choose by my skill level. I choose by time. Who will survive the intervention? Who will take the least amount of time so that I can get to other injured? Who will be the least amount of work?"

That last made her face flush. She'd never admitted it to someone else before—at least not to someone who wasn't a doctor, someone who wasn't really faced with those decisions.

"That's how you pick who's worthy," he said.

His words made her flush deepen.

"Doesn't that bother you? Don't you look at the ones you didn't even try to save, the ones you sacrificed for the others, and wonder about them? Don't you sometimes think you made the wrong choice?"

Her face was so warm now that it actually hurt.

"No." She wanted to say that with confidence, but her voice was small, smaller than she'd ever heard it around him. "If I thought I always made the wrong choice, I couldn't do my job."

"But in the wee hours, when you're alone . . . ?"

She was staring at him. He hadn't looked up once.

After a moment, he shook his head a third time, as if he were arguing with himself.

"Never mind," he said. "I'm just tired."

Which gave her an excuse to leave.

She had no idea it would be the last time she'd see him. The next day, he had left the outpost.

And she never heard from him again.

"I'm sorry," I say after giving her a moment to return from the memory. "I don't see how all of that meant he didn't plan to go to the ceremony. I don't see how this relates to the Room of Lost Souls."

She raises her eyebrows in surprise. I get the distinct feeling she has just decided I'm dumb.

"He wasn't thinking about the future," she says. "He was thinking about the past."

"I got that," I say, and hope the words aren't too defensive. "But he makes no mention of the ceremonies or of the Room. So I'm not sure how you made the connection all these years later."

A slight frown creases the bridge of her nose. "The Room," she says, "is a pilgrimage. Some say it's a sacred place. Others believe only the damned can visit it."

My breath catches. I haven't heard any of that before. Or maybe I have. I used to make it a practice of not listening to stories about the Room because I believed no one could understand that place if they hadn't been there.

"All right," I say, "let's assume he knew that. How do you know he went there next?"

"His crew says so." She crosses her arms.

"I know that," I say. "But you found this interchange important. Enlighten me. Why?"

"Because I was stupid," she snaps. "He wasn't talking about me. He was talking about himself. *His* choices. *His* way of doing things. *His* losses. I'm sure he was reflecting on them because everyone expected him to celebrate the end of the Wars."

"He should have celebrated," I say.

She smiles faintly, then nods. For a moment she looks away. I can see her make a decision. She takes a deep breath and uncrosses her arms.

"I agreed with you back then. I figured he should have been at his happiest. But he wasn't so wrong about our jobs. I spent a lot of years as the chief surgeon on a military ship, and mostly I handled minor injuries and not-so-serious illness. But when we were in the middle of a battle, and the wounded kept pouring in, I just reacted."

I nod, not wanting her to stop.

"I worked my ass off," she says. "And people died."

She leans back, and rests her wrist on the side of the table. "I never, ever counted how many people I saved. I still don't. But I know to the person how many have died under my watch," she says softly. "I'll wager Ewing knew too. And each one of those deaths, they take something from you."

A little piece of yourself, I almost add. But I don't want her to think I'm sympathizing falsely, and I'm not willing to reveal as much of myself to her as she has revealed of herself to me.

"He wouldn't have been talking about death if he was going to go to those ceremonies," she says. "He wouldn't have been looking at the past. He would have been looking toward the future, at what we could build."

She sounds so confident. Yet they were just lovers, in passing, on a military outpost. How well did she really know him, after all?

And how can I ask her that without insulting her further?

So I try a different tack, partly to take my mind off those irritating questions and partly because I want to know.

"You said it's a pilgrimage. You said only the damned can get in."

Her frown grows. "Have you never heard of the Room?"

"I know it," I say, choosing my words carefully. "I just don't know the legends."

And I should. I have learned that the legends are more important than "facts" or histories or stories they can verify. Because legends hold a bit of truth.

"Do the damned go to get cleansed?" I ask.

Her mouth closes. She takes a breath, sighs, then gives me that faint smile all over again.

"Some say the Room bestows forgiveness on those who deserve it." That faraway look appears in her eyes.

"And those who don't?" I ask.

Tears well. She doesn't brush at them, doesn't even seem to notice them.

"They never come back," she says. Then she frowns at me. "You think he went for forgiveness, not to disappear."

I shrug. "The timing works. If he completed his pilgrimage to the Room, he could have gone to the treaty-signing ceremonies."

"With a pure heart," she whispers.

"He was a hero," I say without a trace of irony. "Didn't he have a pure heart already?"

And for the first time, she has no answer for me.

She has led me in a whole new direction. I'm not looking for the remains of a man. I'm looking for something unusual, something special.

A man has a history, and occasionally he becomes a legend. But a man is rarely special by himself. Sometimes he becomes special in a special time. Sometimes he rises beyond his upbringing to become something new. Sometimes he starts a movement, or alters the course of a country.

And sometimes—rarely—he changes an entire sector.

Like Ewing Trekov supposedly did with his friends as they developed a plan for the war.

But that story implies that he didn't work alone. That if he had died before he came to this outpost, someone else would have picked up that mantle. That someone might not have performed as well. He—or she—might have done better. There's no way to know.

But like all humans, Trekov wasn't entirely unique.

The Room of Lost Souls is unique.

No one knows exactly what it is or how it got to be. No one knows where it started or who built it or why.

Places develop myths, become legends in ways more powerful than any human being ever can. Because beneath each legendary human is the reminder that he *is* human, that what makes him special is how he rose above his humanness to become a little bit more than the rest of us.

Not a lot more. Just a little bit.

Trekov was a man who had more children than he could count, who made love to women but apparently didn't love them. A man who cared more about his work than his family.

A man like so many others.

A man who just happened to be the right man for the war he found himself in.

But the Room—the Room existed before humans settled this sector. The Room shows up in the earliest documents from the earliest space travelers.

And because it's so old, and because no one knows exactly how it works or why it's here or how it came to be, myths grew up around it.

People go on a pilgrimage.

Smart people, like Ewing Trekov.

People believe the Room will do something for them. Change something about them. Satisfy something within them.

The legends around the Room are fraught with danger. Space travelers are warned to stay away from it. I remember that much.

I *heard* that much.

But I'm not sure when. Or where. Or from whom.

Still, I need to heed my own advice.

I need to research the thing I think I know the best.

I need to talk to the one other person who remembers it vividly.

I have to talk to my own father.

Much as I don't want to.

SEVENTEEN

My father lives halfway across the sector, on a small planet whose only inhabited continent counts itself as one of the losers in the Colonnade Wars.

He's lived there for nearly two decades—and it's a sign of how out of touch we are that I actually had to look that information up.

My father's house is a maze of glass, stairs, and steel. From the outside it seems haphazard, rooms on top of rooms, but from the inside, it has a wide-open feel, like the best cruise liners, designed not to take you to a destination but to help you enjoy the journey.

He built his house in the center of a large blue lake, so at night the water reflected the skies above. If those skies are clear, it seems like he is in space, traveling from one port to another.

He doesn't seem surprised to see me. If anything, he's a little relieved.

I arrive in the middle of the afternoon, and he insists I stay at his house. I nearly decline until he shows me the guest room. It is at the very top of the house, glass on all sides except the part of the floor that covers the room below. The bed seems to free-float between the blueness of the lake and the blueness of the sky.

The sun—too close to this planet for my tastes—sends light through the glass, but environmental controls keep the room cool and comfortable. My father shows me where those controls are so I can lessen the gravity if I want.

It takes me a while to realize that my father's house is modeled on the station that houses the Room of Lost Souls. We meet in the center room—the room that would be the Room of Lost Souls if we were on that station—and he offers me a meal.

I decline. I'm too nervous in his presence to eat anything.

My father is no longer the man I remember, the man who cradled me when I got out of that Room. That man had been in his late thirties, tall and strong and powerful. He'd loved his wife and his daughter, making us the center of his life.

He'd commanded ships, built an empire of wealth, and still had time for us.

He abandoned everything to figure out how to get my mother out of that place. His businesses, his friends.

Me.

Which makes it so strange to see him now, essentially idle, in this place of openness and reflected light.

He still looks strong, but he hasn't bothered with enhancements. His face has lines—sadness lines that turn down his eyes and pinch the corners of his mouth. He has let his hair go completely white, along with his eyebrows, which have become bushy. His mustache—something I considered as much a part of him as his hands—is long gone.

He makes our greeting awkward by trying to hug me. I won't let him.

He acts like he still has affection for me. He does make it clear that he has followed my career—as much as he can through what little I make public.

But he has respected my wishes—the wishes I screamed at him the last time I ran away from my grandparents—and has stayed out of my life.

"You sent Riya Trekov to me," I say.

I can't sit in the chair he's offered me. I'm too restless in his presence, so I pace in the large room. The glass here opens onto the other rooms. Through their glass walls I can see still more rooms, and at the very end, the lake. Looking at it through all this glass makes it seem far away, and not real. It looks like a holograph of a lake, the kind you'd see on the distance ships of my childhood.

"I figured if anyone could help Riya, you could." His voice is the same, deep and warm and just a little nasal.

I shake my head. "You're the one who has done all the research on the Room."

"But you're the one who has dived the most dangerous wrecks ever found."

I turn toward him then. He sits in the very center of the room. His chair is made of frosted glass, and the cushions that protect his skin are a matching white. He looks like he has risen from the floor—a creature of glass and sunlight.

"You think this is like a wreck?" I ask. "Wrecks are known. They're filled with space and emptiness. They have corners and edges and debris, but they're part of this universe."

"You think the Room isn't?" He folds his hands and rests his chin on his knuckles.

"I don't know what it is. You're the one who has spent his life studying the damn thing."

So much for trying to hide my bitterness toward his choices.

He grimaces, but nods, an acknowledgment that my bitterness has its reasons.

"Yes," he says. "I've studied it. I've traveled to it countless times. I've sent people in there. I've repeated the same experiments that have been tried since it was discovered. None of them work."

"So why do you think Riya Trekov's device will work?" I ask.

"Because I was with her on one of the missions," he says. "I watched people she paid go in and come back out."

"Empty-handed," I say.

He nods.

"Yet she thinks someone can bring her father out."

"She might be right," he says.

"And if he can come out, so can Mother."

"Yes." The word is soft. He lifts his chin off his folded hands. The knuckles have turned white.

"If you believe this and you think I'm the one who can bring a lost soul out, how come you didn't ask me to do this yourself?"

"I did," he says. "You turned me down."

I snort and sink into one of the nearby chairs. He's right; he did contact me. I had forgotten it among his many summonses, all of which I ignored. But this one had been his last, a long plea explaining that he not only had a way into the Room of Lost Souls, he had a way to survive it.

"When I was a kid, you said you never wanted me to go back in there," I say, no longer trying to be polite. "You discouraged me from even going near the place, remember?"

I had been fifteen and full of myself. I'd run away from my grandparents half a dozen times. They were in constant mourning for my mother, and believed I was no substitute. It was pretty clear that they blamed me for her loss.

The final time, my father came after me, and I told him I could get my mother. I was the only one who'd come out alive. He owed me the chance to try.

He had refused.

I left him—and my grandparents—and never contacted any of them again. Although he kept trying to reach me. And I kept glancing at, then refusing, his messages.

"I couldn't risk letting you go in again," he says. "We barely got you out that first time."

"Yet you recommended me when Riya Trekov came to call. Because she has a way out or because you don't care anymore?"

His cheeks flush. "You didn't have to agree."

The chair is softer than I expect. I relax into it. "I know," I say, giving him that much. "Her plea interested me."

"Because of your diving," he says.

I shake my head. *Because I have nothing left.* But I don't say that.

"I recommended you because you're trained now," he says. "Of everyone I know, you have a chance, not just to get out. But to get out with something. You've become an amazing woman."

I no longer know him. I can't tell if he's being sincere or if he's just trying to convince me.

He's still a man obsessed. I wonder what he'll do if he recovers the remnants of Mother. Her "soul" or her memory or even her self. He's lived for decades without her. If she's still alive, she's spent double her initial lifespan inside a single Room.

I came here to find out one thing. So rather than debate the merits of my experience or the point of his obsession, I say, "Tell me what happened. How did we end up at the Room? How did we lose Mother?"

"You don't remember?" he asks.

The lights, the voices. I remember. Just not in any detail.

"My memories are a child's memories," I say. "I want the real story. The adult story. Mistakes and all."

We had no home. I didn't remember that, just like I didn't remember moving onto the ship six months before. My parents had sold our house and had put everything they had into his business, a fleet of cargo ships that ran all over the sector.

The business had become a success when my father stopped caring about the ethics of the cargo he carried. Sometimes he brought food or agricultural supplies to far-flung outposts. Sometimes he brought weapons to splinter groups rebelling against various governments.

He didn't care, as long as he got his payment.

He made so much money, he no longer needed to run the fleet, but he did. Still, my mother begged him to buy land and he did that too. This land, kilometers and kilometers of it, the entire lake and the surrounding greenery.

He promised her they would retire here.

But they were still young, and he loved travel. He commanded the lead vessel because he owned it, not because he was good at piloting or even at leadership.

He tells me about the trips, about the deliveries, about the crew. The ship had a contingent of forty regular with two dozen others whom he hired for larger jobs. Sometimes they worked the cargo; sometimes they repaired the ship. Always they listened to him, whether he was right or not.

But he wasn't the one who commanded them to the Room of Lost Souls. That was my mother. She had heard about it, studied it, thought about it.

She wanted to see it.

She didn't believe a place that old could exist in this part of space.

"She was trying to be a tourist," he says now. "Trying to make all this travel work."

But I wonder. Just like I wondered about Trekov. If my mother had done all the studying, had she been planning a pilgrimage? Because of my father's business or because of some problem all her own?

As I'm sitting there, I realize I know even less about her than I know about my father. I only know what I remember, what her parents told me in their grief, and what my father is telling me now.

"I took her there," he says. "With no thought, no study. I thought it just an ancient relic, a place that we could see in half a day and be gone."

"Half a day," I mutter.

He looks at me, clearly startled that I spoke.

"So she planned to go to the Room?"

"That was the point of our visit," he says.

"And she wanted to take me?" I can't believe anyone who studied that place would bring a child to it.

"You suited up and followed her. You grabbed her hand as she went through that door. I think you were trying to keep her from going inside."

But I wasn't. I was entranced with the lights, as fascinated as she had been.

"I saw you go in," he says. "I called to you both, but the door closed behind you."

"And then?" I ask.

"And then I couldn't get you out."

Minutes became hours. Hours became a day. He tried everything short of going in himself. He smashed at the window, tried to dismantle the walls, sent in some kind of grappler to grab us. Nothing worked.

"Then, one day, the door opened." His voice still holds a kind of awe. "And there you stood, your hands over your ears. I grabbed you and pulled you out, and held you, and the door closed again. Before I could go in. Before I could reach inside . . ."

His voice trails off, but I remember this part. I remember him clinging to me, his hands so firm that they bruise me. It feels like he holds me for days.

"You couldn't tell us anything," he says. "You didn't think any time had gone by at all. You were tired and cranky and overwhelmed. And you never wanted to go in again."

"You asked?"

He shakes his head. "You said. Without prompting. We stayed for a month. We never got her out."

And then he ordered the ship to leave. Because he knew he could spend the rest of his life struggling against that place. And he had a child. A miracle child, who had escaped.

"I dropped you with your grandparents and came back. I figured I could go in and get her. But I couldn't. Except for you, I didn't know anyone who had gotten out."

"Which is why you want me to go," I say.

He shakes his head. "I've found people willing to go inside. Nothing comes out."

"I thought you said you went with Riya Trekov. That she has a way out."

"She does. People go in. They come out. But they're always alone."

Now I ask him. "What'll you do if you get her? She won't be the same. *You're* certainly not."

"I know," he says, and for a moment I think he's going to leave it at that. Then he adds, "None of us are."

We talk long into the night.

Or rather, I listen as he talks.

He tells me what he knows about the Room. He has an almost encyclopedic knowledge of the place, combined with a series of theories, myths, and legends he has collected over the decades.

What it all comes to is what I already know: No one knows who built the Room or the station it's on. No one knows when it was built—only that it predates the known human colonization of this sector. No one knows what its purpose was or why it was abandoned.

No one knows anything, except that people who go in do not come out.

Unless they're protected by Riya Trekov's device.

The device, as my father explains it, is a personal shield, developed by a company that's related to my father's old business. The shield relies on technology so old that few people understand it.

Sometimes I think all of human history is about the technology we've lost. We're constantly reinventing things.

Or recovering them.

Apparently, this device is something reinvented.

How it works is simple: It acts like a spacesuit—creating a bubble around the user that contains both environment and gravity and anything else the user might need.

It has the same flaws a spacesuit has as well: It allows a person to enter an environment but not interact with it—or at least, not interact in important ways.

But the shield is different from a spacesuit as well. From the first discovery of the Room, humans have tried to enter wearing spacesuits, and that has not worked.

So Riya Trekov's device negates something—or protects against something—that a spacesuit does not. Somehow, that device—that bubble it creates—is the perfect protection against the Room.

At least that is what my father wants me to believe.

That's what Riya Trekov showed me briefly on Longbow Station.

But now I have more qualms than before. Because the more my father talks, the more disgusted I become.

He has spent all this time studying the Room. He has made that Room his life's work.

Yet he has never been able to risk that life, not even to pull me or my mother out of the Room.

As he paces around me, I think of all the times I've gone into a wreck, how I've looked for trapped divers, what I've risked to recover their bodies.

I've only failed to recover one.

People have devoted their lives to the mystery that is the Room, and have learned nothing.

Unlike them, I do not want to learn anything. I don't even want to recover my mother or Ewing Trekov—both of whom I consider dead.

I want to see the Room for myself, to satisfy some curiosity that has plagued me since I was ten years old. In that, perhaps, I am more like my mother than my father. If his story is to be believed—and I am not sure it is—then my mother just wanted to see the anomaly for herself.

Which is, in part, what I want to do. But more than that, I want to see, experience, and understand from an adult perspective what had so influenced me as a child.

I want to know how much the Room formed me, the embittered wreck diver, the woman who once believed that preserving the past was more important than any money that could be made from it.

The woman who believed—and maybe still does—that the past holds secrets, secrets which, if understood, can teach us more about ourselves than any science can.

I do not tell my father any of this. I let him believe I'm doing a job. I pretend to be interested in all that he tells me.

And I pretend to be surprised when he tells me he wants to join me.

He says he wants to see the Room one last time.

EIGHTEEN

It takes months to put a team together. The people who want to go to the Room are not experienced divers or experienced space travelers for that matter. The people who do not want to go are the ones I need.

I am able to buy some of them—money goes a long way with people who live on the edge—but I cannot buy all. Most important, I cannot buy Karl.

At first, he won't even talk to me. But eventually, his curiosity gets the better of him. He agrees to meet me in the old spacers' bar in Longbow Station.

I am at the station alone. I told my father that I would not be able to recruit when he was around. He has a reputation for being difficult and for thinking he's in charge. I actually got him to sign legal documents attesting to the fact that he would not run anything on board my ship or do anything to command (or jeopardize) my expedition.

I am using three factors in picking my team: I want people who are creative—both mechanically and intellectually; I want people who have dived the most dangerous wrecks in the sector; and I want people who are honest.

Finding the last two is relatively easy—divers have to be honest or they don't survive. The survivors are usually the ones who have been on the most dangerous missions.

But most divers leave the creativity to the person in charge of the mission. Since, in the past, that was me, I never had the opportunity to work with other dive team leaders.

Except Karl.

He started his business after I quit mine. He took over my routes, and I didn't interfere with him because I believed I would never wreck dive again.

But that isn't the only reason I want him.

I want him because he's trustworthy—and he's dangerous.

I don't know a lot about his personal history, but I do know a few things, things I've observed and things he's told me.

He's ex-military and he's excellent with a knife. He can kill anything—

and has, most recently after he opened his own business and trusted the wrong person.

He's cautious to a fault and yet oddly fearless. I say "oddly" because I've seen him back away from a dive because of worries about it, only to see him conquer those worries and go in.

I respect that about him.

I also know he can get my people back to Longbow if something happens to me.

He can get them back and he can handle my father.

Those elements are more important than creativity, more important than diving ability, more important than survival skills.

He has just come off a run of his own. He won't tell me where, which leads me to believe he has discovered a wreck he doesn't want me to know about.

His angular face has thinned, and his gray eyes seem silver in this light. He looks older, as if leading his own expeditions has taken something out of him.

He wears a thin white shirt over his broad chest. His pants are too loose, suggesting that the thinness in his face isn't my imagination. He's lost weight.

He straddles a chair across from me, using the chair's back as protection between us. He wraps his arms around it and stares at me.

"You have some nerve," he says.

"Yes, I do." I smile.

He doesn't smile back.

Then I sigh and let the smile fade. "I would like to hire you for a run."

"And I would like to tell you to go fuck yourself." But he doesn't move. "But if I do, you'll just keep asking me. So I came to hear what you have to say and to tell you no in person."

I understand why he's angry at me. I also understand if he never works with me again.

"Just hear me out," I say to him.

This time, I tell him everything. I tell him about my past, about my father, about Riya Trekov and her father. I tell him about the Room and its dangers. I tell him about the pilgrimages and the quasi-religious symbolism others have found in the place.

Then I tell him what I remember of the Room itself.

That's when he finally moves. Just a little, but enough so that I know I've hooked him somehow.

And I'm not quite sure how.

"If what you say is true," he says, "this is the second wreck you want to bring me to that's out of time."

My breath catches. I knew that the station and the Room don't belong. I hadn't allowed myself to make the mental comparison to the Dignity Vessel.

"You think it's related to the Dignity Vessel?" he asks.

"I don't know," I say. "There's always a chance. But I worry about preconceptions."

"Yeah," he says dryly. "I remember that about you."

The words sting.

"I might be wrong," I say. "Preconceptions might be necessary. I don't know. I just know I'm going to do this job as if it's a dive, and I want the best team possible."

"You realize the chances of someone dying on this trip are very high," he says.

"Yes." I swallow. That someone will probably be me.

He sighs. He's clearly thinking about the offer. We haven't talked money yet. I doubt money will mean much to him.

"What do you get out of this?" he asks. "Reconciliation with your father?"

I shake my head. "I want nothing from him."

"Yet you bring him along. That could compromise us right there."

I like the word "us." I didn't expect it. But I don't show him that I've noticed.

"I know it could," I say. "I'll need help minimizing contact with him."

"And your mother." He shakes his head. "This is fraught with emotion. You taught me that dives should have no emotion."

And yet our last dive was filled with it.

"I know," I say.

"If I go," he says, "I run the mission."

My entire body freezes. "How can it be my mission if you run it?"

"The dives," he says. "Anything to do with the Room. If I say we pull out, we pull out. If I say we leave someone behind, we leave them."

I bite my lower lip. I'm barely breathing.

"C'mon, Boss," he says. "You know that's why you're asking me to go. I'm the only one qualified, and the only one you'll listen to. You know that when I say we have to leave, I'll be right."

I let out the breath I was holding. Part of me has relaxed. He *is* right. That's why I chose to approach him. Because of our history. Because I know he's more cautious than I am, and because he has nothing at stake.

Except proving to me that I can be wrong.

"No grudges?" I ask.

He smiles for the first time. It's a sad smile. "I've lost two divers in the years since the Dignity Vessel. I don't know if I would have made the mistakes you made, but I've made some of my own. I think I'm finally beginning to understand you. So, no grudges. I'll do what's best for the mission, not what's best for Riya Trekov or your father. Or for you."

I nod. "You haven't even asked about money."

"I know you'll be fair," he says. Then his smile grows. "And I've always wanted to see the Room. The most mysterious place in this sector. I say let's go."

Maybe that's why such places catch and kill so many. Because they capture the imagination. Certainly that's why so many stories spring up around them.

And so many myths.

With Karl at my side, I do even more work. We sort through the repeated histories, and try to find the sources of various legends. We trace the Room in the modern era as best we can, and we ghoulishly make a list of all the souls known to have been lost in the place.

There are more than five hundred—and that's just recorded losses. Who knows how many others there were? No one has kept track of the abandoned single ships found near the station or people on a pilgrimage all on their own.

In passing, I say to Karl that what we've learned isn't worth the time we've spent. And he says what we've learned is that there are no odd recorded stories, things that don't quite fit into the other stories.

Maybe there's even a recognizable pattern. There certainly is to the losses. What happened to my father and his crew is the same as what happened to the very first ship that discovered the place, centuries ago.

"The same," I say, "except me coming out of that Room."

"Except that," Karl says.

In the end, we put together a team of ten, not counting me or Karl or Riya or my father.

Karl will lead the mission once we arrive at the station. Until then, I am in charge. I'll be in charge again when we leave the station as well. It's only when we're docked—when we're near the Room—that Karl will have control.

We use the *Business*. It has never been so full—at least not as long as I owned it. My father has the captain's cabin, which assuages my conscience. I've cut him off from all command and all control, which has to be difficult for him. So I reward him with the best quarters on the ship.

Riya has the third-best cabin. Mine is second best, and with its dedicated hardwired computer, I don't want anyone near it.

The dive team has the rest of the main deck, and Karl has the only room on the upper deck. It has the best views, and is impressive, should anyone visit him. I want him to look powerful and in charge, even before he is.

Some—including my father—believe that I placed Karl in charge of the mission at the station because Karl and I are lovers. The dive team knows differently—it's no secret in the diving community how angry Karl was with me after the events with the Dignity Vessel—but they're under orders not to correct that misperception.

Karl helped me vet the dive team: two women who'd been on some of his previous dives, an old-timer who has more experience than me and Karl combined, three superb and fearless pilots, three young men hired more for their strength than their diving ability, and a woman who had accompanied me on my earliest professional dives.

I have decided to treat this as a real dive, which means that we are focusing on the station, not just the Room. From everything that Karl and I have found, it seems people who have gone to the station have gone for the Room—or only spent time in the Room.

No one has given the habitats more than a cursory examination, not even the scholars. In fact, the scholars have mostly relied on the discovery of others, being too afraid to examine things themselves.

On the first day out, I brief the dive team about our mission. We meet in the lounge. The *Business*'s lounge is not for recreation. I still keep all of my playback and analysis equipment here. Since the Dignity dive, I have bought comfortable chairs as well as two sofas, but they're arranged in an uncomfortable pattern—a semicircle facing the various screens and portholes.

Nine members of the dive team are here, as well as myself and Karl. I have banned Riya and my father from attending any meetings about the upcoming dives. The missing member of the team is the pilot who is currently flying the ship.

The team spreads around the lounge, trying to look casual, but I recognize the emotions here. Everyone is excited. The work is what they live for—

it's what I used to live for—and when they're approaching something new, it's thrilling, not frightening.

I haven't felt the thrill yet. I haven't felt fear either, which I consider a victory. What I am feeling is nervous. I have no idea how any of this will play out.

I'm not sure how I want it to.

Still, I try to maintain an upbeat attitude, like I used to do when I started dangerous dive missions in the past. I walk in front of the screens, looking every member of the team in the eye as I speak.

I am not as honest with them as I was with Karl. I do mention problems—my father, the loss of my mother to the Room, which is why Karl will lead once we get to the station—but I do not mention my own reservations.

Instead, I talk about the history.

"We are not looking for items to resell," I say, although everyone probably knows that. After all, they've signed on to dive with me and Karl, not some salvage divers or treasure hunters. "We're looking for information—anything that will tell us about the station, about who built it, how it came to be here—why it's out here at all so far away from everything—and what its purpose actually is."

"Do we know if the Room is an integral part of the station?" asks Roderick. He's slight but broad-shouldered, a land-bound pilot who somehow became one of the most highly rated in the sector. I supervised his first shift with the *Business* and was impressed. He found my control shortcuts without explanation in a matter of minutes.

"We know nothing," I say. "We don't know if the Room's intentional or part of an accident."

"We do know," Karl says, "that the habitats next to the Room have been destroyed. But we don't know how. We don't know if someone destroyed them trying to block access to the Room or if the Room was something else and an accident or an explosion or something gone horribly wrong created the damage that we'll find around it."

"We're not scientists," says Odette. She's the oldest diver, whom I'd partnered with long ago. She is standing in the back of the lounge near the main exit, her stick-thin arms crossed. She looks delicate against the bulkhead, as if nothing could prevent her from floating off into space. "How are we supposed to know what happened in there or what any of it means?"

"Between us, we have centuries of experience with ancient technologies." I'm mostly talking to her and Karl now, but some of the other divers we hired have it as well. "We'll know as much or more than any scientist we bring out here."

"Besides," Karl says, "we are going to bring back as much information as we can about the station. Our goal is to be the definitive historical mission for the station and the Room."

"Is that why you wouldn't give us a timeline?" asks Tamaz, one of the young male divers we hired for his strength and not for his great experience. He has muscles along his arms and chest that I haven't seen in most divers. He probably had to have a special suit made.

But I wanted his strength in case we have to pull someone out of the Room. We've already established that machines can't do it, but a person might be able to. A very strong, very motivated person.

"We are not giving you a timeline because we can't," I say. "The Room's past history shows that people can sometimes be inside for hours or a day before coming out again."

Although the only history that showed that was mine. All of the people hired by Riya and my father came out within hours of going in, just like they were supposed to.

Both Karl and I felt the dive team didn't have to know this aspect of the Room's history—nor did they have to know the fact that I had already been inside. I did not want to be seen as an expert on the interior, particularly when I can't remember much about it.

"If there's no treasure inside, why would people go in?" asks Mikk, another of the strong young men. He's taller than Tamaz, but otherwise looks very much the same. I would have considered them brothers if I hadn't known otherwise.

"There's treasure," I say before Karl can comment. "But it's not the monetary kind. We warned you about that when we hired you for the dive."

Mikk waves his right hand. It's bigger than my thigh. "I'm not thinking for me. I mean all these five hundred people you say never came out. Why go in in the first place?"

"You're not religious, are you, Mikk?" Davida asks softly. She's one of Karl's hires, a regular wreck diver who has the standard lean physique along with skin so taut it looks stretched over her frame.

"So?" Mikk sounds defensive.

"That's what a pilgrimage is, something religious." Davida sounds sure of herself, but she's obviously not that religious either.

"Pilgrimages have religious connotations, yes," Odette says from her post in the back. This time, the dive team looks at her as if they haven't really noticed her before. "But a pilgrimage is also a mission to a special place, not just a sacred place. One could say this is a pilgrimage."

Her gaze is on mine. She knows some of my family's history, but I don't believe she knows all of it.

"It certainly is for Riya Trekov," I say to cover my own discomfort. "She believes her father's soul is trapped in this place, and she believes we can recover it."

"Do you?" Tamaz asks me.

I think for a moment—the lights, the voices building one upon another, the clutch of my father's arms as he holds me tight.

"No," I say after a moment, "but that doesn't mean we aren't going to try."

NINETEEN

The station is bigger than I remember, bigger than my father's descriptions of it, bigger than anything mentioned in the archives.

It looms ahead of the *Business* like a small asteroid or a tiny moon. It's gray in the constant twilight of space, the reflection of faraway stars making it seem brighter than it actually is.

There are no visible lights on the station, nothing that marks it as a landing site or an outpost or some kind of way station. There are no energy readings, faint or otherwise.

I fly us toward the station as Roderick, Karl, and the other two pilots—Hurst and Bria—monitor the audio bands, trying to find any sign of life coming from the place.

The five of us sit shoulder to shoulder as we work the controls. The cockpit feels crowded, even though it's built for ten or more. The station shows up on my viewscreen and in my controls as well as in the portholes throughout the ship.

Out of deference to my father, we do not dock on the exterior docking ring. This was where his large cargo ship docked—it couldn't go any deeper into the station itself—and this was where the nightmares that have haunted the rest of his life began.

Instead, I pick a smaller ring on the upper level, where the habitats are still intact. From here, it looks as if we've approached a darkened but working space station. Reflections in the exterior windows of the station make it seem like someone is moving inside.

That startles Hurst—he even points it out—but Karl and I have approached so many wrecks, we're used to the phenomenon.

"It's just us," Karl says. "We're seeing our own reflections."

Still, Hurst works the sensors. He's not convinced. He's a small man, younger than most pilots, with black hair that falls to his shoulders and often hides his face.

But it's easy to tell that he's already spooked. I don't like that. I need solid, steady people, not superstitious ones given to outbursts.

I make a mental note to keep him away from the pilot's chair during this part of the mission. And I will tell Karl that later on.

Right now, we settle into work. First we have to use our own equipment to map the station. Then we'll proceed with a dive plan.

"It's bigger than I thought," Bria says. She has steady hands, which I appreciate, and a quick sense of humor. Her dark head is bent over the controls, her hands moving across them as if the *Business* is a ship she's spent her entire life aboard.

"It's a lot bigger," says Hurst. His hands are shaking. He made it clear to us when he was hired that he'd never flown a mission like this. He'd mostly done combat zones. Active danger—shots, explosions—doesn't bother him. He's a quick thinker in that kind of situation, and since Karl and I didn't know what we were facing, we wanted one pilot with experience flying in and out of a constantly changing situation.

"All our previous readings are wrong," Karl says, and that's when I look. He gives me his handheld.

Previous specs showed the station to be one-quarter to one-half the size of this station.

"Are we in the right place?" Roderick asks.

I nod. The coordinates are right. The middle of the station is right as well.

But I don't trust it. I do my own scan.

The readings on the exterior of the station are correct except for the station's size. The strange metal, the age of the station itself, its unusual structure match the past specs.

"What the hell?" Roderick mutters.

Karl has frozen beside me. The hair on the back of my neck has risen.

"There are a million explanations," Bria says, oblivious to our reaction. "You said no one explored the whole thing. Maybe no one mapped it either. You're relying on stuff you've found in databases, which could be corrupted or tampered with or just plain wrong."

"True," Hurst says. "I've run into this all over the sector. Particularly in the lesser-known parts. No one really cares how big something is unless they need to. Most people aren't that accurate."

But this is a place that ships have come to on pilgrimages. This is a place that has been studied.

And my own sense as we approached was that it has become bigger.

I swallow hard, but I don't say anything.

Instead, I get out of the pilot's chair and sweep my hand toward it, looking at Karl's angular face.

"It's your mission now," I say.

He hesitates. Then he takes a deep breath and slides into the pilot's chair. Of the five of us in the cockpit, he is, by far, the weakest pilot, but he knows what I'm doing.

I'm symbolically relinquishing command.

I have to.

I'm already not thinking rationally. I'm making things up based on my past experience.

And that terrifies me.

I leave them to mapping. I go to my quarters and log onto my dedicated computer. I call up files I haven't looked at in years.

Files that I stored after the Dignity Vessel.

Files on stealth technology.

Our weak stealth technology is hard-won. We've been working on it for generations, always seeking to improve it and never doing so.

True stealth technology—the kind that actually makes a ship invisible (and, in some cases, impossible not just to see but to hear and touch)—is extremely dangerous. The kind of stealth that the ancients had actually changed the ship itself (or whatever the stealth was applied to). Some believe that the ship dissolved and re-formed at a particular point. Others think it went out of phase with everything else in the universe. And still others believe that it actually leaves this dimension.

My experience in that Dignity Vessel showed me that it's possible to open small windows in other dimensions. Only in practice those windows don't work the way they do in theory. They explode or get stuck or ships get lost.

People get lost.

Is that what we're facing here? Yet another version of ancient stealth tech?

My skin is crawling.

That would be too simple, and too much of a coincidence.

And it wouldn't explain the voices.

This is why I have given over the controls to Karl earlier than I planned. Although I'm beginning to doubt the wisdom of that. Karl is as familiar with ancient stealth tech as I am and is scarred by it too.

I hope it won't affect his judgment here.

I stand and pace my small quarters, and as I do I remember the other reasons I hired Karl to run things.

Riya.

My father.

My mother.

Those voices.

No preconceptions, that's my motto. And I need to wait until mine are under control before I face the team all over again.

By the time I come out, the station is mapped. It is definitely larger than our research told us it would be. Karl wants to bring in my father, and I can't contradict him even though I don't want to use my father for anything.

We meet in the lounge. Fortunately, Karl has kept Riya out of this meeting. Most of the dive team is here and all of the pilots. The *Business*, safely docked, has its automatic alarms on in case something happens.

Still, this close to a dive, I hate leaving the cockpit unattended.

Karl reminds everyone that he is in charge now. Then he introduces my father—using all of my father's very impressive credentials—and says, "I invited him into this meeting because he's been here before. He knows a lot about the station and even more about the Room."

Karl looks at me. My father is standing next to him, dwarfing Karl. My father, with his planet-bound height and muscle, looks almost superhuman compared to the divers. And even though he's older than everyone except perhaps Odette, he seems much more powerful.

I don't like the contrast.

"The changes in what we're expecting are enough to make me reassess the mission," Karl says.

I turn toward him, shocked. This isn't the man I hired all those years ago. This isn't Karl the Fearless.

He sees my look and holds up his hand to silence me. "I've learned over the years that it's best to talk about the unexpected, and even better to get the dive team's read on it. We're here to take extreme risks, but not *unnecessary* risks."

I dig my teeth into my lower lip so that I don't contradict him—at least not yet. At least not this early in the very first meeting he's called.

Karl explains our findings, and he uses some impressive graphs and charts and diagrams that he's clearly worked on in the short time since he called the meeting. Then he turns to my father.

"What do you make of this?" Karl asks.

My father walks in front of the displays, his hands clasped behind his back like a professor grading a student's work. I get the sense that he likes the attention and is milking it.

"Your worry isn't necessary," he says after a minute. He addresses Karl like the rest of us aren't here. "I've seen this before."

I remain still in the back of the lounge. Odette crosses her arms. Karl tilts his head, obviously intrigued.

"Every time I come here, the station is bigger." My father does not pause, even though he should have. The sentence sends a ripple of interest through the group and would have given him the attention he obviously craves. "I think it's programmed to build new units, which is why the habitable ones are on the outer layers, not in the middle."

It's a plausible explanation, and no one asks him for his proof. I would have. My father is not a scientist, and he doesn't back up what he just said with any statistics or experimentation. Just observation and a supposition.

"So it's normal," says Bria with something like relief.

"There's nothing normal about this place," my father says.

"How do we test the growing theory?" asks Jennifer. She's one of my hires, and she looks at me as she asks this, all wide eyes and innocence. But I've known her for a while, and Jennifer isn't innocent. She's annoyed that I've been forgotten, and she's pointing me out to the others on purpose.

I'm glad for the opening. "We test all theories. That's why it's best to go slow. The more we learn before we go to the Room, the better off we'll be."

"You actually think we'll learn something new about the Room?" Davida asks. She's sitting by Jennifer and Roderick on the couch. They glance at her in surprise.

"Why else come on this mission if you can't learn something new?" Roderick asks.

"It's just that this thing has existed for so long, and no one knows anything about it," Davida says. "That's beginning to creep me out."

"We know some things," my father says, and goes into his lecture on the history of the Room. He doesn't seem to notice that he's talking mostly about conjecture and theory, but some of the others do. They squirm. He's lost the attention he worked so hard to gain.

It takes Karl a while to shut my father down, but he finally does. Then Karl looks at me as if my father's lack of social graces is my fault.

I give Karl a half smile and a shrug.

Karl gets my father to sit. Then Karl sets up the dive roster for the following day—Bria piloting one of the four-man skips (so that our teams don't have to free-dive to get into far sections of the station) and Davida, Jennifer, and Mikk in the upper habitats—with a promise of more when we meet that night.

The team shifts, but this time it isn't because of my father's long-windedness. It's because they're excited.

It's because they're ready.

We all are.

TWENTY

For the next three weeks, we dive the station, making detailed maps, exploring the new and old habitats, sharing small discoveries.

Every night we meet in the lounge and watch the captured imagery of that day's dives. The divers narrate and the others ask questions. That way, we all have the same information.

We learn quite a few things—the built-in furniture is the same in all of the habitats, although in the "new" section, as Karl likes to call it, it's not dented or warped or even scratched.

The new sections contain a few other things—remotes attached to entertainment equipment, equipment that doesn't seem to work "although it might if we can find a good way to power the entire station," my father says. "Maybe the entertainment programming is supposed to come from the damaged central area."

I don't like having my father in the lounge at night. He's not methodical and he's given to supposition. I think supposition is deadly. Karl finds it fascinating, but he can separate out the supposition from fact.

I'm not sure some of the younger divers can. Although they occasionally find my father long-winded, they seem to like him. They may even admire him.

I don't ask anyone what they think of him, not that they would give me an honest opinion. Everyone is aware that he is my father and that we aren't on the best of terms.

Indeed, everyone else talks to him more than I do.

Including Riya, who daily complains that we are wasting her time and money. From the moment we arrived, she wanted us to go into the Room and do nothing else. Fortunately, Karl is in charge of this part of the mission, and Karl must talk to her, reminding her that caution is our byword and that even if we don't recover her father on this trip, the information we gather might make it possible to recover him on the next.

One night, she came to me to complain. I waved her off. "You gave me as much time as I needed," I reminded her.

"Yes," she said. "I gave *you* that, not him."

"And I placed him in charge while we're at the station. I trust him."

She glared at me. "I hope that trust isn't misplaced."

So far, it doesn't seem misplaced. I approve of the way he's handling the team—dividing assignments based on experience and on interest. It soon becomes clear who likes going through debris-crowded destroyed habitats and who prefers a minute exploration of the pristine edges of the station.

He also has kept track of the pilots—who handles the skip best in tight quarters and who is the most observant. And he hasn't lost track of the Room.

Once a week, he and I have gone around its exterior. The first time, we mapped it. The second time, we mapped again to see if it had expanded. The third, we just observed.

The station hasn't grown while we're here. And we've seen nothing untoward about the Room, although on that first dive I was surprised to learn that the Room is encased on all sides.

For some reason, I thought part of it was open to space. I'm assuming that's because I saw the lights and they seemed to lead somewhere. And also, I'm sure I thought the Room had unlimited space because it has taken so many bodies.

When you peer through the main window, you can see none of those bodies. In fact, you can't even see the lights. It looks dark and empty, like the still-intact habitats.

Only when you shine a light inside, it disappears into the darkness. It does not reflect back at you.

My father claims to recognize all of this, which is making Karl grow more and more exasperated with him. At one point, in one of our nightly meetings, Karl snapped at him, "I asked you to tell us everything you knew about the Room."

My father shrugged. "I have."

"Yet each night, you have some new observation, some new memory."

My father didn't seem perturbed at Karl's tone. "You think small details are important, things I noticed but never really thought much about. So when I remember them, I tell you."

Karl asked if there were other things like that which my father noted, things he wanted to tell us.

My father shrugged again. "I'm sure I'll remember when the time comes."

Karl looked at me and caught me rolling my eyes. But I said nothing to him or my father. Karl asked to command this part of the mission because he believed my observations and judgments would be compromised.

He's only beginning to realize that my father's are as well.

The readings have come back from the new habitats. They're composed of the same material as the rest of the station, only it isn't worn down by centuries. It does seem newer, just like the interior furniture does. A lot points to my father's theory—that the structure is being built new—but I am not sure how.

If the station is adding to itself over time, I'm not sure what materials it's using. My father seems ignorant of the law of matter conservation, so he thinks it possible to create something from nothing. I've never seen that happen.

Then, one night, I wake bolt upright on my bed, worried that the matter being used to make the new station comes from the bodies of the dead.

I have to do the calculations just to calm myself down. They show me that even with every part of a body being used, there isn't enough material.

Either the station has some kind of supply, something we don't recognize, or it's bringing matter in from elsewhere.

Or it isn't growing itself. It's revealing itself, like I feared.

And I find a lot of evidence to support that theory. At least, evidence that part of me wants to believe.

I find myself wondering if the station isn't going through the same sort of time split that Junior went through. Maybe the station is stuck in two different time frames. And like some stuck objects, it is slowly sliding out of whatever holds it.

Which would explain how it "grew" each time my father had visited, and why the newer areas don't seem to age. Maybe the time split here is the opposite of the one we'd found on the Dignity Vessel.

Instead of time progressing rapidly in the part we can't reach, it's progressing slowly there—or maybe not at all. That the parts of the station being revealed are in a section between time, between dimensions.

I'm no scientist, and I have no way to test my theories. I don't even want to mention them to Karl. He has enough to worry about.

I do mention one worry, however. I tell him it concerns me that the station has expanded outward, and I make him promise no skip and no diver will travel to the outer edges.

I don't want another Junior. I don't want someone to get stuck between two times or two dimensions or two universes.

I want to be cautious, and in this, as in everything else, Karl agrees.

Everything seems to be going fine, and despite my discomfort, my mood has improved. The divers are enjoying their dives, and no one has had a close call or been injured.

We're not lulled into a complacency, however. We know that the worst part of the dive is ahead, and that it belongs to me.

I've been preparing, and not just in my visits to the Room. I've spent most of my free time examining Riya's device. I've run it through my computers, trying to find its origin, and cannot.

It is made of familiar materials, but they're grafted onto a center that I do not recognize or understand. The materials in that center aren't anything like what I found on the Dignity Vessel or here at the station, and for that I'm relieved.

It doesn't seem to do much when it turns on—I get a small energy spike, and lights run along the edges of the device. But I don't sense the bubble or see a momentary shimmer or something that would imply an actual shield going around me.

But a lot of things work without being obvious. And I'm not testing the device in zero-g. I'm testing in Earth normal, in full environment. I don't want to test it outside the ship, in case I cause problems.

I wish I knew more about the device, but Riya can't tell me much. She says she got the shield through her father's connections.

She can tell me nothing else.

So I memorize the exterior dimensions of the Room, so that I can find the edges even if I can't see them. And I try to ignore the music in my head, which seems to grow each and every day.

"Grow" isn't exactly the right word. The music plays a little longer each time I "hear" it. It isn't louder or any more insistent. It's just harder to shut off.

I'm actually becoming used to it. In the past it would distract me and I would have to concentrate on anything outside myself while the voices sang. Now they're a background accompaniment, and I wonder if I would actually notice them if I weren't planning to go back inside the Room so soon.

The night before I go in, Karl calls me to his quarters. I haven't been up to them since I assigned them. I'm startled to see that he's blocked the view of the station but has left the portals that open to the space views clear.

He's sitting near the clear portals, his back reflected in them. His eyes are wide, and for the first time since I've given him control, I worry that he's not up to it.

Something has unsettled him.

"You okay?" I ask as I sit across from him. My back is to the station. Although the portals are opaqued against it, I can feel it looming, almost as if it's a living entity, one that grows and changes and becomes something else.

"I'm a little uncomfortable," he says, and shifts in his seat as if to prove the remark. "I've put this conversation off too long."

I stiffen. One of the risks of giving him control is that he would keep it, that he would make the mission—and in some ways, the ship—his. I trusted him not to do that, but that trust suddenly feels fragile.

"What's going on?" I ask, careful to keep my voice calm.

"I've been thinking a lot about tomorrow's dive," he says. "I don't think you should do it."

The words hang between us. I make myself breathe before responding.

"Have you seen something that makes the dive untenable?" I ask.

He shakes his head. "The dive is fine. I think we should go ahead with it. I just don't think you should be the one to go in."

My face heats. "That's the whole point of this mission."

"Going into the Room to recover Commander Trekov is the point of this mission—the central point, the one you and I agreed on. But this whole mission is larger than that, and we're learning some great things. We wouldn't have done that without you."

He clearly planned that little speech. It sounds forced.

"Who'll go in?" I ask.

"Me," he says.

"Alone?" The word squeaks out. I'm surprised and can no longer hide it.

"I have the most dive experience next to you," he says.

"Actually, that's not true. Odette does."

"All right, then," he says. "You and I have the most diving experience on dangerous wrecks. She's spent the last fifteen years on tourist runs."

"Like me," I say softly.

"You haven't spent fifteen years at it, and if that were the only problem, I'd ignore it."

I want to cross my arms and glare at him. But I don't. I put him in charge for a reason. I'm going to hear him out.

"So what are the other problems?" I ask.

He takes a deep breath. "Your father, for one."

"I don't like him," I say. "We have history. So what?"

"You have a shared history. And it has to do with the loss of your mother." Karl folds his hands across his knee, then unfolds them. He's clearly nervous.

"We discussed this," I say. "That's why you're in charge."

"I know," he says. "But that loss is significant. It caused the rift between you two, and it changed both of your lives. I've heard your story about the Room, and you were entranced by that place."

"I was happy to get out," I say, repeating what my father told me.

"But you went in willingly. What if the Room causes some kind of hypnosis? What if you're still susceptible to it? It's irresponsible to send you in on the first dive."

I'm about to protest when I register the word "first."

"You think there will be more than one dive?" I ask.

"There has to be," he says. "We do it by the book. We map and observe and then we discuss. If we're going to remove something from the Room, we do so on the final dive."

"So you want to do at least four dives," I say.

He nods. "The problem is that we only have one device, so only one of us can go in at a time. You'll be looking for your mother. You know you will—"

I'm shaking my head, but deep down, I know he's right. Of course I'll be looking for her. And for Commander Trekov, and the others trapped in that place.

"—and you won't be focused on the small but necessary details. I will. I've made a point of not looking at your mother's image or Commander Trekov's. Even if I see them, I won't recognize them. They'll be part of the entire package. I won't be tempted to move too quickly."

I swallow hard. "Why not send someone else in? It's a risky mission. You're in charge. You should stay out here."

"It is risky," he says. "But you'll be out here. And if I can't survive with that device, no one else will be able to either. So you'll abort and get everyone out of here."

"We can make that decision together," I say. "Send in another diver."

"Who? Odette? Mikk? Who are you going to send in, knowing that most people who have gone inside that Room have died? Are you willing to risk their lives?"

I don't say anything. We both know that I wasn't when I hired them. I knew there was only one device and I would be the one to use it. Everyone else was brought in, initially, to help extract me from the Room, not to go in and explore.

"I'm not willing to risk yours either," I say.

"You don't get a choice." He's calmer now. His gaze meets mine. Those gray eyes reflect the darkness of the portals behind me. "You put me in charge."

"But I still have the device," I say. "And I'm not giving it to you."

"No, you don't have it," he says. "That's why I wanted to meet you here. I had it removed from your quarters."

I feel so violated I have to prevent myself from lunging at him. No one goes in my cabin. No one even has access.

Except I gave him command. He has the codes.

He must have looked them up.

"I'm sorry," he says.

My face is so hot that it feels inflamed. I'm gripping my chair, and it takes all of my energy to stay in one place. Fighting him will do neither of us any good.

In handing over command, I also gave him implicit rights to imprison me in my own ship. I'm not going to give him the satisfaction.

"You know this is the right decision," he says.

I'm not going to acknowledge that.

"You're the one who taught me that emotion can be deadly to a dive," he says.

I get up. I trust myself to walk to his door and to get out. But that's all I trust.

Still, I stop. "You will never violate the sanctity of my cabin again."

He nods. "I'm sorry," he says again. "I had Odette wear her recorders and keep them on. She knows if she touched anything other than the device I'll have her hide."

It isn't the touching that bothers me. It's the entering.

That is my private space. No one else belongs in there.

My quarters are so private they almost feel like an extension of myself.

I don't say any more. I step into the hallway, wait until the door closes, and lean against the wall.

A part of my brain already acknowledges that his decision is sensible. I know that when I calm down, I'll agree. Four dives into the Room is actually the minimum for a dangerous area.

Not one, like I'd been planning.

I'd been thinking like a survivor of a disaster, not like a wreck diver.

And Karl understands that.

He's protecting me from myself, yes, but more than that, he's doing his job.

He's making sure the mission is a success.

And I hate him for it.

TWENTY-ONE

I insist on being in the skip the next morning. Karl lets me on board, but he won't let me pilot. I am strictly an observer.

Today's pilot is Roderick. Karl's diving partner—a misnomer, really, since Karl has to go in alone—is Mikk. I've brought my suit just in case, but Karl gives it a filthy look as I enter the skip.

He doesn't want me entertaining any thoughts of diving the Room. I'm along for two reasons: as a courtesy to me, and so that we don't have to explain our plan to my father or Riya.

They've proven more rigid than I could ever be. As time has progressed, they've complained more and more about the habitat dives. They want someone in the Room and they want it soon.

They don't even know we're going in today. In the last several meetings, Karl has not mentioned the diving rosters and locations until my father was gone.

Karl thought I would object to keeping Riya and my father in the dark about the Room dive. But I don't. I haven't liked the access Karl has given them from the beginning. That's more than I would have offered.

Roderick is good at flying the skip in enclosed spaces. We want the skip as close to the entry point as possible. That way, the divers don't have to cover a lot of known ground before going into the important part of the dive. It saves time and could save lives if someone got into trouble.

In this case, the skip will have go into the destroyed habitats. It's not as dangerous as it sounds. Most of the debris has been cleared by time or by scavengers. Roderick flies with the portals closed, which makes me feel blind.

But he focuses on instruments, and he's so good with them that I don't complain. Not that I have any right to, anyway.

Because the distance between the Room and the *Business* is so short, Karl has already put on his suit. It's an upgrade from the days when we dove together, but it resembles the one he had before.

This suit is expensive and a little bulky. It has an internal environmental system, like all suits, but it also has an external one.

Karl used to carry only two extra breathers. Now he has four, and they're larger than the ones he used to have. Apparently the Dignity Vessel experience has had a greater impact on him than he's willing to admit.

Instead of a slew of weapons in the loops along his belt, he carries a few tools and his knife. I find myself staring at it throughout the short journey, wondering what he would use it on inside that Room.

Mikk has also suited up. He'll go as far as the Room's door and wait there—not the best assignment, especially for a young diver. But if Mikk doesn't know patience by now, he'll never learn it. And he swears he understands how long he might have to monitor that door.

Roderick anchors the skip to the remaining wall so that he won't have to use thrust in the small space. He and I will wait on board and will monitor everything through the suit cameras that Karl and Mikk will wear. They'll also have audio in their headpieces.

The dive will follow a strict schedule. Because Karl doesn't have a lot of distance to traverse between the skip and the Room's door, we decided on a two-hour dive—longer than I would have liked, and shorter than he wanted.

It'll only take him five minutes to get inside and, theoretically, five minutes to get back. The rest of the time, he should be observing and mapping.

Provided his equipment works inside. To our knowledge, no one has filmed the interior of the Room, and we don't know if that's because they haven't thought of it or if they didn't succeed when they tried.

Just before he puts on his headpiece, he attaches the device to his belt. Since we don't know much about how the device works, we don't want it inside his suit. We want to give him as much protection as possible.

Then he slips on his headpiece. He hands me the handheld, which will report everything the cameras on the side of his headpiece "see."

We are the least confident in the handheld. The shield device might disrupt the signals the cameras send back. We tested as best we could near the *Business* and didn't have any trouble, but we're not sure if that was an accurate test.

Like so much with wreck diving, this part of the dive gets tested only in the field.

I'm nervous. Karl is not. Roderick hasn't said anything, and Mikk acts like this is a normal dive. While he's curious about the Room, it's an intellectual curiosity. He knows he won't be able to dive it this trip, so it's not the center of his attention.

In some ways, he's along for the ride, even more than I am.

We don't tether to the Room—that would be dangerous with the skip powered down—but we do extend a line. Karl is doing this as a courtesy to me. I won't dive without lines. He has made one alteration. Once he reaches the door, he will attach a tether to one of the loops on his belt. If he loses consciousness in there, we can pull him back.

Mikk and Karl proceed to the airlock. They wave as they step inside.

They wait the required two minutes as their suits adjust. Then Mikk presses the hatch and Karl sends the lead out the door.

It only takes a moment to cleave to the jamb beside the Room's door. We picked that spot because it seemed soft enough to hold the line. Nothing else around the Room's exterior did.

They're stepping out of the airlock. They'll move at a very slow pace because they're good divers. They'll test the line. They'll make sure each part of their suits is functioning. Then they'll travel slowly to that door, and coordinate before Karl goes in.

I take those few minutes to walk into the cockpit. Roderick is sitting in what I consider to be my seat—the pilot's chair—and is already monitoring the readouts. In addition to the skip's cameras, some suit monitors send information directly to the skip itself. And both suits send heart rates and breathing patterns—or will so long as nothing interferes with the signal.

I plug Karl's handheld into one small screen but only look at it to make sure the information is coming to me. Grainy flat images, mostly of the line, appear before me.

Then I look up. Roderick still has the portals opaqued.

"Let's watch this in real time," I say.

He doesn't look up from the instrumentation. "I don't like staring at interior station walls when I'm on a skip."

"I don't care," I say. "We have a team out there. We need our eyes as well as our equipment. We need every advantage we can get."

I shudder to think he's run dives in the habitats on instruments only, and make a mental note to tell Karl that night. It should be a requirement for each dive that the pilot watches from the cockpit. The pilot won't be able to see inside some of the spaces, but he will be able to see if there's a problem between the lead and the skip itself.

"Karl says I'm supposed to make the decisions," Roderick says.

"Well, I have twenty years of dive experience, and let me tell you, only amateurs let their people out of a ship on instrument only."

He winces, then flattens his hand against the control panel. With a hum, all of the windows become visible.

Usually being in the skip with the windows clear feels like you're inside a piece of black glass moving through open space. Right now, it seems like we've crashed into a junkyard. A blown wall opens to space on our left side. Beneath us, the habitat's floor is in shreds. Above us is the sturdy floor of the next level, and to our right is the line, leading to the Room's door.

Karl's already halfway down the lead. Mikk is hurrying to catch up.

I look at their breathing and heart rates. They're in the normal range. But it's not like Karl to move that fast.

I touch the communication panel. "You seeing something?"

"There's not a lot between the skip and the door, Boss." There's laughter in Karl's voice, as if he expected me to ask this question. "Relax."

I take my hand off the panel. Roderick is glaring at me, but in his expression I can see resignation. He knows that I'm going to run this skip while Karl's gone.

Roderick also knows he has no recourse. Even when Karl returns, telling on me won't make any difference. Karl won't ban me from these missions. If he does, I'll declare this entire trip a bust and leave. Then I'll return on my own or with a new team and dive it all again.

Karl reaches the door and tugs on the lead, checking its hold. It seems to be fine. Mikk arrives a moment later. His feet are curled beneath him, but they could just as easily brush against the floor.

This is the part of Mikk's dive that I would hate—floating there, waiting for Karl to do the actual work. For the first time since Karl changed our plans, I'm happy to be in the skip. At least I can pace here.

Karl runs a gloved hand along the door's edge. The cameras on his wrist light up and show what we saw on our preliminary dive—that the edges of this door are pockmarked, not from time or debris, but from people trying to break in. The metal is smoother here than anywhere else, as if countless people have run their gloved hands along the edges in the past.

"It's beautiful, isn't it?" my mother asks me through her suit. She turns her head toward me just a little, and I can see the outlines of her face through her headpiece. Behind her something hums.

Sweat has formed on my forehead. Goddamn Karl, he's right. I would have gotten lost in my own head, in my own memories, if I had gone in alone on this first trip.

I shake my head as if I can free it from the past, then settle into the copilot's chair.

Karl pans the door, making sure nothing has changed since the last time we looked at it. Then his gloved hand slips down to the latch.

My breath catches as the door opens. The lights on his suit flare. He turns toward us, waves again, and then goes inside.

For a moment, I can see him outlined against the Room's darkness. Then he propels himself deeper and he is no longer visible through the clear windows of the skip.

The monitors show that his heart rate is slightly elevated. His breathing is rapid, but not enough to cut the dive short. This is the kind of breathing that comes from excitement and eagerness, not from panic or the gids.

"My God," he says. "This place is beautiful."

"It's even prettier inside," my mother says. Her voice sounds very far away. The lights blink against her suit, making her seem like she's covered in bright paint—all primary colors.

"You should see this," he says.

The cameras have fuzzed. We're not getting any visuals at all. The audio is faint.

"I don't like this," Roderick says as the instruments slowly fail.

I knew it would happen. Maybe I remembered something—or something in my subconscious recalled how faint my mother's voice had become. But I had known.

I had warned Karl and he said he was prepared.

But I'm cold. I'm sitting in the copilot's chair with my arms wrapped around my torso, feeling terrified.

My father said the device worked.

But what if it fails like the cameras are failing?

Riya says a dozen others went in and came out. She showed me evidence.

Showed us evidence.

Karl made this choice.

"I don't like this at all." Roderick's hands are flying across the board, trying to bring up the readings. I glance at the handheld screen. The image is still there, faint and reassuring. Just a blur in all the fuzz.

Karl is moving forward.

But I know better than to tell Roderick everything will be all right. I glance at Mikk through the clear porthole.

He's holding the lead and waiting, just like he's supposed to. And good man that he is, he isn't even peering in the door.

He's following orders to the letter.

Static, a buzz, and a harmonic. A voice? I can't tell. Roderick is still working the instrument panel, and I'm staring through the window at the door beyond.

All I see is blackness.

Karl is probably seeing lights. Hearing voices in harmony. Listening to the blend.

I hope the device protects him.

My arms tighten. My stomach aches. I feel ill.

I catch myself about to curse Karl for being right about my reactions. But I'm superstitious. I can't curse him. Not now.

Not while we're waiting for him to come out of that Room.

TWENTY-TWO

We wait for an hour. Then an hour and a half.

Then two.

At two hours ten minutes, Mikk asks, "Should I reel him in?"

We haven't had any contact. We don't have any readings.

Karl is the kind of diver who never wastes a second, the kind who is always on time.

"How much oxygen does he have without the refills?" I ask Roderick.

"Five, maybe six hours, so long as he's breathing right. He didn't think he needed the larger storage, since the skip was so close."

I would have made the same judgment. My suit can handle two weights of oxygen as well. The backups are in case the internal supply gets compromised somehow, not as supplements to it.

"You want to wait another hour?" Roderick asks. No more pretense at being in charge. We both know I'm the one qualified to make the right decisions.

And oddly, as cold as I am, I'm calm. The emotions I felt at the beginning of the dive are long gone.

It's the two younger members of the team who are beginning to panic.

And that's reason enough to bring Karl in.

"Tug," I say to Mikk. "See if he responds."

Mikk tugs and then grunts as if in surprise. The tether attached to Karl has gone slack.

Roderick looks at me, terrified. Mikk says, "What do I do?"

We have to know the severity of this.

"One more gentle tug," I say. Maybe Karl has let out the line. Maybe he's closer than we think.

Mikk tugs again. I can see how little effort he uses, how his movement should just echo through the tether.

Instead it comes careening back at him, with something attached.

Something small and U-shaped.

"Oh, no," Mikk says.

And I hear the same words come out of my mouth as I realize what I'm seeing.

"What is it?" Roderick asks, his voice tight with fear.

"Karl's belt," I say. "The tug dislodged Karl's belt."

Only, it turns out, my assessment isn't entirely accurate. The tug didn't dislodge Karl's belt.

Karl did. He unlatched it. There's no way to tell how long ago he did so either.

He got disoriented or lost or maybe he was reaching for the tether to pull himself back. Whatever happened, his fingers found the controls holding the belt to his suit and unhooked it.

Mikk shows us the seal with his own cameras, how it's unhooked in such a way that only the suit-wearer could have done. It didn't break and it didn't fall off.

Karl let it go.

"So pretty," my mother says, her voice a thread. "So very pretty."

"Pan it for me," I say, forcing the memory of my mother aside.

Mikk does. The knife is in its holder. So are the backup breathers.

And the device.

Mikk grabs it as I realize what I'm seeing. "I'm going after him," Mikk says, attaching the device to his belt.

"*No*," I say with great force. "You are staying put."

"But we need to get him. He can't be that far in. The tether didn't come back from a great distance."

"I know," I say. "But going in disoriented him, and he's got more experience than you. It'll disorient you. I'm going in."

"He said you're not supposed to dive." Roderick has put his hand on my arm.

I shake it off.

"I've been in there before," I say. "I know what to expect. Neither of you do. Mikk is strong enough to get me out if he has to. We'll double-tether me. We'll hook to my belt and my suit. He'll be able to pull us free."

"Karl says if you lose one diver, you shouldn't send another after him." Roderick is speaking softly. He thinks he's not being overheard, but I have the communications panel lit.

"That's if the other person's dead or dying," I say. "For all we know, he's wreck blind and lost. You want him to float around in there?"

"Can he survive without this device thing?" Mikk asks.

Roderick starts at Mikk's voice, then frowns at me.

"I did," I say. "I didn't have a shield. People do survive the Room without protection. The problem is that most folks don't even realize their companions are in trouble for hours. Maybe the Room doesn't kill them. Maybe the Room disorients them. Maybe, if that's what happens and if someone catches it soon enough, the other person gets out."

"Two point five hours," Mikk says, sounding breathless. "That's quick, isn't it?"

"Do you need to come into the skip?" I ask him as I grab my suit. I strip, not caring that Roderick is watching. I hate wearing the suit over my clothes. "You sound like you're short of air."

"I have plenty," Mikk says.

"You can recover while I'm getting suited," I say.

"His heart rate is elevated, but still in the safe zone," Roderick says. "But if you want to bring him in, then let's do it now."

Abort. Leave Karl. That's what Roderick is saying, in code now that he realizes Mikk—and maybe Karl himself—is listening.

"Stay there," I say. "I'm coming to you."

I have to slow down. I need to dress properly, make sure my suit functions. My own heart rate is elevated, and I'm trying not to listen to the low hum that's been haunting the back of my brain since that damn door opened.

My suit is thinner than Karl's. Body-tight with fewer redundant controls. I used to think he was too cautious. Now I wish I had all the equipment he does.

I check systems, then put on my headgear. I don't bother with extra cameras, although I don't tell Roderick that. I slide on my gloves, grab five tethers, and sling them along my belt hook like rolled-up whips.

I open the airlock and look directly at Roderick. "Now you're in charge," I say as I let the door close.

The two minutes it takes for my suit to adjust seem like five hours. I work on slowing my own breathing, making sure I'm as calm as I can be.

Then I press open the exterior door.

My suit immediately gives me the temperature and notes the lack of atmosphere. It warns me about some small floating debris.

I place my hand on the lead and slide toward Mikk. I can see his face through his headgear.

He looks terrified.

Now I wish we hadn't brought one of the strong divers. I would give anything for someone with a lot of experience.

But I don't have that.

I have the children.

And I have to make the most of them.

TWENTY-THREE

Mikk attaches tethers to my belt, my suit, and one of my boots. I must look like some kind of puppet. I warn him not to tug for at least an hour, unless I tug first. I take the device, turn it off, then turn it on and make sure the lights run along the bottom and sides like they're supposed to.

They do.

I attach it to my belt.

Then I float toward that damn door.

The opening looks smaller than I remember and somewhat ordinary. In my career, I'd gone through countless doors that led to an inky blackness, a blackness that would eventually resolve itself under the lights of my suit.

But right now, I have those lights off. I want to see the interior as I remember it. I want to see the light show.

Only I don't. There are no lights. The persistent hum that I'd been hearing since we arrived has grown.

It sounds like the bass line to a cantata. I freeze near the door and listen. First the bass, then the baritones and tenors, followed by altos, mezzo sopranos, and sopranos. Voices blending and harmonizing.

Only they aren't. What I had identified years ago as the voices of the lost is actually some kind of machine noise. I can hear frequency and pitch, and my mind assembled those sounds—or to be more accurate, those vibrations—into music, which as a child was something I could understand.

Now I understand what I'm hearing, and for the first time since I go into the Room, I'm nervous.

"Your heart rate is elevated," Roderick says from the control room.

"Copy that," I say. I don't tell him that these sounds, these vibrations, are familiar. I also don't tell him that I heard them just a few years ago, faintly, and interpreted them as a hum.

When I was on the Dignity Vessel, trying to save Junior.

The thought unnerves me. I have to concentrate on this moment. On now.

I block the sounds as best I can, then I flick on my suit lights. They illuminate everything around me. There's a floor, a ceiling, the window that we'd already observed, and walls.

A completely empty room.

Except for Karl, floating in the middle of it.

I let out a small breath, relieved to see him. Part of me expected him to have vanished.

Or to be stuck, like Junior.

But he's not. He's free floating. His face is tilted toward the floor, his legs bent, his feet raised slightly. Occasionally he bumps against something and changes trajectory.

He's either unconscious or—

I don't let myself complete that thought. I use a nearby wall to propel myself toward him. I grab him by the waist and pull him toward me. His bulky suit is hard to hold; I undo the tether on my boot and attach it to his right wrist.

That's not normal procedure—you could pull off the arm of the suit if you're not careful—but I don't plan to let go of him. Instead, I tug my remaining tethers, and hope Mikk is strong enough to pull us both out.

It takes a moment, and then we're moving backward. I shift slightly so that I can see if we're about to hit anything.

I expect to hit something. I expect to see a pathway to somewhere else or maybe a visual reflection, something that might convince me the emptiness is an illusion.

But it's not an illusion.

Karl and I are the only things in the Room.

Ever since Riya hired me, I imagined the Room filled with shades of the people lost. Or their remains. Or maybe just a few items that they had brought in with them, things that had fallen off their suits and remained, floating in the zero gravity for all time.

The previous divers wearing the device said they couldn't recover Commander Trekov—that he wouldn't leave. Were they lying? Or had they seen something I hadn't?

The open door looms. I kick away from the wall and float a little too high. I have to let go of Karl with one hand to push away from the ceiling.

Then we slide through the door and into the destroyed habitat. Mikk still clings to the tethers.

I shove Karl at him, then reach behind me and grab that damn door.

It takes all of my strength to close it. There's some kind of resistance—something that makes the movement so difficult that I can't do it on my own.

I'm not going to ask Mikk for help, though, and I'm not going to leave the door open. I grunt and shove, then brace my feet and pull that door.

It takes forever to close. I'm sweating as I do, and my suit is making little beeping noises, warning me about the extreme exertion. Roderick is cautioning me, and Mikk is telling me to wait so that he can help.

I don't wait.

The door closes and I lean on it, wondering how I can close it permanently, so no one ever goes in there again.

I can't come up with anything—at least, not something I can do fast—so I make sure it's latched, and then I turn off the gravity in my boots. As I float upward, I grab the lead.

I wrap my other hand around Karl and pull him with me. Mikk is protesting, repeating over and over again that he can bring Karl in.

Of course Mikk can bring him in, but he won't. I'm the one who brought Karl here. I'm the one who put him in charge. I'm the one who didn't protest when he wanted to go into that Room alone.

He's my responsibility, and I need to get him back to the skip.

It only takes a few minutes. It's not hard to move him along. Mikk moves ahead of us and pulls open the skip's exterior door. Together we shove Karl into the airlock and then follow him inside.

I detach the lead. As I close the exterior door, I hear Mikk gasp.

I turn.

His body is visibly trembling. He's looking into Karl's faceplate.

I walk over to them and look.

Karl's face has shrunken in on itself. His eyes are gone, black holes in what was once a handsome face.

"He's dead," Mikk says and he sounds surprised.

That's when I realize I'm not. I think I knew Karl was dead when his belt appeared at that door. Karl's too cautious to lose his extra breathers, his weapons, and the device.

"What happened to him?" Roderick asks from inside the skip.

I touch Karl's faceplate. It's scratched, cloudy, marred by the passage of time. The suit is so fragile that my grip has loosened its exterior coating.

He didn't just die. He suffocated. Or froze. Or both. His suit ran out of oxygen. The environmental systems shut off, and he was left to the blackness of space as if he were outside the station, unprotected.

"Is it something catching?" Roderick's voice rises.

"No," I say. At least, not yet. Someday we'll all die from the passage of time.

"Then what is it?" Roderick asks. I realize at that moment that he's not going to open the interior door until I tell him.

“The device malfunctioned,” I say, and that’s true. It didn’t protect him, although it protected me. “The Room killed him.”

“How?” Mikk asks, his voice nearly a whisper.

All I have is a working theory at the moment, and I learned long ago not to let others know my theories. It causes problems, particularly if I’m right.

“I don’t know exactly how,” I say, and that’s not entirely a lie. I don’t know the mechanics of what happened exactly, although I do know what caused it.

That Room has a fully functional stealth system. Ancient stealth, not the stuff we invented. The kind we found on the Dignity Vessel. Only here, it works, and has continued to work over time.

That’s why we couldn’t find an energy signal, like we did on the Dignity Vessel. Because the stealth tech is strong here. It’s not a barely functional stealth system. This one is hard at work, masking everything, including itself.

But there are problems. The station isn’t growing. The stealth shield is degrading. The exterior parts of the station move in a slower time frame. The interior part, nearest the stealth tech itself, is moving at an accelerated pace.

That’s why Karl died when the device malfunctioned. Time accelerated for him.

I wonder if that was when he saw the lights. Time passing, things appearing and changing, like the light from stars long gone, seen over a distance.

At least he hadn’t died frightened.

Or had he? Thinking he was alone in that big empty Room.

Thinking we had abandoned him.

Like all the other souls lost in that horrible place.

TWENTY-FOUR

We get him inside. It's harder in real gravity; he's heavier than I expected. Roderick and Mikk want to remove the suit, to see what really happened, but I talk them out of it.

We'll do it on the *Business*.

We fill out logs, download information, remove equipment—all the things you're supposed to do at the end of a dive. We do it without speaking, and while trying not to look at the body on the floor behind us.

Then Roderick goes to the cockpit. Mikk sinks down beside Karl, as if staring at him will bring him back. I take out the device. It's still on. The lights run along the bottom in the same pattern they did when I picked it up from Mikk.

I shut it off again, then turn it on. I can feel no vibration, nothing to signal that the thing is working. Nothing changes around me—no visual shift, no audio hallucination.

Nothing.

Just like before.

I should have seen that as a warning.

But I didn't.

It was my fault for trusting technology I didn't understand.

TWENTY-FIVE

Moments later, the skip arrives at the *Business*. Roderick sends the signal and we ease into the docking bay. The doors shut behind us, and the countdown begins until the atmosphere inside the bay gets restored.

No one here knows that Karl is dead. No one knows how spectacularly we failed.

I tell Roderick and Mikk that Karl has to remain on the skip. We'll send in some of the other crew to retrieve him while I look up the forms he filled out so that we can take care of his body according to his wishes.

I also tell them not to say much until we meet tonight in the lounge.

Then I take the device, tuck the handheld into my pocket, and leave the skip. I'm going to meet the team first, and I'm going to tell them what went wrong.

My father and Riya are standing near the door. No one else is with them, and I have the distinct impression they've prevented the rest of the team from coming here.

My father is smiling. Riya is looking hopeful. Somehow they know we were in the Room.

All of my good intentions fade.

I toss the device at them. "This damn thing malfunctioned."

It skitters across the floor. My father is staring at me. Riya bends down to pick it up. As she stands, she frowns.

"Obviously it didn't fail," she says. "You're here."

"*I'm* here," I say, "but Karl is dead."

"Karl?" Riya glances at my father as if he understands what I'm talking about and can explain it to her.

And to his credit, he does. "You let Karl go into the Room?"

"I didn't let him do anything," I snap. "He's in charge."

Or he *was* in charge. But I don't correct myself.

"He chose to go in. He decided last night."

"You let him?" my father repeated.

Behind me, I can hear the door to the skip snap shut. Footsteps along the floor tell me that Roderick and Mikk have joined us, but have stopped just a few meters back.

"How irresponsible of you." Riya shakes her hand. "I gave this to you with the express understanding that you would use it."

"Really?" I say. "You gave it to me so someone could access that Room and recover your father, which isn't possible, by the way."

"You were supposed to go. That's the basis for our agreement." She's still shaking the device at me. "You were supposed to go."

She doesn't react to what I said about her father. Maybe she hasn't understood me.

"What you want," I say slowly, as if I'm talking to a child, "is not possible. Your father is not recoverable. Didn't the previous people who went in tell you that? Didn't they tell you how empty that fucking Room is?"

"It's not our responsibility that he died," she says. "You didn't follow my instructions."

I know she heard me the second time. And it's clear she doesn't care. She knew what was in that Room. She knew that her father—or some kind of ghost of him—wasn't there.

I snatch the device from her hand. "What happens if I break this thing?"

"Don't," my father says, but he's not scared. He is looking at my face, not at the device in my hand.

I turn and toss it to Mikk. He catches it, looking surprised. He holds it like it burns him, even though it's cool to the touch.

Then I advance on my father. "Tell me what's really going on here."

"You were supposed to go in," he says.

"I did," I say. "I went in and recovered my friend."

"He's like almost mummified," Roderick says, his voice shaking. "What does that?"

My father looks at me, then looks at Riya. She is staring at Roderick.

"They both went in?" she asks. "Together?"

"The boss already told you," Mikk says. "She had to recover his body. He went in alone. It was a smart dive move. He was going to map everything. He thought he'd be clearer headed than everyone else."

"You shouldn't have allowed it," my father says.

"Maybe if I'd had all the information, I wouldn't have," I say. "What aren't you two telling me? Besides the fact that you knew the Room was empty."

"It's not our fault," Riya says. "You didn't listen."

"I listened," I say. "You wanted us to recover your father. You wanted me to treat it like I would treat any other wreck, and your father would be salvage. That's what you offered. You came to me because I'd gotten out of the Room before and you figured I wouldn't be scared to wear the device. . . ."

My voice trails off as I listen to what I had just said. *I had gotten out of the Room before.* That's why they hired me. Not because of the device. Not because of her father.

Because I had escaped once before.

"The device doesn't work, does it?" I ask. "It's just pretty lights and nothing more."

"No," my father says, but Mikk takes the device and rips it apart. He takes out the center piece, the part I couldn't quite place, and stomps on it.

The lights still run along the outer edge of the frame.

"Son of a bitch," he says.

Roderick takes the device, turns it over, then crouches and looks at the pieces on the floor of the bay. Whatever that circle piece was, it was solid. There were no component parts, nothing that could be built into an engine or a chip.

"What were you people thinking?" he asks my father and Riya. "Why did you do this?"

"You were testing something else, weren't you?" I'm looking at my father. "This is something to do with your business, not with Mother, isn't it?"

He doesn't answer. He takes a step back. His cheeks flush.

"The others who went in, the ones you say tested the device, they're all survivors too, aren't they?" I ask.

Riya looks at my father again.

"I thought I was the only one still alive," I say.

My father is staring at me.

"But there are others, aren't there? And you found them. You sent them in. And they came out again. Didn't they?"

I take a step toward Riya, and I let her see how angry I really am.

"Didn't they?" I ask again.

"Yes," she says.

"With a fake device. A handful of us can come and go as we please, can't we?"

"Yes," my father says.

"Why didn't you just tell us?" I ask.

"Would you have gone in then?" Riya asks.

"What does my getting into that Room prove?"

"That some of us can do it," my father says. "Some of us are designed to survive."

He clings to me. His helmet hits mine, and a crack appears along my visor. He covers it with his gloved hand, and I can hear his voice in our comm system: Hurry, hurry, I think her suit is compromised.

He holds me so tight I can't breathe. We go through the door back to the single ship someone has brought and they stuff me inside. My dad can barely fit beside me. He checks the environmental system in the single ship, then pulls off my helmet and shoves a breather in my mouth.

C'mon, baby, c'mon, *he says*, don't die on me now.

My lungs hurt. My body aches. I look up at him and he's terrified. He keeps glancing out the porthole at the Room.

I had no idea, *he says*. I didn't know or I wouldn't have let her go in there. I certainly wouldn't have let her bring you.

But I can't think about it. I can't think about any of it. The hum is too loud, the voices echoing in my head. I close my eyes, and I refuse to think about it. About the way she stopped talking, the way her hand slipped from mine, the way her faceplate shattered as her body slammed into the wall.

Then I wrapped my arms around my knees, waiting. My daddy would come. I knew he would come.

I stayed there for what seemed like days, listening to the voices, feeling my mother's body brush against mine, as she got older and thinner and more and more horrible.

Finally I couldn't look anymore. I closed my eyes and wondered when the voices would get me.

Then my father grabbed me and pulled me out.

And I was safe.

I look at him now. His eyes are wide. He has made a verbal slip and he knows it.

"My God," I say. "You know what's in there."

"Honey," my father says. "Don't."

I turn to Roderick and Mikk. "Go get the others. Bring a stretcher so that we can take Karl out of here with some dignity."

"I don't think we should leave you here," Mikk says. He's catching onto this quicker than Roderick.

"I'll be fine," I say. "Just hurry back."

They head to the door. Riya watches them go. My father keeps looking at me.

"You tell me what you know," I say, "or I'm going to have the authorities come get both of you for fraud and murder. You clearly brought us out here on false pretenses, and now a man is dead."

Karl is dead. My heart aches.

"Call them," Riya says. "They won't care. Our contract is with them."

My father closes his eyes.

I look from him to her. "For stealth tech. This is all about stealth tech."

"That's right," she says. "You're one of the lucky few who can work in its fields without risks."

Lucky few. Me and a handful of others, all of whom were conned by this woman and my father. For what? A military contract?

"What are you trying to do?" I ask. "Consign us to some imperial hellhole?"

My father has opened his eyes. He's shaking his head.

"No, you're just the test subjects," Riya says, apparently oblivious to my tone. "Before they approved our project, they wanted to make sure everyone who got out before could get out again. You were the last one. Your father didn't think you would work with us, but I proved him wrong."

"I signed on to help you recover your father," I say to her.

She shrugs one shoulder. "I never knew him. I really don't care about him. And you were right. I already knew he wasn't in that Room. But I figured telling you about him would work. I'm not the only one in this bay who was abandoned by her father."

My father puts a hand to his forehead. I haven't moved.

"I thought this was a historical project," I say, maybe too defensively. "I thought this was a job, like the kind I used to do."

"That's what you were supposed to think," she says. "Only you weren't supposed to send someone else into the Room. You're the only one with the marker."

Marker. As in genetic marker. I turn to my father.

"That's what you meant by designed. I'm some kind of test subject. I have some kind of genetic modification."

"No," he says. "Or yes. Or I'm not sure. You see, we think that anyone on a Dignity Vessel had been bred or genetically modified to work around stealth tech. Then the ships got stranded and the Dignity crews mingled with the rest of the population. Some of us have the marker. You do. I do. Your mother didn't."

He says that last with some pain. He still grieves her. I don't doubt that. But somehow he got mixed up in this.

"There were no Dignity Vessels this far out," I say. "They weren't designed to travel huge distances, and they weren't manufactured outside of Earth's solar system."

"Don't insult my intelligence," he says. "We know you found a Dignity Vessel a few years ago. I've seen it."

Because I salvaged it and got paid for it. I couldn't leave it in space, a death trap to whoever else wandered close to it.

Like this Room is.

I salvaged the vessel and gave it to the Empire so they could study the damn stealth tech.

And now my father has seen the vessel.

"That's how I knew how to find you," he says.

"You didn't need me," I say. "You had the others."

"We needed all of you," Riya says. "The Empire won't give us a go unless we had a one hundred percent success rate. Which we do. Your friend Karl simply proves that you need the marker or you're subject to the interdimensional field."

Karl and Junior and my mother and who knows how many others.

"How long has the Empire known?" I ask. "How long have they known that the Room is a stealth tech generator?"

She shrugs. "Why does it matter?"

"Because they should have shut it down." I'm even closer to her than I was before. She's backing away from me.

"They can't," my father says. "They don't know how."

"Then they should have blocked off the station," I say. "This place is dangerous."

"There are centuries' worth of warnings to keep people away," Riya says. "Besides, it's not our concern. We have scientists who can replicate that marker. We think we've finally discovered a way to work with real stealth tech. Do you know what that's worth?"

"My life, apparently," I say. "And my mother's. And Karl's."

Riya is looking at me. She's finally understanding how angry I am.

"Don't," my father says.

"Don't what?" I ask. "Don't hurt her? Why should you care? I could have died in there. Me, the daughter you swore to protect. Or did you abandon that oath along with your search for my mother? Was that even real?"

"It was real, honey," he says. "That's how I found this. Riya and I met at a survivors' meeting. We started talking—"

"*I don't care!*" I snap. "Don't you understand what you've done?"

"You wouldn't have died," he says. "That's why we approached you last. Once we were sure the others made it, then we came to you. Besides, you've done much more dangerous things on your own."

"And so has Karl." I'm close to both of them now. I'm so angry, I'm trembling. "But you know what the difference is?"

My father shakes his head. Riya watches me as if she's suddenly realized how dangerous I can be.

"The difference is that we chose to take those risks," I say. "We didn't choose this one."

"I heard you tell the team," Riya says, "that someone might die on this mission."

"I always tell my teams that," I say. "It makes them vigilant."

"But this time you believed it," my father says.

"Yeah," I say softly. "I thought that someone would be me."

TWENTY-SIX

And that's the crux of it. I know it as soon as I say it. I thought I would die on this mission, and apparently I was fine with that.

I thought I'd die in multicolored lights and song, like I thought my mother had died, and I thought it a beautiful way to go. I'd even convinced myself that I would die diving, so it would be all right.

I would be done.

But it's not all right. Karl's dead, and I can't even prove fault, except my own. Only when I review the decisions we made, we made the right ones with the information we had.

The thought brings me up short, and prevents me from slamming Riya or my father against the bay wall.

Somehow I get out of that bay without killing either of them.

I don't speak to them as the *Business* leaves the station. I don't speak to them when I drop them at the nearest outpost. I expressly tell them that if they contact me or my people again, I will find a way to hurt them—but I don't know exactly how I would do that.

Riya's right. The Empire will back them because they're working on a secret and important project. Stealth tech is the holy grail of military research. So she and my father can get away with anything.

And—stupid me—I finally realize that my father has no feelings for me at all. He never has. The clinging I remember is just him pulling me free of the Room, leaving my mother—my poor mother—behind.

I can't even guarantee that we weren't part of some early experiment on the same project. While my father was telling my mother's parents to care for me while he tried to recover her, he might have been simply trying to recoup his losses from that trip, experimenting with people and markers and things that survive in the strangest of interdimensional fields.

After we leave my father and Riya on the outpost, we have a memorial service for Karl. I talk the longest because I knew him the best, and I don't cry until we send him out into the darkness, still in his suit with his knife and breathers.

He would have wanted those. He would have appreciated the caution, even though it was caution—in the end—that got him killed.

As we head back to Longbow Station, I realize that I have to stop them—my father, the Empire, all those naïve scientists like Squishy once was. I have to take the functioning stealth tech away from them.

I have to make sure they never fully understand this technology.

I have to make sure they never ever win.

PART THREE

THE HEART OF THE MACHINE

TWENTY-SEVEN

My task isn't as hard as it sounds. It's much easier to destroy something than it is to understand it or to re-create it or even to find it.

But before I start my mission, I need some questions answered.

I need to find Squishy.

Squishy lives in Vallevu, a pretty little town high in the mountains of Naha. She calls herself Rosealma now, and she works as a doctor in a small clinic specializing in family practice.

I am surprised by all of it—by the fact that she has chosen a quiet life, by the fact that she lives in gravity, by the fact that she never dives. When I arrive at her home, I am surprised by one more thing.

The children.

The house is full of children.

It's warm here, and the air is thin. We're five thousand meters above sea level. The house is built on the crest of this part of the mountain and appears to have 360-degree views. Mostly, from my vantage, I can see only clouds and sunlight and bluish purple sky, but even that is enough.

It's stunning here. It almost seems like this point is floating, as if it's traveling through this thin air to somewhere else, like a skyship.

The area offers the illusion of freedom and travel.

Until you look at the house itself.

The house is big and square, with many windows. It dominates the landscape. There are five stories, each smaller than the other, until the fifth is little more than a balcony with a tower in the center.

The house has a wide, rock- and grass-covered yard, with trees and bushes and plenty of places to sit. Paths thread through flowers and foliage.

A front porch rises out of the plants like it has grown from them and attached itself to the house.

An elderly woman sits on the porch, watching the children play hide-and-seek in the yard.

I can't count how many children there are—maybe ten, maybe more—but they are all of different ages, and they all seem very comfortable in front of Squishy's house.

The woman watches them as she sips on a glass of brown liquid. She doesn't move as I come up the main path, but I sense that her gaze has switched from the children's games to me.

"Hello," I say in my friendliest tone. "I'm looking for Rosealma. The people at her clinic say I can find her here."

The woman doesn't respond. She sips from that glass

"I'm an old colleague," I say. "I just need to talk to her for a few minutes."

The children have stopped playing. Several more pop their heads out of the bushes and watch me. It feels eerie, as if they're not quite human. But they are human. I can smell the child sweat mingling with the minty sweetness of the plants and see the impish grins that pass from face to face when they think I'm not looking.

None of these children have been raised in space. They all have the strong bones and thick musculature of children who have grown up in normal gravity.

They make me nervous.

"Please," I say, "if I can just talk to her . . ."

The woman doesn't answer, but one of the older children—a girl, I think, but I can't really tell—ducks under the porch and disappears.

My stomach clenches. I can dive abandoned ships all by myself in the vastness of space, but I'm afraid to cross that last bit of path. I don't want to walk through that crowd of staring children, and I don't want to step onto that porch with the silent woman.

All of this—heat, children, plants—is so far from my everyday life that it stops me from doing anything at all.

Even though no one speaks, it's not quiet up here. The air buzzes faintly—insect noise, I suppose—and far away, something chirps at irregular intervals. If I were on the *Business*, I'd check out that chirp, see if it was an equipment malfunction.

But here, I suppose, it's something alive, something that makes such a noise for reasons I can't understand.

Or maybe there are machines here as well, machines I can't see.

I lick my lips. "Ma'am," I say—

And then the main door on the porch bangs open. The child who disappeared under the porch comes out first. It is a girl, reedy and strong, the lines of her face just beginning to slide into adolescence.

Another woman stands behind her, and it takes me a moment to realize that the new woman is Squishy.

She's not thin anymore. She's rounded, softer, her cheeks chubby and red-tinged. Only her eyes remain the same, flat and distant and frightening.

"What do you want?" she asks.

I've practiced this moment a million times, and I've come up with a million answers. What do I want? To reverse time, Squishy. To go back to the original discovery of the Dignity Vessel and that very first meeting, with you and Karl and Turtle and Jypé and Junior. I want to tell you all what I think we've found, and I want you to tell us how dangerous it is and I want all of us to vote on whether or not we go inside, and then when we do vote . . .

I'll go in anyway.

I shake my head just a little. I don't say any of that, just like I don't say the countless other things I could say. Like: I found more stealth tech. Like: Karl's dead. Like: I need your help.

Instead, I say, "I owe you an apology."

The girl stands in front of Squishy like a shield. I can't see Squishy's face. The woman on the porch acts like nothing is going on.

The children watch. They know something is happening here, but they clearly don't know what that something is.

"Yeah, you do owe me an apology." Squishy hasn't moved. The girl looks over her shoulder at Squishy, and that's when I see the resemblance. The girl looks like a younger version of the Squishy I met. A younger, gravity-bound version.

I'd never thought of Squishy as someone with a family. I'd always thought of her as someone like me, someone who abandoned her family when she realized they never really cared about her.

"To say I'm sorry is inadequate," I say. "But I am sorry. Deeply sorry."

Squishy steps past the girl. She puts a hand on the girl's shoulder and stares at me. Squishy's gaze hasn't changed. It's still flat and dismissive.

Neither of us move for the longest moment. The air continues to buzz around us, like a circuit going bad. A child moves, rustling some leaves. A purplish scent fills the air, so strong that I have to hold back a sneeze.

"That's it?" Squishy says. "That's the apology?"

I nod.

"Then you can leave," she says.

I take a deep breath. "I can," I say. "But I shouldn't."

"Shouldn't?"

The girl is looking up at Squishy again. The woman still hasn't moved, but for a moment she doesn't seem quite as solid as she had. I finally realize that she's not real. She's some sort of projection, maybe a part of the game the children were playing, maybe a holographic nanny, or maybe a low-tech security program, designed to chase intruders away just by her presence.

I make myself focus on Squishy's voice. It's as flat as her gaze. She doesn't want to show any emotion. She's being deliberately calm—too much so. Which is almost like showing emotion, to me anyway.

It shows me that she's afraid of how she feels, afraid that if she lets those emotions loose they'll be inappropriate to the place or the time. Or maybe she's hiding emotions so strong that the only way to control them is to deny them.

I make myself take a deep breath. That thick scent gets caught in the back of my throat and I cough.

"Because of what I did with the Dignity Vessel," I say.

"Because of what I forced you to do," Squishy says.

The girl in front of her is frowning.

"No," I say. "Because I found it, and we dived it . . ."

I can't go on, not in front of the children. I have to censor what I was going to say about Jypé's death, about Junior's corpse.

I swallow against that tickle, wishing that smell would fade back.

"Because of the way I had us dive it," I say, "I put some things into motion, things that I can't take back. But I can stop those things, with your help."

Squishy raises her chin slightly. Her expression doesn't change. The girl watches her, but the other children watch me.

Finally Squishy sighs. "Come with me," she says. "We'll go somewhere private and talk."

Somewhere private turns out to be a gazebo far from the house. The gazebo is on a ledge that extends over the valley below. Plants crawl up the gazebo's walls and cover its roof.

The entire thing looks unstable to me—the ledge extending off the mountainside, and the plants covering the building like some kind of decay.

But the chairs inside are clean, and oddly, so is the floor. The gazebo has no windows—only archways completely open to the outside. Yet the interior is cool. A breeze that I hadn't noticed near the house blows through here, and the shade is pleasant.

I don't like standing in the sun.

Squishy stands at the farthest edge of the gazebo, the part that overhangs the valley, and clings to the wall.

I sit on some kind of couch that appears to be made of sturdy woven sticks. The sticks are painted white, and they look new.

The entire thing creaks as I move, yet I'm somehow confident in the couch's sturdiness.

Squishy and I didn't talk as we walked up the path. The girl wanted to come with us, and Squishy told her no. Squishy told her that she had to watch the other children.

The girl made a face, but she stayed behind.

A few of the other children followed, until Squishy turned on them and glared.

They ran back to the house, laughing. Apparently they had wanted that reaction.

The air doesn't buzz here. The only noise comes from the creaking furniture, and the breeze, rustling the leaves on the plants.

I know so little about plants. I don't know if these are native to Naha or if they are transplanted from Earth. Until I got here, I had no idea that plants could grow on buildings—or that people didn't mind when the plants did.

"Somehow," I say to break the silence, "this isn't where I would have imagined you."

"You've imagined me?" Squishy doesn't turn around. She seems like Squishy and not like Squishy. The extra poundage on her is muscle, not fat, yet she doesn't seem stronger to me. It seems like she softened, eased into life here, lost her edge.

"I think about you a lot," I say. "I should have listened to you."

"Yes," she says. "You should have."

I sigh. This isn't going to be easy. I knew that when I came. However, I didn't expect Squishy to make it even harder.

"Please," I say. "Sit down. Let me tell you what happened."

Finally, she turns around. "You mean something's happened since the Dignity Vessel."

"Oh, yeah," I say. "Way too much."

TWENTY-EIGHT

I tell Squishy everything. I leave nothing out.

I tell her about my father, about Riya Trekov, about the Room of Lost Souls.

She sits on a chair that matches the stick-woven couch. She has her hands folded in her lap, her legs crossed at the ankles. The breeze plays with her hair. She looks like a woman who is listening politely to a story that has nothing to do with her.

Until I get to Karl.

Then she closes her eyes.

Just for a moment, but it's long enough.

"So now," she says before I finish, "you want revenge."

Of course I want revenge. I dream of it sometimes, of going after my father, of shoving Riya Trekov into the Room of Lost Souls, then following her inside so that I can watch her die.

Yes, I want revenge.

But I'm smart enough to know I'll never get it. Not really.

"I want to stop them," I say.

"From taking others to the Room of Lost Souls?" she asks.

"No," I say. "I want to stop them from solving the mysteries of stealth tech."

Squishy's hands tighten. She leans forward. I have her attention now.

I tell her about the genetic markers. I tell her about the "designed" humans loose in the population. I tell her that the Empire now has several people who can work in stealth tech without dying.

She lets out a small breath.

"And," she says as if this has been a conversation instead of a monologue, "they have working stealth tech."

"Yeah," I say. "The Room."

"And the Dignity Vessel that I gave them," she says.

"That we gave them," I say.

She sighs. "What exactly do you want to do?"

"I don't want them to have a breakthrough," I say. "If the Empire gets stealth tech, they'll be able to conquer the Nine Planets Alliance within weeks. At first, the Alliance won't even know who's attacking them."

The Empire never made it to the Nine Planets in the last war. The distance was too far for the Empire to sustain. But the Colonnade Wars frightened the planets and they formed an alliance, planning to fight the Empire if it tried to overtake any of them.

The Alliance has kept the Empire out of this part of the sector so far. But stealth tech would change everything. The Empire could defeat one part of the Alliance before it ever had a chance to send for help.

"So give the Alliance some stealth tech," Squishy says.

"And people with markers? And a way to create those markers?" I roll my eyes. "You make it sound like there are Dignity Vessels all over the sector."

She just looks at me. I wonder if I've said something wrong. Finally, she sighs. "Why did you come to me?"

"I want you to tell me my options," I say.

"You know your options," she says. "You destroy that vessel."

"And the Room?" I ask.

She looks at me for the longest time. "I'd need to see it," she says.

I swallow hard. I'm not going back there. I'm not going to go inside that Room ever again. I'm not going to look at the habitats or the docking areas or the station, looming out of the darkness.

"You said you mapped it," she says.

I let out a breath.

"I have a place we can view things. Did you record inside the Room itself?"

"No," I say. "But Karl did."

There isn't much. The cameras on his suit quit about the time he died. Roderick and Mikk tried to recover the information.

I didn't help at all, and I didn't want to. I didn't want to look at the last minutes—the last few *days*—of Karl's life.

But I will, with Squishy.

Because she's right.

I have to.

Her setup is inside her medical practice. There are several rooms set up for holographic projection, some of which re-create patients on surgical tables. Apparently she uses this place to review what she or others have done.

It reminds me of the lounge in the *Business*, only this setup is more efficient.

Nothing else happens in these rooms except viewing. Viewing and learning and understanding.

It takes a while to make my recordings compatible with her system. I let her worry about all of that. While she does it, I wander the practice, trying to figure out who Squishy is now.

The practice itself is comfortable. Patients enter a waiting area that tailors itself just for them. When I walk inside that room, it becomes a replica of a space ship's cockpit. The cockpit is generic—it has a fake star map outside its portals and the guidance equipment is out of date—but I'm instantly comfortable.

The room takes information from my various chips and re-creates the environment I'm in the most often.

As I stand there, not taking the pilot's chair, the room seems to think I'm uncomfortable. A holographic list appears before me. A soft female voice tells me I can reprogram the room to one of these other places.

One of them is a spaceport bar.

Obviously, I've spent too much time on Longbow Station.

I leave the waiting area and investigate the examination rooms. They're as patient-specific as the waiting area. Because I haven't logged in, the rooms want to know if I'm a visitor, a family member, or a patient.

I don't answer.

I back out quickly and wander the corridors. The private areas are locked.

No one else is here, except for me and Squishy.

So I go back to the viewing area.

Squishy is still fiddling with the machinery. I lean against the wall and wait.

This woman is different from the one who left the *Business* years ago. The weight isn't the only thing that's changed. The military posture is gone as well.

I understand the medical practice—she has found a new way to expiate all her guilt from those deaths—but I don't understand the children.

I asked her about them as we walked down to the village.

She shrugged. Then when I pressed her for an answer, she said, "Everyone needs a place to go."

"That girl, the one who got you," I said, "she's clearly family."

Squishy gave me a sideways look—one I couldn't read.

"Oh," she said softly. "They're all family."

And she wouldn't say anything else.

Now she stands, puts a hand on her back like it hurts her, and turns around. "Got it," she says.

I take a deep breath. I'm not sure I want to see this.

"You can leave, you know," she says.

But I can't. She needs me to explain what she's seeing. She needs context, and only I can provide it.

✦

The station looks small. Nothing we recorded shows the vastness of the place, the sense of emptiness that we all felt when we first examined it.

Not even the *Business*, locked into one of the docking rings, gives it a real sense of perspective.

At first, Squishy and I discuss size, measurements—both the ones that my team took when it arrived and the ones my father claimed he had.

I explain again that my father's information isn't trustworthy, that he has lied to me all along.

But Squishy waves her hand to silence me.

"We can download more information when we need it," she says. "Others have been to the Room as well."

We. I'm not sure how I feel about the word "we." I don't want us both to investigate anything. I just want her help repairing the damage I've already done.

I want to know my options.

Squishy is acting like we have a mission.

For three nights, we examine the footage of the Room. Fortunately, Squishy has turned down the audio. Karl does start to talk about twelve hours in, speculating, wondering if we can find him or if he's entered another dimension.

Mikk listened to the audio on the way back, hoping to figure out what went wrong. He's as haunted as I am, only he blames himself. I keep telling him that what happened is my fault. Odette forcefully told him that it's my father's fault, but Mikk blames himself.

I do understand that. When you're part of a mission, you believe that you have to do everything you can to make it go well.

When it doesn't go well, you review, make certain things will go well the next time. That's part of our training.

When things go horribly awry—when someone dies—then you review as well. Only you carry the burden of that death, and the what-ifs become even more powerful.

You become more powerful. You imagine what would have happened if you spoke up a moment sooner, or tugged the line earlier, or refused to participate in the mission.

You try to find the one way the mission would have worked, and of course, you can't. Or worse, you can.

I know what went wrong on the Dignity Vessel. *I* went wrong. So did Squishy. If I had told my divers it was a Dignity Vessel, they would have acted differently. If Squishy had told them that she worried the probe was stuck in an ancient stealth field, we never would have gotten near it.

Divers died because we did things wrong.

Jypé and Junior died.

But Karl died because my father and Riya Trekov lied to us. Much as I want to review that and change the decision to go with them, I know I would have done nothing different. All of my actions were correct—except, maybe, going in after Karl. That was reckless.

But I'm glad I did it.

Mikk's actions were right too. We just can't convince him of it.

And listening to Karl talk to himself in what, to him, was the last few days of his life, made Mikk feel even worse.

Squishy says she doesn't need to hear it, although I know she's making herself a copy of the imagery. I have a hunch she will listen when I am not around.

And I am grateful for that bit of sensitivity.

There isn't much to see. The others told me that Karl claimed he heard music and saw lights, but none of that shows up on the imagery. I do explain the music and lights to Squishy. I give her my theories.

She pauses the imagery as I talk. "You heard sound?" she asks.

I nod. "It's almost unbearable in the Room. It sounded like a faint hum on the Dignity Vessel. I noticed it when we went to get Junior."

"Not before?"

I can no longer remember what I heard and when. Junior has woven his way into my dreams. My nightmares, actually. I still see his face behind that clouded helmet. Sometimes he speaks to me. Sometimes I watch him age and can do nothing about it.

Often I watch him try to free himself. I try to tell him that he can't, that he's stuck in time, but he won't believe me.

After a moment, I answer Squishy. "I don't know when I first noticed it on the Dignity Vessel."

"That took a lot of thought," she says with no sympathy at all.

I shrug. "I could have told you after we found the body. But some of the details are gone now. I just know that the hum and the music are related, and I only hear them around ancient stealth tech."

She taps a finger against her chin and looks at the image in front of us. It hasn't changed much as we watch. Sometimes Karl explored the edges of the Room. Sometimes he tried the door. But he could never leave, for reasons I can only guess at. Was the door in another dimension? Out of time with him? Or was there something else going on?

I do know it was difficult for me to close that door after I pulled him out. Clearly, for whatever reason, it was impossible for him to open it.

"Sound," Squishy repeats as if she's mulling the concept. "In all the time I worked on stealth tech, no one reported any sounds."

"Do you think that's what was missing?" I ask.

"Sound?"

"Whatever the sound really is," I say.

"Clearly," she says. "Because you've been inside one working stealth tech system and near a malfunctioning one, and both times you heard something unusual."

"But did I hear it because I can function in stealth tech?"

"Karl heard it," Squishy says.

"When he was trapped inside of it," I say. "But I heard it even outside the stealth tech. I heard it from the moment we arrived on the station."

She's frowning at me. "You never asked if anyone else heard anything?"

I shake my head.

"That's not like you, Boss," she says, and that's the first time our conversation feels like one of our conversations of old.

"Nonsense," I say. "You left because I hadn't told you enough. Isn't this just one more case of not saying anything?"

"No," she says slowly. "Because you connect the sound to the stealth tech, so you would have asked others about it. You didn't."

"I didn't make the connection until late," I say.

"Still," she says. "After you got out of the Room, you would have said something."

I didn't say much of anything when I got out of the Room. I was afraid if I said too much I would lose what small grip I had on my temper and go after my father and Riya.

"It wasn't a normal mission," I say.

"Clearly," she says again.

That's a new habit of hers, and one I'm not sure I like. It's a bit condescending. But it's obvious that she's been in charge here for a very long time. She's been the one people have confided in, the one who told them how to take care of themselves, how to live their lives.

On our missions, that had been my function, even though I listened to her and the other members of the team. Only now, she's not acting like a team member.

She's acting like Rosealma Quintinia, the doctor in Vallevu, the woman I really don't know.

"I'm going to have to check my notes," she says.

"You kept notes?" I ask. "On stealth tech? They let you do that?"

"They didn't let me do anything," she says. "I just did it. I had qualms from the beginning. I wanted to keep track of everything I learned, and I didn't want it for their view only. I wanted to have the opportunity to think and speculate without those speculations becoming fact."

I have a hunch, from her tone, that too many of those speculations became fact anyway. Or at least played some role in the experimentations.

"What do you think is important about the sound?" I ask.

"I don't know," she says. "I think something is. But you've brought me so much information, I'm not sure where to start."

"Start?" Now I'm the one who is confused. "Start with what?"

"Figuring out stealth tech."

She sounds almost fanatical. There's a light in her eye I haven't seen before.

"I don't want to figure out stealth tech," I say to her. "I want to prevent my father and the Empire from figuring it out. It's dangerous."

"I know," she says softly.

"I want to destroy it," I say.

"You've told me that," she says.

"Yes, I have," I say, "but you don't seem to understand. *I* want to destroy it. By myself. At no risk to anyone else."

This time, she heard me. She looks at me, a slight frown creasing her forehead. "If that's the case, why did you come to me?"

"Remember our conversation about the Dignity Vessel?" I ask. "Remember how you asked me to blow up the ship?"

"Yes," she says. "You wouldn't."

"For a variety of reasons. I wasn't going to because I wanted that ship. I loved the mystery of it, the history in it. I loved how challenging it was, and I found it beautiful. I didn't want to destroy it. I wanted to explore it."

"I know," she says, crossing her arms.

"But I asked you a question about destroying the Dignity Vessel, remember? I asked you what would happen if we bombed it. Would we do some kind of damage? Open a rift in that dimensional field that the ship traveled in? Would we leave the stealth tech intact while destroying the ship?"

"I told you it didn't matter," she says.

"But it does," I say. "Because ships do travel through there. And the last thing we want is for them to go into some kind of weird anomaly that we created."

She stares at me. "And that's somehow worse than the Empire getting stealth tech? Tell me how."

She's seeing something I'm not. "People will die," I say.

"Do you know how many people will die when the Empire fully develops its stealth tech? The Colonnade Wars aren't really over. They're in hiatus. The Empire still believes the rebels are traitors. It'll attack the Nine Planets Alliance, and it'll be impossible to defeat. That's why the Empire wants this. You know it's important. You called it the holy grail of military technology, and you're right."

It's my turn to stand. I know some of what she's saying, but there's a recklessness to her words, a recklessness born of deep conviction. She believes it's wrong, so we can take any measure to destroy stealth tech, damn the consequences.

If dealing with stealth tech has taught me anything, it has taught me this: Actions have consequences. And some of those consequences can be prevented with thought and preparation.

I say, as calmly as I can, "I came to you, Squishy, because you understand stealth tech—"

"No one understands stealth tech," she says.

I clear my throat, irritated. I have to take two deep breaths before I can continue.

"I came to you because you know more about stealth tech than I do—"

"I'm not sure that's true," she says.

"Do you want to hear me out or not?" I snap.

She looks startled. No matter what has happened between us over all these years, I have rarely lost my temper at her.

"I'm sorry." She uncrosses her arms and threads her fingers together. She adopts a posture of someone who is trying hard to listen, and while I don't doubt her sincerity, I do doubt her ability to hear me.

She's fanatical about stealth tech, just like I was fanatical about that Dignity Vessel.

"You understand the science of stealth tech," I say.

She's about to object, but I hold up one hand.

"Or," I add, "you understand more of it than I do, and probably more than I ever will. I don't have a scientific mind. I'm suited toward history and exploration, not contemplation."

She moves slightly. I sense impatience, but she doesn't say anything.

"I want a real, scientific examination of what can happen if we destroy that Dignity Vessel. I want to know the best case and the worst case, and everything you can think of in-between. I want to know if we're going to unleash something awful into the universe. I want to know if we're going to do what we're trying to prevent the Empire from doing."

She waits. I nod, indicating that I'm done, at least for the moment.

"What about the Room?" she asks.

"What about it?" I ask.

"Do you want to destroy that too?"

"Yes," I say. "But I think we have to pick our targets correctly. Right now, scientists are working on that Dignity Vessel. Anyone can go into the ship. It's just one small area that keeps them out. So the study is easier. But I know no one is working the Room yet. It's still too dangerous."

"You said they can create that marker," she says. "Soon they'll have scientists inside of it."

"I don't know if that's a lie or not," I say. "Riya Trekov told me that, and I got the impression that finding the genetic marker and making one that works is still in the experimental stages. Think about it, Squishy. Would you go into that Room knowing how many people died in there, just because someone promises you that the untested marker they've given you might work?"

"You went in with a lot less."

I turn away from her. She's right, of course. I had gone in with a lot less. But I had no desire to come out.

I haven't told her that part.

"So did Karl," she adds.

"I can't speak for Karl," I say. Then I realize how harsh that sounds. "When you put it in those terms, however, it does seem out of character for him. He was always cautious. I have to think he thought everything through."

"Everything except the fact that the device might not work."

I shake my head. "We talked about that. We knew going into the Room might be suicide."

"I can understand why you would want to do it," she says. "Your mother died in there. You probably felt guilty about that, figured you might deserve to die."

I don't move. She's close, but not as close as she thinks. Because I wasn't feeling guilty about my mother. I was thinking of Jypé and Junior and the other divers I'd lost over the years.

My failures over the years.

My failures. Not my parents' failures or things that had happened to me as a child. But the things that I had done wrong.

"But Karl didn't have that dark side to his personality," Squishy says. "At his core, Karl was an optimist."

I wouldn't have called him that, but we each have our perceptions. And Squishy's perceptions of me are closer than I like to think. So maybe she is close with Karl too.

"He was also an adventurer," I say. "That's his job. And as cautious as he was, he was cautious in the context of a job that could have killed him every time he put on that suit."

She pauses. "True enough," she says after a long moment.

"Most scientists aren't risk takers. They—"

"That's not true," she says.

"But it is," I say.

"Scientists take risks every day," she says over me. "That's what their experiments are. Daily risks."

"In a controlled environment. With data that can be quantified and measured and moved forward. Every scientist I know hates it when something unexpected happens. *You* hated it, Squishy. That was one of the reasons you left the military program."

Her face flattens. She gets that expression she had when I first saw her in Vallevu—protected, guarded.

Angry.

"No scientist is going to go to an uncontrolled environment like the Room—an environment none of us completely understands—and run experiments. That could compromise the experiments. You know that, Squishy."

She stares at me.

"But scientists like you," I say, "scientists who are also adventurers would go into the Dignity Vessel. People without the marker have gone into that ship and come out alive. They can send probes into it, maybe some kind of countermeasures. They can work with that level of stealth tech, but not the fully functional level of stealth tech."

She doesn't move for the longest time. Finally she glances at the image she has frozen. It's just a corner of the Room, and it looks hazy because—well, I'm not sure why. Because something was happening to Karl's equipment, maybe, or because the equipment couldn't capture everything the human eye could see.

"You're taking a lot of risk based on some supposition," she says after a moment.

"What do you mean?" I ask.

"What if you're wrong? What if you destroy the Dignity Vessel and leave the Room intact, and the Dignity Vessel isn't what they were interested in? What if the Room is?"

She has a good point. She always makes good points.

But there's only so much I can do. And even though I'm an adventurer, there's only so much I'm willing to risk.

At least at first.

"If we can successfully destroy the Dignity Vessel," I say, "then we can consider destroying the Room. Let's do this methodically. Let's see what a small explosion will do before we contemplate a larger one."

"We?" she asks.

"Me," I say, "using some technology you've designed for me."

"You want me to build a bomb?" She looks around the room we're standing in. Her office, in a doctor's quarters. She has spent the last several years saving lives. Now I want her to make something that might take them.

"Yes," I say. "Haven't I been clear?"

"Not that clear," she mutters. "You haven't been that clear at all."

TWENTY-NINE

Squishy shuts off the images from Karl's suit. Then she sinks into a nearby chair. She suddenly looks tired.

I'm not sure what she thought I wanted. It's clear how involved she is in her life here. The children, the medical practice, the lovely house. It's all something that radiates contentment.

Although Squishy doesn't radiate contentment at the moment.

"Obviously we haven't been communicating," she says softly. "Tell me again why you're here."

I grab a nearby chair and sit down. "Before you left the *Business*, you insisted that we destroy the Dignity Vessel. I got the sense that you knew how to do it. I just wasn't willing to listen."

She nods.

"So now, I'm willing to listen. I'm going to destroy that damn ship, but I don't know how to do it. I'm afraid if I do it wrong, I'll make things worse. Or maybe I'll just blow another hole in the hull and it won't hurt the stealth tech at all. That piece will stay intact."

She isn't looking at me. She nods again, as if she understands what I'm saying.

"What I want from you," I say, "what I'm hoping you can give me, is a foolproof way to destroy that ship."

"Without destroying whoever takes the bomb inside," she says.

I shake my head. "I'm taking it in. Alone. If I die, I die. But I don't want to take a bomb in and die in vain. Do you understand now?"

She doesn't say anything. She extends her hands and studies them as if she's never seen them before, as if they belong to someone else. She's hunched into herself, and I have the sense that I've disappointed her yet again.

"What did you think I came for?" I ask.

She shakes her head slightly.

"Squishy," I say, "what did you think I was asking?"

"I want to destroy it," she says after a moment. "I *deserve* to destroy it. After all, it nearly destroyed me."

I can say nothing to that. Squishy doesn't look destroyed to me. She looks like a successful woman, a pillar in her community. People love her here. I've discovered that in my few days in Vallevu. They love her and they don't understand why I am here.

I'm beginning to wonder that myself.

I leave her because we have reached an impasse. She won't help me destroy the ship if she can't place the charges. And I'm going to be the only one who places the bomb.

Too many other people have died in my place. Some of the early divers I've lost, I lost because we didn't know how to properly run a dive. I can cope with that. We made mistakes, and any one of us could have died.

A few others died because of their own stupidity. I don't blame myself for that either. I'm not responsible for every stupid act someone pulls.

But Jypé and Junior died for my greed, because I thought I knew best. I didn't investigate enough. If anyone should have died in that wreck, it was me.

Only, as I later discovered, I couldn't have died there. I was the only one on board who could have investigated stealth tech, and I was the one who didn't dive that wreck enough to get to the tech first. I could have survived the tech. I could have pulled the debris away from the field and found the probe. I would have seen the danger, and warned the others away.

No one would have died.

I blame myself for their deaths, for not giving them enough information about the dive, and for not listening to Squishy.

But that's not the death that bothers me. Karl bothers me. He died in my place, doing my job. Granted, we had discussed the dangers, and we both thought we understood them. But Karl had no chance of surviving the Room. Even without knowing the information my father and Riya Trekov kept secret, we knew that I had a chance of survival because I had survived the Room before.

I don't know how to tell Squishy about these things. I can't let her go into that cockpit. I can't let her plant any bombs. She would be going in my place, no matter how much she says she deserves it, and I can't let her do that.

I can't let someone else die in my place.

Too many have died already.

I pace my hotel room, trying to think of a way to get Squishy to work with me instead of trying to take over the mission. The hotel room itself is uncomfortable, partly because it's on land.

I've had several nightmares here, each worse than the last. First I see my mother drift. Then I hear the music for hours, and I wake to silence, clutching my ears. Finally, I dream repeatedly of Karl, his voice slowing as he realizes that he's trapped and we'll never find him, even though he's only a few meters away.

In my nights here, I switch between the bed and the couch. The bed is soft and covered with blankets. It looks inviting. After I found Squishy, I napped here and forced myself awake as the first nightmare came on.

So I moved the half dozen pillows to the couch in the front room of the suite and slept there, thinking I wouldn't get comfortable enough to sleep soundly. I dreamt more in that half sleep than I would have in a full sleep, so I moved back to the bed again.

The room itself has a view of the mountains and the sky. I can program everything from thousands of plays and holovids and readings that play on the wall across from the bed to the bed itself. I can make it softer or firmer, raise it up or let it flatten against the floor. I can even change its length and width—within the confines of the room, of course.

But the one thing I can't program is the environment. Sure, I can change the temperature and the humidity. But I can't change the gravity, and I can't make the room feel like it's on a ship, hurtling through space. If I could do that—if I could make the room feel like it's traveling far from here—I would be able to sleep.

Being in the room only adds to my frustration. I leave, heading to the restaurant across the street.

The hotel has its own restaurant, but it's like restaurants in a thousand other places, with a generic menu designed to appeal to people from all over the system. The restaurant across the street has local cuisine, using local ingredients, and I have fallen in love with one of the omelets, made with homegrown tomatoes and mint. I don't recognize the cheese placed on top, but it adds a tang that only accents the mint.

The restaurant never closes. On my first night in the hotel, I came here after fighting the nightmares and ordered the best meal in the house, letting the chef decide what that was. He asked me what I needed, and I said comfort food, and somehow he figured out the kind of meal that soothed me.

From then on, I was hooked on the place. I've come often enough to become known as Rosealma's friend. No one here calls her Squishy, and I'm careful not to. I don't want to explain how she got the nickname.

To the people here, she's a nice woman, a good doctor, someone who cares for the children.

And the children are the issue. Late one night, when I couldn't sleep, I asked the owner about Squishy's children. It wasn't as abrupt as it sounds. The owner, a tall, slender woman who has a knack for listening, was doing an inventory—which mostly meant carrying a handheld and letting it examine each shelf.

The work wasn't engaging her, so she asked me questions: Who was I? Why was I visiting Rosealma? How long had it been since I'd seen her?

I answered some questions truthfully. I told her that I ran my own business and that Squishy (although I said Rosealma) had once worked for me. I needed to get away after the sudden death of a colleague, and I realized that Squishy probably hadn't heard the news.

Rather than send her an impersonal message, I brought the news myself, as an excuse to travel here and see the Vallevu I had heard so much about.

I don't know if the owner believed me. But when it became clear that she wanted to know more than I was willing to tell her, I gradually shifted the conversation away from myself and onto Squishy.

"She worked as a medic for me," I said. "Yet I was surprised to see she had a private practice here."

"She's a good doctor," the owner said. "People love her. I got the sense she hated field medicine."

"She did," I say, "because you can only work with what you've brought and what's at hand."

The owner was quiet for a moment after that. I wasn't sure if she was listening to her own memories or if she assumed I was stuck inside mine. Or maybe she was done asking me questions, having gleaned enough information to pass onto the locals about the strange friend of Rosealma's who arrived in town unexpectedly.

"The children surprised me too," I said. "Some of them are too old to be Rosealma's."

"They're all hers," the owner said. "She cares for them. She's raising them."

"They can't all be hers," I said.

The woman gave me a withering look. "Biologically, they're not," she said. "But Rosealma loves them as her own."

"Orphans, then?"

She shrugged a shoulder and the conversation ended there. No matter how many times I tried to engage her, on how many future nights, I wasn't able to.

Now I'm hunched over my omelet, a cup of the best coffee I've had steaming beside my hand. The owner sits at the counter. She's watching me, and I get the sense that she wants to ask me a question but doesn't know how.

"Go ahead," I say tiredly. "Ask whatever you want."

She smiles slightly. Then she grabs two pieces of pie, puts some kind of cream on top, and brings them to the table. She keeps one for herself and gives the other to me.

I'm not ready for it. I still have half an omelet to go.

"They say you and Rosealma are working on a project together," she says.

I shrug. "I asked her to review information from our friend's death."

"It's more than that," the owner says. "She's searching for a replacement at the clinic. She wants to leave."

This news both startles me and doesn't surprise me at all. Of course, Squishy hasn't told me that. She is taking care of her business here, which is none of my concern. Until our discussion a few hours before, she thought she was leaving with me.

She thought she wasn't going to come back.

"She's not coming with me." I finally finish the omelet. I set the plate to one side, but I don't take the pie, not yet. I want the food to settle. Instead, I grab the coffee.

"Good," the owner says. "Because we can't spare her."

"I would suppose doctors are hard to find here," I say.

"That's not why," she says. "We got by before; we could get by again."

"Then I don't understand," I say.

"The families here are former military," she says. "Vallevu isn't a natural community. We were given this land and the money to build on it."

I freeze. I don't want to be anywhere connected to the military. "After the Colonnade Wars?" I ask, trying to pinpoint this in time.

She shakes her head. "We haven't been here that long."

I wait, but she doesn't say any more. Instead she picks at her own piece of pie.

"How long?" I ask.

"Technically," she says, "I'm not allowed to talk about that."

I sigh.

"But," she adds, "I was twenty-five when I came here. I'm fifty now."

She gives me an odd smile, as if she's begging me to understand something I'm only getting glimmers of.

"Are you one of the founders?" I ask.

"Not quite," she says. "A few people have been here longer than me. Maybe by five years or so."

"And Squ—Rosealma?"

"She was invited, but she never came. Until a few years ago."

After she left the Dignity Vessel. The glimmer of understanding is finally beginning.

I start, "So the people who retired here—"

"Actually, no one retired here," the owner says. "This was a base at first."

"A base," I repeat. The housing doesn't look like base housing. It's too nice for that. "The Empire dropped quite a bit of money here."

Some nervousness must echo through my voice, because she smiles. "Relax," she says. "The base closed long ago."

"But this is still imperial property," I say.

She shakes her head. "Abandoned and purchased legally by the families who live here."

"Who are former military." I wrap my hands around my cup. The coffee is now cold. "I suppose I have enough information to figure this out, but I'm dense. I don't know your name—"

She starts to tell me, but I wave her off.

"—and I don't want to know. I can't tell anyone if you broke confidentiality, and aside from your employees, we're the only ones in the place. So tell me what I'm missing."

She gets up and takes the cup out of my hand. She pours out the remaining coffee. For a moment, I think she's subtly telling me to leave. Then she grabs the coffeepot and pours me a refill.

She brings the cup back to the table.

"You don't know the history of Naha, do you?" she asks.

"I don't know the history of a lot of things," I say. I don't know the history of any planets. I can barely handle the history of the sector, and then only vaguely. I need some details so that I know which ships should be where, when, and who was piloting them. But if the information didn't affect surrounding space, it didn't interest me.

"We used to have a military base in orbit," she says. "It was classified, so it doesn't surprise me that you didn't know. It was also hard to miss, since it was so large."

"And the families lived on the planet?" I ask. I know enough about military history to know that's strange.

"It was a science base. People used to speculate that they were making weapons up there."

"Were they?" I ask.

She gives me that odd smile again. "That's classified."

"I thought we dealt with that," I say.

"The kind of classified that could get me, a former military worker who lived on that base, in trouble."

"Oh," I say. She is trying to tell me what she can without getting herself in too much trouble. I have to pay more attention. She's giving me the information in an order that won't get her in trouble but that will make her meaning clear.

If I'm quick enough to catch on.

"So," I say after a moment, "people believed they were making weapons."

She nods.

"And it was military scientists who worked up there," I say.

She nods again.

"While their families were down here, for safety's sake."

"At first," she says.

"And then?" I ask.

"What do you know about hazardous duty pay?" she asks.

I hate elliptical conversations. They're the opposite of what I believe. I believe in being blunt and honest and straightforward. This conversation is going to give me a headache before the night is through.

"I know that hazardous duty pay is a great deal more than regular pay," I say tentatively.

"With bonuses should the soldier die in the line of that hazardous duty."

I blink.

"It sometimes takes years to declare someone dead," she adds.

I'm frowning now. I have to put this together with—what? If you have a dead body, then it shouldn't be hard to declare someone dead.

But if you don't . . .

I let out a small breath. On the *Business*, all those years ago, Squishy said to me, *Why do you think I like finding things that are lost? Because I've accidentally lost so many things.*

Things? Karl had asked her. He was in that conversation, as were Jypé and Junior. And me. Such ironies.

And she answered him. *Ships, people, materiel. You name it, I lost it trying to make it invisible to sensors.*

People. She said people.

It sometimes takes years to declare someone dead.

Particularly if they've been lost.

"Rosealma was assigned to that military base, wasn't she?" I ask.

"Until her tour was up," the owner says.

I let out a breath. Squishy worked on stealth tech in orbit around this planet. And somehow, this community was tied to it all.

"Then she left," I say.

"She didn't have family," the owner says.

"Did you?" I ask.

Her eyes narrow. She shakes her head. "I was given a medical discharge. I'm no longer combat worthy."

"May I ask why?" I ask.

"I'm afraid of the dark," she says softly.

My gaze meets hers. She knows why I'm here. She knows what happened, maybe not to Karl, but to Jypé and Junior. She knows about the stealth tech.

"You're one of Rosealma's good friends," I say.

She nods. "You've upset her."

"I'm sorry for that," I say.

"You asked about the children," she says.

Days ago, I wanted an answer, but now I don't. "Yes."

"They're hers. And mine. And everyone's. We care for them."

"Where are their parents?" I ask.

"Lost," she whispers.

Lost. Like ships and materiel. I shiver. "You made it sound like Rosealma was the only person who cares for them."

"The children love her best," the owner says. "They would be devastated if something happens to her."

"So would I," I say. "Believe me, so would I."

THIRTY

"You didn't tell me this was a military base," I say to Squishy the next evening. We are in the viewing area of her medical practice, where we've been the past few nights. Only on this night, there is no image of Karl's surrounding us.

For the first time, I feel like we're alone.

"It's not," Squishy says.

"But it was," I say. "It's on imperial property."

"The families bought this land," she says. "They've invested a fortune to clean it up."

"To clean up what?" I ask.

Her lips thin. Then she smiles, as if she's had a private joke with herself. "What does it matter if I tell you?" she says. "Of all people, you're not going to say anything."

I feel my cheeks heat. Was that why the restaurant owner didn't tell me much? She was afraid I would run to the authorities?

I only know one person in Vallevu who ever did that, and it wasn't me.

"The families cleaned up everything legally," she says.

"Legally?" I ask.

"They effectively sued to own this place," she says. "Then when they got it, they scrubbed the record. In no way can the military reclaim this land. In fact, it should be off their books as well."

I frown. "Why?"

"Because," she says, a slight color building in her cheeks, "the families believe someday their loved ones will come back."

I feel a deep horror, something I thought I was past. The families here believe like the families did at the Room of Lost Souls. Someday their loved ones will return to them. Someday, their loved ones will come back.

Only unlike the Room, where no one could stay for a long time, simply because of its location, these families remained at the site of their loved ones' disappearance for years.

"Shouldn't they be in orbit instead of down here?" I ask.

She looks at me sharply. "Diana talked to you," she says.

"I don't know any Diana," I say. And that's true. I never let the owner of the restaurant—if, indeed, that was Diana—tell me her name.

"Yeah," Squishy says in a tone that implies she doesn't believe me.

"You didn't answer my question," I say.

She nods. "They should be in orbit, yes. On the military science station. We had an entire wing for our work. And they should be waiting somewhere near it. Only it's gone."

I saw many things in orbit when I approached Naha. There were a few obvious tourist resorts—places where people stayed so that they could get a lovely view of the planet without traveling too far from home—and a few other things that I'm sure were classified. But I didn't see anything obviously military. I would have noticed, I'm sure.

"Gone," I repeat, just to make sure we're being clear this time.

"The military took the base apart. The equipment went other places. I'm not sure what happened to the parts of the base itself. I know some people thought it contaminated." She shrugs. "This is all after my time."

"So they can't stay in orbit, so they stay here."

"If you believe that someone can return from stealth tech—or whatever it was that we created—then yes, this is the second most logical place to be. The soldiers who took part, they knew their families were here. So they would come here. If they could ever come home."

It's clear from the way she says that that she doesn't believe they will ever return.

"That's how the families ended up with this place," she says. "They were supposed to leave when their loved ones were declared legally dead, but they wouldn't. A bunch of them wouldn't even participate in the call to declare their loved ones dead. The military had to do it over their protests."

I stare at her. "There was a battle over Vallevu?"

"Yes," she says. "And in this case, the families won."

"The children," I say. "They're orphans of soldiers who were . . . lost?"

Her face closes down again. "The children aren't any of your business."

"Actually, they are," I say. "They're the reason you can't go to that Dignity Vessel."

Her expression is flat. She doesn't want me to see how she feels. But now I'm getting to know that expression, and I've come to realize she puts it on when she's the most frightened, and the most upset.

"I want to destroy that ship," she says.

"You can," I say. "You build the bomb. I'll place it."

"I'm going to place it," she says.

I shake my head. "You can't. You don't want those children to lose you too."

"I'll be fine," she says.

She sounds like me at the Room. Or me just before going to the Dignity Vessel. All bravado and denial.

But I don't tell her that. Instead, I say, "Squishy, look. You can build the bomb. You can even come with me on the trip to the Dignity Vessel. You just can't dive the wreck."

"I want to go onto that wreck."

"Serve as my science officer and medic," I say.

She shakes her head.

I'm getting irritated. She's being stubborn—again. I don't want her to be stubborn.

"If we fail," I say, "and we both die, then what? The Empire continues with its program. More family members will disappear. Or worse. The Empire will get stealth tech."

She raises her chin slightly. I know I have her attention now.

"But if I go in," I say, "and if I fail, then you'll live to fight another day."

"I'll just go in the next time on my own," she says.

"But I won't be alive to see it," I say. "Then it'll be your choice."

"It's not my choice now?" she asks.

I shake my head. "It's my choice. My mission. My father's behind this, Squishy, and all he's interested in is money. He sacrificed my mother to it."

"You said you don't know that for sure," she says.

"You heard my story," I say. "What do you think?"

She looks away.

"I saw you with those children," I say. "They care about you. You're different with them. Warmer."

"Nicer," she says.

I smile. "That too." Then I let my smile fade. "Don't you think that's worth coming back for?"

"Others can take care of them."

"But everyone tells me the children prefer you."

She stares at me. "I can come?" she asks.

"If you swear to me you won't dive the wreck," I say.

Her jaw clenches. She moves away from me. She walks around the furniture, then stares at the wall where we watched the images that Karl recorded.

She's clearly thinking about it. The question is, even if she agrees, can I trust her to keep her word?

I don't know the answer to that. But I do know that I need her. I don't have the expertise to make weaponry. I suppose I could make some kind of bomb or buy something that might be effective. But I'm not sure it'll work on the Dignity Vessel.

The mysterious Dignity Vessel that is out of time and out of its proper region of space.

In some ways, I am more superstitious about that ship than most people are about the Room. That ship seems almost magical to me, and because it does, it seems indestructible too.

I need Squishy not just for her expertise, but for her common sense. If I were to tell her I thought that the ship was somehow immortal, she would laugh at me.

She stops pacing. She glares at me as if I've participated in the discussion she's been having with herself.

"All right," she says with barely contained anger. "I'll take your conditions."

"I want you to swear to me you won't go into that wreck," I say. "Not for any reason."

She crosses her arms. For a moment, I think she won't agree. Then she says, "I swear. I'll stay out of the damn Dignity Vessel. And I'll help you blow the fucking thing up."

THIRTY-ONE

We leave Vallevu three days later. It will take us a while to get to Longbow Station. That's where I've left the rest of the team that dove the Room with me. They want their revenge on my father and Riya Trekov, and while I know that revenge isn't always the best motive for something like this, right now I'll take what I can get.

On the trip to Longbow, Squishy starts her work. Right now, she's just doing theory, but she will need some kind of scientific station, somewhere safe where she can do a few small experiments and build her bomb.

Obviously she can't do that on Longbow. She won't work at Vallevu either—*those people have suffered enough*, she says. What she wants is a decommissioned military science vessel. Those things are designed with disaster in mind.

The science workstation detaches from the main part of the ship, so if some experiment gets out of control, the crew can jettison the laboratory and send it into space.

Only trying to find such a vessel would get us noticed.

So instead, Squishy suggests that we modify the interior of one of the skips. She and an assistant (not me) will leave Longbow, take the skip out of the space owned by Longbow, and do their work.

They'll be within view of the station, but should anything happen to the skip, not close enough that an explosion will damage Longbow.

It isn't until she makes these conditions that the entire project becomes real to me. I want to blow up the Dignity Vessel, but I don't want anyone harmed in the process. The fact that Squishy's work might destroy even a small section of Longbow terrifies me.

We are half a day away when I finally talk with Squishy about this. We're having a meal I prepared in the *Business*'s galley. Usually I don't cook for anyone else. If someone else is on the ship, I either hire a cook or, if I have a large team, I make sure someone on that team doubles as chef.

I never thought Squishy would come back with me, so I didn't hire anyone to take care of us. She has to eat my food which, although it lacks sophistication, is at least filling.

This afternoon I serve the leftover soup I made from some meat (whose name I forgot) from Naha, and cornbread that I made fresh. I can bake, which often gets me through long trips on the *Business*, but I can't do much else.

Squishy eats like a former prisoner, hunched over her food, one arm circling it. She claims it comes from eating rapidly with others on military vessels. Since I've never served, I don't know. I do know that Karl, who had also been military, had eaten the same way.

Still I find it a disconcerting habit. I keep the gravity at Earth normal on the *Business*, so eating is never an issue. I lean my chair against the galley's wall, hold my bowl against my stomach, and eat slowly. I will have my piece of cornbread for dessert.

I don't know how to approach her about her work. Finally, I just decide to be honest.

"I'm having second thoughts," I say.

"I knew you would." She doesn't look up at me. She keeps her bowl close to her chest, the spoon scraping against the bowl's sides. "What part worries you? Or are we just going to abandon the whole idea?"

Her moods have fluctuated since she got on board the ship. Some of it I understood: She got instantly homesick for Vallevu and her life there. But some of it I did not. Every time she goes into the cabin we set aside for her research, she stops at the door, as if she is the one having second thoughts, not me. Sometimes she comes out calm, and sometimes she emerges furious.

Once she left the cabin in tears.

"We're not going to abandon the whole idea," I say. No matter how many qualms I have, I cannot stomach the idea of the Empire having stealth tech. "I just need to know what you're doing."

"You're having second thoughts about me, then," she says, setting her bowl aside. It's completely clean, as if no soup has been inside it at all.

She's making me defensive. I forgot how good she is at that. "No, not exactly," I say, and then realize I lost control of the conversation the moment I said "second thoughts."

So I decide to try another tack.

"When you said you need to experiment, I thought I understood. Then you said that you can't do it on Longbow, and I got concerned. And when you mentioned that the skip might blow up—"

"You've never built a bomb," she says.

That's true enough. I've never built anything large, and certainly not anything large and destructive.

"No, I haven't," I say. "Before I went to see you, I figured I would simply buy one for this project."

My language is so clean, as if I'm discussing a dive or a new piece of equipment.

"If we were facing a regular ship, you could have done that," she says. "But we're not. The very thing that brought you to me is why I need to be as far from Longbow as I can and work."

"Obviously, I don't understand," I say.

She gets up and cuts herself a large piece of cornbread. She doesn't put it on a plate, but instead cups it in one hand, using the other to break pieces off of it.

"I have to make sure the bomb works," she says, "not just in theory, but in practice."

I let out a small breath. Whatever I had expected her to say, it wasn't that. "That's not possible," I say. "We don't have any real stealth tech."

"I know," she says. "And if my research determines that we can use a conventional explosive, then I won't need to work on the skip. But if we can't, then I'm going to need to see how certain types of matter interact with each other."

I grab her bowl and place it in the washer. I add mine to that, then cut myself a large piece of cornbread, place it on a plate, and grab a fork. I start some coffee, less because I want it than because I want the time to think about what she just said.

"I thought you can't replicate stealth tech," I say.

"We did some bottle experiments," she says. "They didn't work, but we didn't know as much as I do now. I want to try one of those, and see what happens."

"No," I say.

"No?" She sounds shocked.

"You're not doing any kind of experimentation. The only time you detonate anything is when we get to the Dignity Vessel."

"I thought you said I can't go in."

"You can't. You'll teach me what to do," I say.

She shakes her head. That very movement makes me angry.

"You're not replicating stealth tech in even the smallest way inside my skip," I say. "You're not experimenting with anything. You and I are going to decide on the most effective possible bomb and we are going to use it. Once. On that vessel. There will be no test run. There will be no experimenting."

Her cheeks are red. "But it might not work," she says.

"That's the risk we're taking. You're here to figure out what we need."

"That's what I'm trying to do," she says.

"*Not*," I continue, "as a scientist. As a diver, an adventurer, and a human being who wants this stuff out of our lives."

"If that Dignity Vessel is on a base somewhere," she says, "then we could take out hundreds of innocent lives."

"It's not on a base," I say.

She pauses, pieces of cornbread dripping from one hand into the other. She looks like a little girl, making a mess because she doesn't know how to properly eat that particular food.

"It's not?" she asks. "How are they working on it, then?"

"I'm not sure they are yet," I say. "All I know is that they've set up a guard."

"That's it?"

I shrug. I've sent Mikk and part of the team to check it out from a distance. They were on that mission while I came to Naha to see Squishy.

"I'll know when we get back," I say.

I told Mikk not to get too close. If he got caught, he could say he was traveling nearby and had no idea there was something important in that part of space. He was going to treat it as if he were taking a bunch of people on a tourist dive (not that my team would ever be tourists) and let the Empire think he was just a bit ignorant.

I hope it worked.

"See why I'm not too worried about blowing up the ship?" I ask. "It's in the middle of nowhere."

"I'd have to test—"

"No," I say. "You can read about Dignity Vessels. I gave you the numbers for the component parts. You know what the ship is made of. We destroy it, and most likely, we'll destroy the stealth tech."

"Most likely," she says, and takes a bite of cornbread.

I am simply repeating her argument back to her, but now she doesn't sound convinced.

"You were worried," she says, "that we'd create an even larger stealth tech field, even with the ship gone. Aren't you still worried about that?"

Of course I am. I'd be foolish not to worry about it. "Of course I'm still worried about it, Squishy," I say.

"If I do a bottle experiment, I might figure out—"

"No," I say. "First of all, you could die. Second, you could open a rift near Longbow. And third, if we do create something nasty, we'll start rumors and warn people away from that part of space."

"If we survive," she says.

I nod. "If we survive."

THIRTY-TWO

I am relieved to see Longbow. I am even more relieved to find that Mikk and the team have returned from their mission to the Dignity Vessel intact. Their little ruse worked.

We meet in a small restaurant that I have rented for the evening. The proprietor has set out a full meal for us—meats, cheeses, breads, fruits and vegetables grown in one of Longbow's hydroponic gardens—and he has left us alone. That too is by my request. He'll return in two hours, serve desserts, and then usher us outside.

I don't mind. It's the privacy I'm after, not the food.

The team is already waiting for me. They're milling around the long table in the middle of the restaurant. Everything here is done to look authentically Old Earth—wooden tables, wooden floors, wooden walls, big thick wooden signs, and a wooden bar off to one side.

None of the wood is real, of course, and I have no way to judge if any restaurant on Old Earth ever looked like this. But it has always felt authentic to me.

The food sits in the center of the long table on thick white plates. The same spread appears on both sides of the table, so things don't have to be passed very far.

Most everyone already holds a plate, loaded with a different variety of snacks. Full glasses of various liquids sit near different spots on the table where people have already staked their claim.

There are only two spots left, one at the head of the table and the other to the right of the head.

Apparently Squishy and I have assigned seating. I glance at Mikk. He smiles at me. He's done this. He has really stepped into a leadership role since Karl died, and I appreciate it.

Mikk sets his glass to the left of the head of the table. Then he puts his plate down. Everyone else comes to the table as well.

Odette takes the foot. Her presence surprises me. She was so angry after we dropped my father and Riya Trekov off the *Business* that I thought she wouldn't work with me again.

As we all thread to the table, there's only one person I don't recognize. She's too thin. Her hair is so short I can't tell its color.

It's not until she stops beside me that I realize who I'm looking at.

Turtle.

"Turtle," I say, and hug her. She feels brittle. "I thought I'd never see you again."

She hugs me briefly, then steps back. She looks to my side, her gaze finding Squishy.

"I contacted her," Squishy says. "Just before we left Vallevu."

"I couldn't believe I heard from you." Turtle tentatively touches Squishy's arm. "Thanks for letting me know about Karl."

Squishy moves away ever so delicately.

"You told her in a communication?" I ask. I can't believe the insensitivity of that. Karl and Turtle were friends. I figure that such news is always better told in person.

"I told her to meet us here and to find some of your divers," Squishy says to me. "They'd let her know what happened."

Turtle gives Squishy another longing look, and then steps back. "I'm so sorry about Karl," Turtle says to me. "It sounds awful."

I remember the feel of him in my suited arms. How I could close my arms around him and gently tug him backwards, getting no resistance at all. How, in that moment, I knew that the Karl was gone, even though his body remained.

"It's probably worse because Karl would be alive if it weren't for her dad," Mikk says. "If Boss hadn't stopped me, I would have killed the bastard. Hell, I'm still not sure we shouldn't."

I give Mikk a sideways look—a silent "not now."

He shrugs.

Turtle stays close to my side. She's still peering at Squishy.

"You look different," Turtle says to Squishy.

"Boss says I'm nicer now," Squishy says. Then she smiles. "I'll work on fixing that."

Mikk smiles, but no one else does. Instead, we go to the table. I sit at the head, as I'm expected to do.

I look around the table. No one is missing. Roderick sits between Bria and Jennifer. Hurst looks tiny next to Davida and Tamaz. Turtle actually looks like she belongs.

Only Squishy seems out of place.

There is also one empty chair, and I'm not sure if that's accidental or by design. The chair is even kicked out a little and turned at an angle, just like Karl would have done if he were actually sitting there.

My heart twists. To cover that sudden surge of emotion, I wave at Odette, who, at the other side of the table, seems impossibly far away. She actually smiles at me, and waves back.

I make the introductions. I tell my most recent team that Turtle and Squishy dived the Dignity Vessel with me, and they're familiar with it. I also tell them that Squishy won't be diving it this time.

"She's our medic," I say. "She's also in charge of destroying the damn thing."

"How can she destroy it if she doesn't dive?" Mikk asks.

I glance at Squishy. I don't know how much of her past she wants me to tell them.

She tilts her chair slightly. "I'm former military," she says. "I worked in the stealth tech program. Boss thinks I can blow the ship up."

"Do you think so?" Hurst asks.

"Boss won't let me test my equipment," Squishy says as if this were a democracy, as if she can convince the others to vote for her way of doing things.

"You would want to test an explosion?" Davida asks. I can hear the horror in her voice. "Where would you do that?"

"On one of the skips," Squishy says. "It would be controlled—"

"If it were going to happen," I say. "Which it's not. Squishy is going to figure out exactly what components we need and how much we need. Then I'm going to take it into the wreck."

"That wreck is big," Mikk says. "You can't dive it alone."

"I'm going to," I say.

He shakes his head. Apparently he thinks this is a democracy too. "It's too dangerous. I think a team can safely go in there with you—"

"You haven't been inside," I say. "It's better if I go by myself."

"I've been inside," Turtle says softly. "I never went into the cockpit, though, where we lost Junior. That's where the stealth tech is. I think if you stay away from that part of the ship, you'll be fine. I mean, I'm okay, and so is Squishy. Nothing harmed us while we were there."

Everyone is watching her, looking more than a little confused.

She gives a small shrug. "I'm just trying to say that I think Mikk's right. It's better if a team goes in, just in case there's a problem."

I feel a thin band of anger start in my stomach. "I know what I want to do here," I say, "and it doesn't involve any other divers."

"Maybe you should hear us out first," Mikk says. "You don't know what you're facing."

"I know what's inside that ship," I say, and realize I sound as stubborn as Squishy did when I was talking to her on Vallevu. "You haven't been inside. Have you?"

I ask that last with an edge in my voice. He was under strict instructions *not* to dive the wreck. If he didn't follow those instructions, I will not bring him along on the new trip.

"No, I haven't been inside," he says, "but you haven't asked what we've found."

I lean back slightly. I'm not used to Mikk talking back to me. Give him control of his own mission and he believes he's in charge.

But he's also right. I need to know what happened when he went to the Dignity Vessel, and I need to know before we make actual plans. Everything could change depending on what he saw.

"You're right," I say. "We shouldn't be arguing procedure until we have all of the information."

Squishy and Turtle both look at me, with matching stunned expressions on their faces. Apparently they've never heard me utter that sentence before.

Mikk doesn't notice their response, although Odette does. She grins, apparently understanding what they're thinking.

"We left just after you did," Mikk says. "I rented a ship—I figured it would give us more verisimilitude—and I took Jennifer and Hurst with me."

He took the younger-looking members of the crew. They were good choices if Mikk didn't plan on diving. It would seem to a stranger boarding the ship that everyone on board was naïve and new to diving.

"We brought rented equipment and stashed ours in the cargo hold, figuring no one would ever look for it, not with the rented stuff sitting out. Then we charted half a dozen courses, and began each one of them, veering off course every time. Hurst got us 'lost' so that it really looked like we had no idea where we were going."

"I was beginning to think we didn't," Jennifer says.

Everyone laughs, but I don't think she meant it as a joke. I think she had gotten nervous.

"The Dignity Vessel is a long way from nowhere," I say.

Mikk nods. "I think that's why they're not too worried about it."

"What do you mean?" I ask.

He holds up his hand. "Let me explain," he says.

They drifted in, like a group that's tired and not sure where it's supposed to be. They let the rented ship—called *The Seeker*—drift once they got close.

The one thing *The Seeker* did have was an excellent scanning system. Hurst used it to see what was in the vicinity. They located three military-class vessels, none of them warships. Two were quick maneuvering skips, and one was a command vessel. They formed a loose circle around one point in space.

The active vessels made it impossible for Mikk or Hurst to lock in on the Dignity Vessel's signal, the thing that drew me to it so long ago, but they surmised it was there, just by the way the other ships surrounded it.

"There were only three ships," Squishy says, interrupting the narrative. "And one of them was a command vessel?"

Mikk nods. He doesn't seem irritated by the interruption.

I would have been.

"That's not a lot of firepower," Squishy says. "A determined someone could come into that area with the right equipment and drag that Dignity Vessel out of there."

"It doesn't sound possible to me," I say.

"It is." Odette speaks from the other side of the table. "There's an easy maneuver to make the odds in your favor. But I want to hear what else Mikk found."

She sounds a little annoyed. I'm getting a sense she's not fond of Squishy. They've both been around diving a long time, so it's possible they've met before and have a history.

It can also be that Squishy's abrasive nature has already rubbed Odette the wrong way.

"We had to get a lot closer to see if the Dignity Vessel was actually there," Mikk continues. "We drifted *The Seeker* in, as if we weren't paying attention."

Hurst knew how to do a casual mask of the scans, so it wouldn't seem like they were looking for something. If they did get caught, he planned to say that the ships made him nervous and he wanted to know if they were a threat.

The three vessels didn't seem to notice *The Seeker*. They didn't come after it and they didn't say anything to it.

Finally, the small team got a reading on the Dignity Vessel. They were even able to get a holographic image of it. They compared that image to the images I gave them before I left, and figured that not much has changed in the intervening years.

They even saw the probe.

Hurst wanted to go in closer. Jennifer agreed. It was Mikk who wanted to come back.

"I figured we were too exposed," Mikk says, "but Hurst reminded me that Boss wanted a recon, and if we had to send another ship, then the people surrounding the Dignity Vessel might get suspicious."

"I'm confused," I say. "Those ships *surrounded* the Dignity Vessel? I thought they were small."

"They were small," Jennifer says. "But they were constantly moving around it."

"The two skips were, anyway," Hurst says. "The command vessel stayed in place."

"You're sure that was a command vessel?" Squishy asks.

Hurst nods. "I don't think it could've been anything else."

Neither of us tell Squishy that Hurst used to pilot ships in combat zones. He's as familiar with military procedure as she is.

She shrugs skeptically, looking away. I'm not skeptical at all, and it's my opinion that counts.

"I knew they were watching us," Hurst says. "And I figured we should continue our ruse. We're just a lost band of wannabe divers. Then we see the Dignity Vessel and we want to know more about it. We figured we would go in closer."

"Did you?" Turtle asks.

Hurst nods. "I wanted to get into a better scanning range. I didn't believe what we were seeing."

"I thought there had to be more ships," Squishy mutters.

"It's not the ships," Mikk says. "There were only three. But the readings we were getting of the Dignity Vessel were odd."

"Odd?" I ask.

"I think they were feeding us scans off their own ship's systems," Hurst says. "They added some stuff."

I hold up a hand. "What did they add?"

"Radiation," he says. "The ship was giving off the strongest radiation signature I've ever seen."

"Every ship gives off radiation," Squishy says, "especially if it's spent some time in space."

"We know," Mikk says gently.

I give him a sharp look. He gets softer and more gentle when he's irritated. He doesn't meet my gaze. He knows I'm sensing his mood.

"The readings we were getting off the Dignity Vessel were off the charts," Hurst says. "The kind of readings you'd get if the ship had been in some kind of firefight. You know, with ancient radioactive weapons or something."

"The implication," Jennifer says, "is that the ship is so contaminated no one dare go on board, even in an environmental suit."

"We didn't get readings like that *ever*," Turtle says in surprise.

I fold my hands together. "But it's a great way to keep passersby away from the ship, and it also explains why the military is there. They're trying to clean up some kind of toxic mess, which they generally only do when they're the ones who cause the mess."

"Well," Mikk says to me, "you never said anything about radiation, but we knew about stealth tech, and we thought maybe it went haywire or something and caused the readings."

"We reviewed your information again," Hurst says. "From what we can tell, you got no radiation readings from the stealth tech at all."

"We weren't in the cockpit very long," I say. We weren't thinking of taking radiation readings. When Karl and I were in the cockpit, we were trying (hoping) to save Junior.

"Not just the cockpit, Boss," Turtle says. "Karl and I never noticed anything on our first dive, and believe me, I would have monitored for it. I'm terrified of radiation."

"She is," Squishy says, and they look at each other from across the table. For a moment, the old attraction between them becomes obvious to everyone.

Then Squishy looks away.

Turtle makes herself look at the others. Her cheeks are flushed.

"The readings had to be false," Mikk says. "We argued about that a little. Hurst wanted to get closer, and I have to say, I was the one arguing for caution."

"But Boss wanted to know what we were facing," Hurst repeats. I'm beginning to sense that was his mantra on this trip with Mikk and Jennifer. It must have annoyed them after a while, but I'm relieved that Hurst listened.

I did—I do—want to know what we are facing.

Mikk nods. "We got really close and took our own scans. That's when it got dicey."

One of the smaller military ships broke away from the Dignity Vessel and headed straight for *The Seeker*. As the military ship came, it demanded that everyone on *The Seeker* identify themselves and why they were in the vicinity.

"We thought about lying," Mikk says.

"Be honest," Hurst says. "*I* thought about lying. I didn't want them to know I was a vet."

Squishy looks at him in surprise. She has underestimated him, and she finally realizes it. She gives me a glance, as if I should have protected her from herself.

I say nothing. I let them continue with the story.

"But I decided it was better that I tell the truth," Hurst says.

"Or as much of the truth as we could," Jennifer says. "We agreed to answer questions directly, but not to embellish."

"I wanted to do most of the talking," Mikk says.

"And so he did," Hurst says with a small smile.

The military ship took their identification and then demanded to board them. The entire crew had expected that. So they agreed to the boarding and crowded near the airlock to wait.

It didn't take long. The military ship grappled onto theirs, holding it in place. Then four soldiers boarded, coming through the airlock with weapons drawn.

"I've never seen anything like that," Jennifer says. "It scared me worse than any dive."

"Except the Room," Hurst says softly.

She gives him a sad look. Then she nods. "Except the Room."

The four soldiers crowded into *The Seeker*'s cockpit. Their weapons—laser rifles—were long and looked more powerful than anything Mikk had ever seen. Hurst believed they were newer models than the ones he'd trained with, powerful guns that could kill from a great distance—and if the settings were right, wouldn't do any damage to a ship's hull.

"Scary," Turtle mutters.

Half the people around the table nod.

Squishy just crosses her arms, as if she already knew about this sort of thing.

"They asked us to identify ourselves all over again," Jennifer says. "So I introduced us."

"It was a nice effect," Mikk says, "because her voice was shaking."

"It wasn't an effect," she says. "I was scared."

The soldiers muscled their way in. They searched the ship, found the rented diving equipment, and asked a lot of questions about where the team planned to go and what they planned to do.

Jennifer told them that the team had been looking for a specific wreck, but couldn't find it. They'd gotten turned around several times.

"All four soldiers were men," Mikk says, "and Jen's doing this little lost girl thing with them. They believed it."

"*I* believed it," Hurst says, "and I knew she was lying."

"They checked our logs and our trips report, and they offered to help with plotting the correct course," Jennifer says. "Then Hurst got all defensive with them, and I got worried. I thought he was going to ruin it."

"But it turns out that was the thing that turned the tide," Mikk says. "They might have thought it was a setup if it weren't for Hurst saying he knew better. They pushed him aside and proved to him he was wrong."

"I pretended like that hurt my feelings." Hurst laughs. "Instead, I used the time they were searching through my equipment to do a quiet scan on them."

"Did you learn anything?" I ask.

"Nothing I didn't expect. These were real soldiers, fighters, career military. Their work was classified, but they were strong and battle-ready." Hurst looks at me. We both know that's significant.

When we go to the Dignity Vessel, we have to be ready to fight.

Squishy squirms beside me. She has realized that we must fight as well, and she clearly doesn't like the idea.

I turn my chair slightly so that I don't have to see her. She's distracting me.

"It took a while," Mikk says, "but they accepted our story. Then they told us to leave immediately."

"I did ask them about the ship," Jennifer says.

"But she was smart about it," Hurst says. "She did that lost little girl thing again, talking to the big bad soldiers."

"It wasn't as bad as all that," Jennifer says.

"No, she wasn't acting like a little girl," Mikk says. "She was flirting."

Jennifer gives him a fond smile. "I asked them if they were worried about being that close to so much radiation."

"And one of them says to her, 'It's not as bad as it seems.'" Mikk laughs. "The guy next to him whacks him on the arm, as if he'd done something wrong. Which, essentially, he had. He told us that the radiation wasn't really a problem."

"But the way he said it, you could interpret it as he was just being a tough soldier," Hurst says. "That's what Jen did. She saved our butts."

"She got us a lot of information," Mikk says.

"Like what?" I ask.

"The ships have a minimum complement of soldiers," Jennifer says. "They aren't paying a lot of attention to what's going on around them. I even got the sense that it took them a while to see us."

"All the time we thought we were being watched, and they probably hadn't even noticed us," Hurst says.

"They consider it the worst duty in the sector because it's so dull," Jennifer says.

"It makes sense," Hurst says. "They were trained for battle, and there they are, circling some abandoned ship for weeks, with nothing really to do."

"What about the command ship?" Squishy asks.

Mikk looks at her. His expression is measuring, as if he doesn't really want to talk with her. Squishy is not making herself popular with my team.

Hurst is the one who answers her.

"The command ship is the one detail we weren't able to figure out," he says. "They didn't tell us why it was there, and we couldn't ask."

"I tried," Jennifer says. "I said something dumb like how come it wasn't the big ship that came for us, and they said that the big ship rarely does hands-on work. But that's all they said about it."

"They probably didn't dare say anything else." I scan the table. Everyone is watching Jennifer, Mikk, and Hurst. Apparently they haven't told this to the team—or if they have, they haven't told the story in its entirety.

"Then what?" I ask. "Did they detain you?"

"They talked a little bit," Jennifer says. "They wanted to know about diving."

"We had to be careful," Hurst says. "We didn't want to sound too knowledgeable."

"But we did want to seem enthusiastic," Mikk says. "I think we achieved that."

"I don't think they cared," Jennifer says. "I think they wanted something to do. Imagine circling around that wreck, waiting for something to happen."

"They'll be itchy," Squishy says. "That's dangerous."

Turtle nods. So does Hurst.

Odette leans forward. Her movement is so abrupt that it's an interruption all by itself.

"You were on a fact-finding mission," she says to Mikk, sounding like she's the leader instead of me. I let her take this. Odette can be quite forceful if need be. "You discover three ships—two small military vessels and something you call a command ship. Four restless soldiers who really didn't investigate you all very deeply from what I can tell, and a manufactured scan of the Dignity Vessel. Is that all you found?"

"It doesn't sound like much when you put it that way," Hurst says.

"You've given us details, but no understanding," she says. "For us to make plans, we need understanding."

"I have to add one more detail," Mikk says. "We did get a good scan of the Dignity Vessel. One of our own."

We all look at him.

He spreads his hands as if he's apologizing. "It's not too different from what you found. But . . . Squishy? Is that really your name?"

"It's what Boss calls me," Squishy says, "and that's good enough."

He sighs as if he doesn't approve. "They never fixed the hole where the probe is. The ship is still open to space. They haven't put anything on it. The radiation readings were in the normal range."

"With the hull still open to space like that, then that means they didn't get the ship's internal environment up and running," Turtle says.

"The ship is the same vessel you found," Mikk says to me. "Same low power reading, same openings. If anything, the hull is even more pock-marked, but I can't say that for certain."

"They haven't done anything with the Dignity Vessel?" Squishy asks.

"Not that we could tell."

"No life signs on board or anything?" Squishy asks.

"*The Seeker*'s equipment wasn't that sophisticated," he says. "We couldn't get life sign readings from any of the ships."

"The military vessels were shielded," Squishy says.

"I figured," Mikk says in that gentle dry tone that implies he's humoring her. "But we couldn't get anything from the Dignity Vessel either, and I doubt they shielded that."

"It would've been too risky," Turtle says, taking him seriously.

Squishy just frowns at him. "I can't believe they're not working on the vessel."

"I told you," I say. "They're waiting for my father and Riya Trekov to finish their experiment."

"I thought they did, with you," Squishy says.

"Things move slowly in the Empire," Hurst says. "As former military, you should know that."

She glares at him, then leans back.

"Maybe that's why the command vessel was there," Turtle says. "Maybe something is happening. Or am I misunderstanding what a command vessel is?"

"You're not," Hurst says. "That's the mystery of the place. With two tiny military vessels, they didn't need a vessel that big. We couldn't get any information about it, and they certainly weren't going to tell us why it was there."

"Do you think they're bringing in more ships?" Bria asks. "Maybe that's why it was there."

"You'd think the ships would arrive before the command vessel," Hurst says.

"It's all speculation," Odette says. "We need facts."

I agree with her. We need facts.

"Here's what I understand," I say. "The Dignity Vessel is exactly where we left it. They have a small team of guards surrounding it. Two small military vessels with a crew complement of—what?"

I look at Squishy, then at Hurst. I'm hoping they know.

Hurst shrugs one shoulder. "I can't imagine more than eight soldiers on each of those ships."

"They're built for ten," Squishy says. "But if this is easy duty, the military isn't going to waste twenty soldiers on some wreck in space. There might only be four on each vessel."

"You mean we saw the entire crew?" Jennifer says. "That makes no sense. Someone had to remain with the ship."

Odette nods. "It makes sense to me. Five. That's half what the ships will bear. If you have five on each, then you have a redundant system. Something can happen to one ship, and you haven't lost your entire crew. But you're not fully staffed, so you're not wasting money either."

"What about the command vessel?" I ask.

"I'd like to see the specs," Squishy says. "Maybe it's a scout vessel."

Finally, Hurst gets annoyed. "Believe me," he says, "it was a command ship."

"That's a minimum of thirty," Squishy says to me, as if she hasn't noticed his irritation.

"On the command ship?" I ask.

She nods.

"So we have forty soldiers, minimum, maybe fifty," I say, "and God knows how many nearby."

"We didn't register any," Mikk says, "but they could've been in stealth mode."

"I don't see the point of that," Odette says. "Especially if nothing has happened to that vessel in years. I think we have to assume there were only the three ships."

"All right," I say. "Three ships. Maybe fifty soldiers. No one on the Dignity Vessel. And probably no one is doing long-range scans or they would have come to get *The Seeker* much sooner. They wouldn't have let *The Seeker* get that close."

"I agree," Squishy says.

"They may be itchy," I say, "but they're also complacent. It'll take them a while to get up to speed on any situation. The question is time."

"Time?" Mikk asks.

"We need time to plant that bomb. We haven't dived the Dignity Vessel in years. We could get to the heart of it within about fifteen minutes, if my memory serves, but we can't do that now."

"Why not place the bomb in that hole in the hull?" Jennifer asks.

Squishy shakes her head. "We want the bomb outside of the stealth tech. Close, but not close enough to be in the stealth tech field."

"Still, planting it outside seems the logical thing to do," Jennifer says.

"That also makes the bomb obvious to the military," I say. "I'd rather put it in the cockpit."

I want to obliterate that place from my memory. I'm not sure a bomb will do it, but I hope it will.

"We need some kind of diversion," Odette says. "We need those military vessels out of the area for at least an hour."

"An hour?" Hurst says. "You think that'll be enough?"

I shake my head. "We're better off planning for two or three hours, and even that might cut it close."

I put my hands on the table and stand up, effectively ending the meeting. More hard facts aren't forthcoming, and speculation will only confuse the issue. Squishy hasn't finished the bomb yet.

Up to this point, the bomb is all I've focused on. Now I have to get us past military vessels and find time to dive. That'll take a lot more planning than I'm used to.

I wish Karl were here. This is a mission he would be able to lead much better than I would. His own military background and his innate caution would guarantee success.

"Let's think on this," I say. "We have time. Let's make sure we do this right."

THIRTY-THREE

Odette pulls me aside later. I am heading for my berth. She insists on walking with me.

The corridors in this part of Longbow are narrow and cramped. They're designed to discourage people who've been drinking and eating in the nearby restaurants from venturing in this direction. There is barely enough room for both of us to walk side by side, even though neither of us is large.

Before she speaks, Odette looks over her shoulder. When she is satisfied that we're alone, she says, "I think you should let Squishy go."

"I sought her out," I say.

"I know," she says, "and I'm not exactly sure why. She's not trustworthy."

I clasp my hands behind my back. "She knows a lot about stealth tech."

"You've asked her for her expertise in that area, and she's given you what she knows. At least, as much as you can tell."

We go around a corner, and I stop. I want to see Odette's face as we talk. "You don't like her, do you?" I ask.

"Do you?" Odette asks.

It's a fair enough question. "We were friends once."

"Once," Odette says. "Then she betrayed you. To the Empire, no less. *She*'s the reason they have that Dignity Vessel in the first place."

"I know," I say. I'm not likely to forget that betrayal.

"Have you ever asked her why she turned you in?"

"I know why," I say. "She thought stealth tech was too dangerous for us. For any layperson, really. She wanted the Dignity Vessel removed from that site."

"Which didn't happen," Odette says. "You'd think Squishy would know that it couldn't happen."

I think about that for a long moment. Odette has a point. And I never asked Squishy to clarify her reasons. She hasn't apologized to me for reporting the Dignity Vessel, nor has she said she made a mistake.

I'm not even sure she considers her actions a mistake, given what she knew at the time. She figured no one could work in stealth tech. She probably figured giving something that dangerous to the Empire might save lives.

"She fought me pretty hard on that Dignity Vessel dive," I say. "If she wanted to stop me—and anyone else—from diving the vessel, she made the right choice. She didn't report us until Jypé and Junior died. I assumed—hell, I know—she couldn't take it anymore. She didn't want to be part of any more deaths."

"Yet she gives the ship to the Empire, which guarantees there will be more deaths," Odette says.

"What choice did she have?" I ask. "She didn't want others to stumble onto the wreck, and I wasn't listening to her."

Odette frowns. She looks at the empty corridor as if making certain we're still alone. When she looks back at me, her frown seems to have deepened.

"She's delaying you now," Odette says. "She wants to test everything. She wants to tell others what to do. She invited her old lover and is now ignoring her. All of this will cause troubles on the mission."

I got into this position the first time by not listening to one of my team members. After Jypé and Junior died, I vowed I would listen. I have to struggle right now to follow my own vow.

Which is odd, since I've known Odette a long time.

"Have you worked with Squishy before?" I ask, recalling the stray thought I'd had during the meeting.

"My opinion remains the same," Odette says. "She's trouble."

So she has worked with Squishy.

"I'm not doubting your opinion," I say. "I just want a little more information."

Odette sighs. She leans against the wall, something I would never do here, since these corridors are filthy.

"I worked with her," she says. "I helped train her to dive."

"A long time ago," I say.

"Boss, you're being dismissive," she says.

Normally, she would be right. What I'm saying may sound dismissive, but it isn't.

"I'm trying to get a sense of how long ago this was," I say.

"When Squishy came out of the military," Odette says. "Before you gave her that ridiculous nickname. We called her Rosealma, but she wasn't fond of that either. She was very military."

"Meaning?"

"By the book. She didn't like change or variables. Even after the training, I thought she was a dangerous dive partner."

"Why?" I ask.

"Because she wanted everything just so," Odette says.

That wasn't the Squishy I dived with. But most divers were by the book in the beginning. If they remained by the book, they could never go beyond tourist dives.

I would never take an inflexible by-the-book diver on my wreck dives. But if I tell Odette that, she'll think I'm being defensive again.

"Did you have other trouble with her?" I ask.

"I never knew exactly where she stood," Odette says. "Like now. Is she working for the Empire? Is she working for you? Or is she working on something else?"

I smile. "She's not working for me, and she's certainly not working for the Empire."

"How can you be sure?" Odette asks.

"Because I've been to her home. I've talked with the locals. That's an antigovernment place."

"So they tell you," she says.

"The research I did after I left backs it up," I say.

She nods once. "If she's not working for you or the Empire, who is she working for?"

"Herself," I say. "Just like the rest of us."

"That doesn't reassure me," Odette says.

"I didn't think you were asking for reassurance," I say. "I thought you were talking about Squishy."

Odette studies me. She knew me back in my beginning days too. She obviously feels like I've changed enough to lead a team. This will be the second time she trusts me to lead her somewhere dangerous—and the first time did not go well.

"Do you trust her?" she asks me.

"No," I say.

"Then why bring her along?" Odette asks.

It's my turn to frown.

"She convinced me on that first dive into the Dignity Vessel that she knew a lot about stealth tech. I wanted that expertise," I say.

"And now?"

I shake my head. "I guess I expected more from her. I expected her to find a way to destroy the tech only."

"She hasn't done that?" Odette says.

"She won't, not without experimentation," I say.

Odette nods. "And you won't allow the experiments."

"Would you?"

She studies me for a moment. Then she says, "No."

We're both quiet. I'm about to head to my berth—alone—when she says, "I think you should send her back where you found her."

I sigh. I can feel my own reluctance. I think about it for a moment and realize where it's coming from.

"No," I say. "She stays. She's as determined as I am to destroy the Dignity Vessel."

"But you can't trust her," Odette says.

"I can trust her on that," I say. I nod to Odette and start down the corridor, thinking the conversation is over.

But Odette follows me and grabs my arm. "You're giving her too much credit."

"If I fail, what does it matter?" I ask.

"You haven't thought about this, have you? Your failure? What's the best way to guarantee it?"

"Not go to the Dignity Vessel," I say, half seriously.

"Make sure the bomb doesn't work at all," Odette says. "Or make sure it detonates early."

Which would kill me. I can't imagine Squishy killing me. But then, I couldn't imagine Squishy leaving the team years ago either.

I feel cold. "What do you suggest?"

"Let her work on her bomb," Odette says. "Let her think she's part of this. But let me get you something big, something that'll take out the entire ship."

"You know where to get a bomb like that?" I ask.

"I didn't always wreck dive," she says. "I worked salvage in my early days."

"With Squishy?" I ask.

"Before Squishy," she says. "But I still have a lot of friends who salvage."

"You mean full destruction salvage," I say.

She nods.

Full destruction salvage works like this: The divers go in and strip the ship of its valuables. They also take important parts, like engine parts and computer chips. Sometimes they take things like screens or certain types of exterior material, particularly if the ship is made of expensive components. Then the divers blow the ship up. They don't just destroy the ship. They obliterate it. Unless you arrive in the area shortly after the explosion, you have no idea anything even happened in that region of space.

I stare at Odette. "I didn't know that about you."

She shrugs. "I made a lot of money. Then we found a beautiful old ship, one of the loveliest things I'd ever seen. Everything was carved and molded. It was stunning. I tried to buy it from my friends, but they wouldn't hear of it."

She looks down the corridor, but this time I know she's not checking to make sure we're alone. This time, she's seeing that old wreck, the one she thought was so lovely.

"I cried when we blew it up," she says.

She turns back toward me.

"There isn't a day that goes by without me thinking of that ship." She gives me a half smile. "I often wonder if I could have done something else to save it. I've never seen another one like it. It was someone's baby, and we destroyed it."

She shakes her head.

"That's when you stopped working salvage," I say.

"Yeah," she says. "But I've kept my connections. I can get us something that will obliterate that Dignity Vessel."

I study her. She's serious.

"We're going to need weapons too," I say.

"I figured as much," she says. "Have you ever used a weapon on a dive before?"

"No," I say. "But I've been prepared to."

Her expression tells me being prepared to use a weapon and using that weapon are not the same thing.

But I know that. And she doesn't insult my intelligence by reminding me of it.

"You're going to need guards," she says.

"Guards?" I ask.

"People to flank you when you go in. You're going to need a team to watch your back. Preferably someone who has fired a weapon before."

"Like you," I say.

"Like me," she says. "And Hurst."

"Sounds like a good team to me," I say.

She can sense that I'm about to leave again. She takes my arm. "There are a lot of logistics, Boss," she says.

"I know," I say.

"No, you don't," she says. "When you blow a ship, you don't want to be near it. You don't want to be caught destroying it."

I guess I knew that, but I hadn't thought it through. It makes sense. Still, I taunt her a little. "Even if you obliterate it?"

"Especially if you obliterate it," she says. "Especially then."

THIRTY-FOUR

It takes us weeks to put all the pieces together. Odette contacts her friends and suddenly we have weapons. She tells me we have our bomb as well, but I do not ask where it is.

I research everything that I can, from the military vessels Hurst saw (their maximum crew complement is ten) to the command vessel. None of the images of command vessels I show Hurst are the one he saw, but we can't find an image of that ship. For all we know, it's a new model. At least we have a general size. I still can't figure out what its mission was, but I at least know how many people we might be facing.

I even visit the rental ship, *The Seeker*, and investigate its scanning equipment myself. It's a primitive version of the *Business*. We won't need to get nearly as close to the Dignity Vessel as *The Seeker* did to do a proper scan. We might even be able to scan the military vessels, particularly before they know we're there.

Squishy works on her bomb too, something delicate and sophisticated, something—she tells me—that will take out the stealth tech only, leaving the Dignity Vessel intact.

She thinks that pleases me, and it might have, years ago. But I want the Dignity Vessel all gone. I don't tell her this. I've decided to use Odette's weapon, but I tell no one that.

Not even Odette.

In the last week, I have become obsessed with the actual mission itself. How we'll get in, how we'll distract the military, how we'll buy ourselves enough time.

I also want to make sure we don't take anyone else out when we obliterate the Dignity Vessel. While I'm okay with a charge of destroying imperial property, I don't want to be charged with murder.

Hurst becomes my primary tactician. He's flown combat missions, and as Odette reminded me, this is a combat mission.

In some ways, this is the first step toward war.

All the way along, people remind me of that. Of the huge step I'm taking. Of the risks involved.

I pretend to care. Sometimes I mouth political slogans—the Empire has gotten too big since the Colonnade Wars; too much power in one place creates a great danger; stealth tech doesn't belong to anyone except the ancients who knew how to use it. But mostly, I'm not thinking of politics.

Mostly, I'm thinking about my father.

I see his face—not just the man who recently betrayed me, the one whose face has become mostly planes and angles accented by silvering hair, but also the face of the man who held me close outside of the Room, who put his hand over the crack in my helmet and urged whoever was with us to get us out of there quickly.

I try to remember the man from my childhood, not just the man who grabbed me when I left the Room, but the man who took me and my mother on that trip, who let us go into the Room alone.

I cannot see that man's face. It's as if he doesn't quite exist. He's more of a sense than a person, or maybe a construct, someone I want him to be rather than who he was.

But the man I can see clearly, besides the one who traveled with us to the Room, is the one who came to my grandparents' house on that last visit.

She's always angry, my grandmother said to him that day. *She's sullen and sharp-tongued and not very nice at all.*

My father answered, but I didn't hear what he said.

Whatever it was, my grandmother didn't like it. *She's your child. There's nothing of my daughter in her. Find her someplace else to go. We don't want her here.*

I have no other place for her, my father said. *You agreed to take her in.*

When we thought she'd be normal, my grandmother said.

Normal. Whatever that meant.

Those raised voices caught my attention, and I slipped out of my room. I stood at the top of the stairs, waiting for my father to defend me.

I have no idea what I wanted him to say, only that I wanted him to say something. Something about me. Something that showed he cared. Or at least understood.

What he did say was, *You signed a legal agreement, saying you would care for her until she came of age.*

We want out, my grandmother said. *We're too old to take care of a child, particularly one as troubled as she is.*

To this day, I do not know what those troubles were. I performed well in school. I had friends. Yes, I talked back to my grandparents, but I followed their rules. I lived as quietly in their house as I could.

They just expected me to be like my mother, and clearly, I was nothing like her. Maybe I had been my father's daughter.

Or maybe I was a desperate, lonely child who had never come to terms with her mother's horrible death.

A death I had witnessed.

A death no one else wanted to talk about.

I can't take her with me, my father said. *She'd just get in the way.*

And that was the moment it all ended for me. Any idea of family, of love, of caring.

She'd just get in the way.

We thought she'd be normal.

I went back into my room and packed what few things I had. I took the money I had earned through odd jobs, and I sat on the edge of the bed, waiting for someone to come talk to me.

But my father left without a word. My grandmother didn't come upstairs. Finally, I left my packed bag near the bed and went down.

Is Dad coming back? I asked.

Eventually, my grandmother said.

Tonight? I asked.

No, she said.

My heart twisted. I don't know if she lied. I'll never know. Later, I realized it was just like her. My anger was often provoked by her harsh words, her insensitivity. Sometimes I think she liked to poke at me to get the response she expected, something harsh or sullen or just plain mean, from me.

I'd like to see him, I said.

Well, she said, *you missed your chance.*

It seems I always missed my chance with my father. Or maybe I never really had one.

I left that night, and I never came back. For years, my family had no idea where I was. Odette was the one who convinced me I had to let them know I wasn't dead, although I'm still not sure why. I wish I hadn't now.

I wish I had truly let them go.

I know my decision to destroy the Dignity Vessel, as high-minded as I make it sound, is about my father. I want him to pay. Not just for ignoring me, although there's a part of me—the young part, the girl who stood at the top of those stairs—who does want him to pay for that.

No, what I really want him to pay for is my mother's death.

And Karl's.

THIRTY-FIVE

We approach the wreck in stealth mode: lights and communications array off, sensors on alert for the military ships around the Dignity Vessel. I've never traveled in a convoy before, but I am doing so now. In addition to the *Business*, we have rented *The Seeker* again, and one other ship, the *Space King*.

The Seeker is a compact vessel that has maneuverability and some sophisticated systems. The *Space King* is a pleasure ship, designed for short luxurious travel from one part of the system to the other.

Mikk and Jennifer pilot *The Seeker*. They have their rented dive equipment, plus some salvage supplies. Turtle, Davida, and Bria are on the *Space King*, in the finest clothing we can afford. Their diving equipment is in storage on the *Business*; I doubt they'll have any use for it.

But they do have weapons.

We all do.

And I've insisted that we learn how to use them.

Hurst pilots the *Business*. When he and Odette escort me onto the Dignity Vessel, Roderick will pilot the ship. Tamaz and Squishy will remain on board with him. Tamaz's only job is to guard Squishy—something Squishy does not know.

Nor does she know that I will not be using the bomb she's developed. I've decided to use the more powerful explosive Odette acquired at great expense.

I've done some research myself, and while I don't understand the fledgling science of ancient stealth tech (not that the Empire has let much information out about it), I do know a bit about explosives.

The Dignity Vessel is old and large. The metal hull, with its rivets and its dents, is fragile compared with modern ships. But its very size makes it difficult to destroy completely.

That, more than anything, made me decide to go with Odette's explosive. Hers is designed to obliterate. Squishy's is targeted to the cockpit, designed to destroy the stealth tech and little else.

We spoke of it briefly when she finished. Apparently I had an odd expression on my face when she talked about the device's subtleties.

I thought you'd be pleased, Boss, she said. *You don't like destroying historic things.*

I don't. If I could think of a way to keep the Dignity Vessel intact, I would. But sometimes, you have to make sacrifices for the greater good.

Or, at least, this is what I tell myself.

As we approach, I can't tell if what I'm feeling are understandable nerves, regrets, or a desire to abort the entire mission. I pilot, thinking that being hands-on will calm me.

It does give me a chance to reflect: I actually think about how I would feel if we turned around right now and headed back to Longbow.

I think I would be relieved in the short term.

The long term would depend on a few things. If the military and my father's people solve the mysteries of stealth tech and change the balance of power in the sector, then I will regret not taking advantage of this moment.

If they never solve it, then I might be all right with the decision to turn around.

Although once again, my father would continue to make a profit off death—my mother's and Karl's.

Karl. He would stand beside me urging caution. But he would go into the Dignity Vessel at my side, like he did when we searched for Junior. Karl had no qualms about taking care of threats.

And if he had had all the proper information, he would have seen my father as a threat.

We pass a small area of space that I have secretly designated as the point of no return. My fingers don't even hover over the navigation system. I pilot us forward as if I have no qualms at all.

We are not turning back.

The mission is about to begin.

We have set up the mission in three parts. We designed the first part to separate the military ships from the Dignity Vessel. The second part sends me and my team into the Dignity Vessel, and the third part gets us out of the area before the explosion.

Oddly enough, it's the first part that makes me the most nervous.

Perhaps because I have no control over it at all.

When we reach the designated coordinates just past the point of no return, the *Space King* breaks away from our convoy. The *Space King* speeds away on a perpendicular course from us, its modern stealth mode still on.

When it reaches another designated set of coordinates, it will modulate its speed and shut off its stealth mode. It will also create an echo in its sensors. The echo will show a different route for the *Space King*, a leisurely one that comes from a resort-heavy area some distance from here.

As we were researching vehicles to rent, I learned that the *Space King* is a high-end luxury rental. In addition to all its amenities—cabins the size of apartments on Hector Prime and a galley stocked with the most expensive (and best) food from areas around Longbow—the *Space King* has one of the fastest engines ever designed as well as an array of defensive weapons.

Apparently, a ship like that attracts space pirates, and the owners of the *Space King*—a high-end luxury rental firm which caters to the wealthiest among us—want to make sure they don't get sued by renters who get ambushed and can't defend themselves.

We rented the *Space King* for its speed. The weapons are a luxury that we hope we won't have to use.

The *Space King* zooms away from us, and I silently hope they'll be all right. We're basing our actions on Hurst's memory of military tactics and Squishy's occasional sarcastic opinion about things the military will and will not tolerate.

We travel for another hour before *The Seeker* breaks away. It will find the path it used a few weeks before, when it first investigated the Dignity Vessel. Mikk and Jennifer have loaded *The Seeker* with alcohol and sex aids. They've also added some broken rental diving equipment (which the dive shop gave us at no extra cost), and have scattered it through the cargo space so that it looks like there was a fight.

They are going to come back, pretending to be drunken adventurers. If asked, they will claim they got into a fight with Hurst—ostensibly about coming back to the Dignity Vessel, but really over relationships. Then just to prove him wrong, they're going to ask the military to let them dive the old ship or at least inspect its exterior.

We actually made a security recording of part of the so-called fight that they had. Hurst, the ex-military member of their team, argues that the military won't let them close. Mikk claims they will. He says they want the ship nearby because they need something to do, and he will provide that something.

We're hoping that one military ship will approach *The Seeker* and the other will investigate the *Space King*. The *Space King*'s speed and ability to maneuver should draw the command vessel as well, when it becomes clear that it can outrun the smaller military ship.

We figure we need to keep all three ships busy for a few hours. We're going to monitor the Dignity Vessel. When the first two ships leave, Odette, Hurst, and I will get into the skip. We're going to fly in close and wait, in stealth mode, until the third ship leaves.

Then we're going in.

THIRTY-SIX

We stay just outside of sensor range for two hours after the other ships have left us. Hurst worries that the military's scans have improved since he left the service. Squishy says no one thinks about improving scans, but I rely on Hurst's caution.

When our planned two-hour window is up, we move to the very edge of sensor range. We stay in stealth mode, and we scan the area around the Dignity Vessel.

And get a surprise.

There are only two military vessels, both small. We find no evidence of the command ship.

"They're doing that to fool us," Hurst says. "Like they're doing with the false Dignity Vessel radiation information."

I concur, but I have no way to prove it without going closer. I don't want to draw attention to ourselves, not while our friends are drawing the smaller ships away.

We're going to have to wait until we think it's safe to go in, and then we're going to have to do another scan.

An hour after we arrive, one of the military vessels flies off in the direction of the *Space King*. We're huddled in the cockpit, staring at our sensor information as if it is a lifeline—which, for all we know, it is.

"Let's hope they can give those bastards a run," Roderick says, with uncharacteristic force.

I look at him. He still seems too young and green to me to have the experience he claims, but I've seen him pilot ships and I trust him.

Tamaz stands behind Squishy, watching the monitors, but also keeping an eye on her. I get the sense that he trusts her less than Odette does, and I wonder if someone (Odette herself?) has talked with him about Squishy.

Squishy radiates calm. She's watching the proceedings as if she already knows the outcome. I wonder if this is how she doctors in Vallevu, pretending calm in a crisis, just to keep the others from panicking.

Odette sits in the copilot's chair, even though I don't let her touch the controls. Odette has never piloted anything larger than a skip, although she's navigated ships the size of the *Business* on occasion. She has threaded her fingers together. She keeps looking at all the sensors, checking them one against the other as if they're lying to her.

We all suppose that they are.

"I think you should run the readings again, Boss," Hurst says. He's standing just behind me, hovering the way I usually hate my crew members to hover. He clearly wants to handle the controls himself, and I won't let him.

"I don't want to do too many scans," I say.

"I know," he says, "but we registered that first ship leaving, and if we're looking at a false scan of military vessels, we shouldn't have gotten that reading."

He has a point. We might be looking at things in real time after all.

I'm tempted to run the scan, but I'm not going to. I don't want to give the second military vessel any excuse to stay in the area.

Of course, if there are only two, will they both leave their posts to go after stray ships?

I can only hope so.

"Boss," he says, urging me.

I shake my head. "We're going to wait," I say. "I know it's hard."

I resist the urge to tell him to be patient. He knows he has to be patient. We all know it. And that's the most difficult part of this early section of the mission.

Forty-five minutes after the first ship left, the second ship moves out of its little orbit of the Dignity Vessel. It comes toward us, making my heart skip a beat.

"I thought we're in stealth," Squishy snaps, sounding decidedly not calm.

"We are," I say. "But they might have upgraded their scanning equipment like Hurst said before we left."

"You should move this thing back out of scanning range then," Odette says.

"First," I say, "if they have upgraded their system, how do we know what scanning range is? And second, if they haven't, I don't want to give them a ghost."

A ghost is a blip in their scanning systems, one that shows just a hint of a nearby ship, which is usually caused by movement. The ghosts are precisely one of the things that the military hates about current stealth tech (one of the things we all hate).

Since modern stealth tech only masks us on instruments, ships do better when they remain stationary. Especially ships with the lights and communications down, like the *Business* is right now.

We're dark, and even if someone looks out a portal, they might not see us. We have a good chance of blending into our surroundings. If we move, we might catch someone's eye.

We also might show up as a brief blip on the sensors—a bit of an energy signature or a slight blur of motion that shows up for a half second.

That half second might be enough to blow our cover.

We watch the military vessel bear down on us. My heart is pounding. I'm beginning to wonder at my own wisdom. Maybe I should have moved when Odette urged me to.

Behind me, I can hear Hurst's ragged breathing. Odette has leaned forward, her hands still clutched so that she doesn't touch the board. Roderick paces.

Only Tamaz and Squishy remain in place. Squishy is pretending at calm again, and Tamaz really seems calm. Or maybe he has found some deep place inside of himself where he goes when things get difficult.

At the last moment, the military vessel veers off. It heads on a path that should take it to *The Seeker*.

Roderick lets out a relieved whistle.

"That was closer than I like," Odette says.

"Can we move now?" Squishy asks, once again her voice betraying her true emotional state—which is quite a bit more agitated than I realized.

I don't answer her. Instead I move us forward—slowly—and I double my scans.

First, I search for energy signatures and ghosts. I haven't ruled out the possibility that the command ship is cloaked, just like we were. I get as close as I dare, but I'm not seeing anything.

I set up my own sensors to monitor the area around the Dignity Vessel. I want notification of the smallest anomaly.

"If we can't find that command ship, are we going to abort?" Hurst asks.

I don't know the answer to that. So I don't say anything.

I do know that if we don't go into the Dignity Vessel on this trip, we have blown our chance. Any way to get those military vessels away from the ship will have been barred from us—that is, if we don't want an actual firefight.

At this moment, I wish we had strong weaponry. The weapons on the *Space King* are the most sophisticated that civilians can legally buy. Squishy tells me that they aren't strong enough to destroy the Dignity Vessel. After some study, Odette concurs.

But I do some investigating on my own and realize that there's nothing that we can shoot at the Dignity Vessel that will do the kind of damage that we want.

We can destroy part of its hull. We can open yet another section to space. We can even (probably) destroy the cockpit.

But I want that thing obliterated.

And to obliterate, we have to go in.

Of course, that doesn't stop me from wishing we could just send a barrage of weapons from here, destroy the Vessel, and fly off as if we had no involvement at all.

I scan the Dignity Vessel. I expect to get the fake scan, the one that tells me there's too much radiation.

But I don't. I get a new image of the Dignity Vessel, which tells me that the military ships were the ones creating the false image, and they're gone.

"I think we can go in," I say.

"We have to hurry," Squishy says.

I turn. This is precisely the kind of thinking that I don't want on this mission.

"We're going to do this right, Squishy. We're following the plan we set up. We're not going to hurry."

She licks her lower lip, then nods. "I just meant that we need to act now."

She's eager. She wants this done as much as I do, maybe more. I can feel the depth of her desire to finish this mission.

"Stay calm," I say to her. It's a not-so-subtle dig at her posture and her fake manner.

She doesn't snap at me like I expect her to. Instead, she nods once.

"All right, Boss," she says. "Looks like we're finally under way."

THIRTY-SEVEN

I pilot the skip toward the wreck. Odette and Hurst are already partially suited up. They don't know who is going to accompany me inside. I left that decision to the last minute, wanting to be flexible, and now I'm glad that I did.

As we come in, we aren't in stealth. The skip really doesn't have an effective stealth mode, and I don't want to be blind.

No command vessel comes toward us. No one tries to communicate with us. There isn't even an automated message to warn us away.

This tells me that Jennifer's initial impression is correct. These soldiers guarding the wreck are waiting for something to happen. They've gone days, maybe weeks, maybe months, without seeing another ship.

The fact that two have shown up on the same afternoon doesn't bother them, because they know that the chances of yet a third ship showing up are extremely remote.

The soldiers aren't being vigilant, because the time they've spent out here has taught them that they don't need to be.

So far, this is working in our favor.

"The command ship should have come after us by now," Hurst says.

"I know," I say.

I have placed the cockpit windows on clear. The Dignity Vessel looms ahead.

It looks bigger than I remember, and for a moment, I worry that it's growing, like the station around the Room. So I run yet another scan, checking its size against the specs I logged years before.

I get the result I'm hoping for: The Dignity Vessel hasn't changed.

Only my perception has.

My heart is pounding. If Squishy were here, she would warn me about the gids. I can hear Karl's voice, telling me this dive will be too emotional for me.

For a moment, I consider sending Odette and Hurst in without me. Then I realize this dive will be emotional for them too—and they've never been inside a Dignity Vessel before. Even with a map, they won't know exactly where they're going.

Once inside, they might move wrong, and then what would happen? They might get stuck in the stealth field, just like Junior did.

No. If we're going to do this, I need to dive the wreck.

I need to lead my team.

I need to be the boss.

My two team members are staring at the Dignity Vessel. Hurst isn't even looking at the controls, getting the latest readouts from the sensors. His mouth is open slightly. Odette is chewing on her lower lip, something I haven't seen her do since our earliest days diving together.

"It's so big," Hurst says.

I don't like his tone. There's too much awe in it.

"You saw the specs," I say.

"I know," he says. "They just didn't translate into this kind of size in my mind. I've never dived a wreck this big."

I make myself take a deep breath. Clearly, I'm not the only one who's nervous.

"Odette?" I say. "Is your device powerful enough for this ship?"

She nods. Then she turns. Of the three of us, she seems the most calm—even with the lip biting. "I *have* dived something this big before," she says.

"A Dignity Vessel?" I ask.

"Old freighters," she says. "They're larger than this. They're like miniature planets."

I've seen them, and they are large, although not as large as she says. Certainly as large as the Dignity Vessel, though.

I grab my environmental suit. I strip, then slip it on. It clings to my skin. I haven't worn it since I pulled Karl out of the Room, but it feels like an old friend.

"Hurst," I say, "you're staying here. I need you to monitor the area."

"I thought we were all three going in," he says.

Both Odette and I look at him. "Then who will keep an eye on the skip?" she asks.

I'm glad she asks him, because my tone certainly wouldn't have been as polite.

"We're going to be tethered," she continues. "If one of those ships comes back and severs the tether, we die. They won't even be responsible. They'll plead ignorance, thinking someone was in the skip and had tied to it to rob it."

She sounds so positive about this that I wonder if this scenario played out when she was working with the scavengers. And then I remember: What she describes is an old pirating trick. It's a way to steal a diving vessel when all the members of the team go into a wreck.

I tilt my head slightly. Odette might be more of an asset on this trip than I realized.

"You have your device?" I ask.

She nods.

"Finish suiting up." I pick up the laser pistol I brought for personal use. I have never dived with any laser weapons, even though I know how to shoot one. But I'm not the best shot, and for that, Hurst might be a better choice. His military experience gave him a lot of weapons training.

But there aren't any ships around. We've bought some time. With luck, we'll go in and out without using the laser pistols at all.

I also strap a knife to my belt. It's the same model knife as the one Karl always carried, although it isn't his. His is still attached to his body, floating somewhere near the Room.

My knife is in a thick sheath, since I have dived with a knife before, and I know that the greatest danger is cutting into my own suit. I stopped carrying knives early in my career when I watched one of my dive partners slice open the seam on her thigh. We managed to seal it up, but the entire dive was compromised.

Still, I'm carrying the knife for two reasons: It's the weapon I'm most familiar with, and I want to honor Karl on this dive.

Since I have nothing of his own to carry with me, I need to carry something that reminds me of him. Divers are superstitious, after all.

Although on the outside, my knife looks nothing like his. The sheath makes it look like another breather. I'm already carrying one weapon that someone can take away from me and use against me.

I don't need two.

I pick up my helmet. Then I nod to Odette. She's finishing with her suit. She has four breathers on her hips, as well as her own laser pistol, and something extra on her front.

That extra thing is the bomb itself.

My heart pounds so hard I think that the others can probably hear it.

"I've left Squishy's bomb on the skip," I say to Hurst. "If something happens to us, you bring it back to her and tell her to find a way to use it."

His eyes are big. He nods.

"I've watched those vids from your previous dives here," he says. "I won't be able to communicate with you."

"Not when we're inside the wreck," I say.

"But what if the ships come back?"

I shrug. There isn't much he can do. But if I don't give him something, he'll panic now. He was expecting to go in, and now that I've deprived him of the adventure, his imagination has kicked into overdrive.

"There's not much you can do," Odette says before I have a chance to speak. "The skip has no weapons."

"We're going to be on a strict timetable," I say. "Twenty to get to the cockpit, thirty in the cockpit, and twenty to get out. If we're close to those numbers, stay here. We might make it back before they get here."

"If not?" he asks.

I look at Odette. She looks at me.

"After an hour ten," I say, "you have to get out."

"I'll wait for you," he says.

Odette shakes her head. "You can't. You might die. You have to get clear of the Dignity Vessel."

His mouth opens again, and then closes tightly in disgust. While he's been thinking of the dive, he's clearly forgotten the point of the mission.

"If you can," I say, "you warn those military ships away. I don't want collateral damage."

"They'll go in," he says. "They'll try to remove that bomb."

"They won't be able to," I say. "Not in the time they have."

And suddenly my mouth is dry. The potential for collateral damage is great. I don't want to cost lives—any more than I already have.

"If they show up, hold them off as long as possible," I say, trying to make myself feel better.

"By doing what?" he asks. "Leaning out the airlock and shooting at them with my laser pistol?"

I grin in spite of myself. "If you actually think that'll work."

Then I look at Odette. She has her gear on, her helmet under her arm.

"You ready?" I ask.

"As I'll ever be," she says.

"You can back out now," I say. "I can do this alone."

"No, you can't," she says, and puts on her helmet. It makes her head look twice as large as it is, which makes the package attached to her front look small.

I hope that thing won't trigger as we maneuver our way into the ship. She says it's easy to operate and not something to fear, but I do worry.

I worry about everything.

"Keep an eye out," I say to Hurst, and then I put my helmet on.

We head to the airlock as he extends the tether between the skip and the Dignity Vessel.

Here we go, I think, but do not say. *Here we go.*

THIRTY-EIGHT

We reach the wreck in less than five minutes. I stop us as we touch the hull. I want to make certain we haven't moved too quickly.

"Check your monitors," I say to Odette.

She tilts her head. The clear part of her helmet reflects the lights from the skip. "Heart rate normal," she says. "Breathing normal. I'm fine."

My breathing is up and so is my heart rate, but I don't tell her that. Because my elevated heart rate is also normal for me every single time I return to diving after a layoff.

Of course, I also don't mention that the elevation is the highest I've seen on a return dive. I chalk that up to the fact we're about to do something illegal.

Something illegal and something that would normally go against every principle that I have.

"Good," I say. "Because now we're at the tough part."

I lead her to the hatch and am surprised to find that it's open. I have no idea if Karl and I left it that way, not that it matters. I'm sure military divers have been inside.

For the first time, I cringe, realizing we might find other bodies—newer bodies—in that cockpit.

I make myself take a deep breath. I'm glad I've brought along extra breathers, because I'm using a lot of oxygen at the moment. Hurst, bless him, has said nothing.

This is the last time he could speak to us before we go into the wreck, and he doesn't. He doesn't remark on my elevated heart rate or my breathing. Maybe he's not monitoring them.

Given how nervous he was when we left, he might only be monitoring the surrounding space.

Which is probably good enough—considering. If something goes wrong, he can't come and rescue us anyway.

I turn on the lights under my boots. I know better than to light up like a tourist on her first dive—I remember how blinding that was in the small space that leads into the ship—but I'm tempted. I'm very tempted.

I slide into the hatch first. I'm going to lead the way to the cockpit.

I've reviewed the directions. I've also put them on a small map that can run in front of my faceplate if I press the right button. The map will overlay on the plate, leaving my field of vision clear, but helping me maneuver.

I hope I don't have to use it. I will have part of it on when we go inside, however. If I get turned around, I want the navigation system to beep at me so that we don't waste time being lost.

The hatch is wider than I remember, but the ladder seems even more fragile. I grip it with my gloved hands, and it seems like the rungs are loose.

As I go down, I check the bolts. They don't seem to be screwed in as tightly as they had before.

Or maybe that's my memory again.

I thought my memory of this place was clear, but maybe it's not. Maybe the overlay of trauma has heightened the wrong things. I'm glad I decided to use the special map and the guidance system. I'm beginning to worry that I'm wrong about a lot of things.

Some things are different. The particles that floated around us like snow are gone. Maybe that's because the hatch has been open to space for a long time. Or maybe enough military divers have gone in and have knocked things loose.

"I thought you said this thing was narrow," Odette says. Her voice sounds a bit hollow through her suit system and into mine.

"It is," I say.

"You haven't seen narrow," she says, and she's right. By some dive standards, this is wide open. I have been in situations so tight that I was afraid I would get stuck.

But I don't call those places narrow. I call them dangerous.

Still, I can understand her initial worry and her relief. She's got an extra half meter of material attached to her front.

"This is as narrow as it gets outside the cockpit," I say.

"Good."

We make it to the bottom. The corridors open away from the entry, just like I remember.

Just like I dream.

The nightmares of Jypé and Junior joined the nightmare of my mother's death shortly after they died. Only the Jypé-and-Junior nightmare is less a distortion of what happened than a memory of it.

My stomach clenches. It almost feels like I'm back in the dream. I make myself move forward.

I'm surprised I remember where the handholds are and where we pushed off from. But my navigation system never beeps at me, and we move quickly down the corridor.

As we do, I hear voices. Faint voices. They're whispering. I make myself focus on them, reminding myself that these aren't voices at all, but something to do with stealth tech.

The focus enables me to separate out the sounds. Not whispering, but a soft thrum. Several soft thrums on different levels.

I get an idea.

"Do you hear anything unusual?" I ask Odette.

"Just my own breathing," she says. "That's the only part of diving I hate. Why? Do you think someone's here?"

There's an edge to that final question, as if she's afraid we're going to get attacked while we're inside the vessel. If we do, we'll never get out.

Surprisingly, that thought calms my own breathing. My heart rate has slowed now that we're inside.

"No," I say. "It's just that there's a sound I associate with stealth tech. I thought maybe if you heard it too, you have the marker."

"Oh." She's following me, careful to put her hands where mine have been. "That doesn't sound very scientific."

"It's not," I say.

The corridors seem cleaner. Except "clean" isn't quite the right word. They're not as dismal. They're just as dark, but it almost looks like someone has scraped off a layer of dirt—or something—that accumulated over time.

Although I have no idea how dirt could have formed way out here in the middle of nowhere. Just like rust couldn't form without oxygen.

Yet everything seems just a little shinier, just a little newer. The words and numbers running along the doorways are clearer.

I'm becoming more and more certain, as we move, that this isn't a fault of my memory. The Dignity Vessel is different.

People have been here.

A lot of people, during the time I was gone.

We reach the final corridor. I check with Odette.

"Everything still okay?" I ask.

"Fine," she says, but she doesn't add anything. I don't know what she thinks of the ship.

I'm not sure I should know what she thinks of the ship, given what we're about to do.

So I don't ask for her opinion.

However, I do check the time.

Less than five minutes to the hatch. Less than eight minutes to get here. We should make it to the cockpit with five minutes to spare.

I slow us through that corridor. I want to make certain we're both calm. Because this is the tricky part.

Odette has walked me through it before, but I'm still nervous. I've never set an explosive device.

She's offered to do it—it doesn't have to be near the stealth tech, given the power of the explosive—but I want it to be there. If anything gets obliterated, I want it to be those stealth tech controls.

I want to shut the whole thing off.

Or, at least, send it to oblivion.

I swallow against a dry throat. The corridor widens a little.

We're here.

And now I have confirmation that the military has spent a lot of time in this Dignity Vessel. Modern signs litter this part of the corridor.

Danger.

Do Not Pass without Authorization.

Warning: To Unapproved Personnel, the Field Inside These Doors Can Be Lethal.

The signs begin about six meters from the entrance, and grow more and more insistent the closer we get. But there is no barrier, nothing the military has constructed to prevent illegal entry.

I wonder if they couldn't get anything to work here.

Just like our communications devices don't work here.

For the first time, I worry that I've made a mistake bringing Odette's device.

Maybe it won't work here either.

I make myself take a deep slow breath. It'll work. If I keep it outside the stealth field. It'll have to work.

Odette has slowed down. I look at her. She's doing something to the packet on the front of her suit.

"I think I'm going to stay out here," she says.

"You're going to have to come closer than that," I say. "You have to talk me through setting the device."

She takes such a deep breath that I can hear it. "I'll do it through the door," she says.

That's fine with me. As long as she can see what I'm doing, then we'll be all right.

Provided we can get through the door. The signs make me worry that someone has locked it—the old-fashioned way, with some kind of padlock.

The thrumming is stronger. If I don't pay attention, it sounds like a chorus of hums. If I concentrate, I can hear the different sounds at the different levels.

The sound isn't giving me a headache like it normally does. Instead, it's lifting my spirits. I was worried that I'd back out once I saw the interior again, that my preservationist instincts would collide with my desire for revenge and I would back away from destroying the ship.

But the thrumming keeps me on edge, reminds me why I'm actually here. If anything, my feelings about destroying the stealth tech have grown stronger.

"Here," Odette says to me.

She hands me the packet. It seems smaller now that it's not attached to her suit.

I don't attach it to mine. Instead, I clutch it in one hand. My heart rate is increasing again, and I make myself breathe evenly so that I stay calm.

"Come with me," I say. "It's not far."

And indeed, it isn't. It only takes us a minute to get there.

My worries about the padlock weren't justified. The door is propped open. Someone has braced it open by attaching it to the wall.

Apparently, whoever did this was afraid of being trapped inside.

"If it's so dangerous, why would they do that?" Odette asks.

"So you can get out quickly," I say. I add the "quickly" mostly for her sake. Because the real answer is that they just want to make sure they can get out.

We peer in. The cockpit looks very different. All the debris is gone. What remains is broken edges and hints of places where the furniture had once been. Lights, activated by our movement, have come on around the controls.

But no lights come on near the stealth tech field. I automatically look in that direction.

I was afraid I would see Junior, still horizontal in the debris field.

He's no longer there. Someone—the military probably—removed his body. I knew they would

But I was afraid just the same.

I let out a small sigh.

"It doesn't look threatening," Odette says.

In fact, it's even more dangerous now. Because the debris field marked where the stealth tech was. It's harder to determine now where the stealth tech begins and the regular part of the cockpit ends.

"Stay back," I say.

I stop just inside the door. It's easy to see through that hole open to space. The hole where our probe is. I resist the urge to go to it and peer out.

Now I'm hearing the same soft harmonies I heard when I came here with Karl. They're soothing instead of distracting.

"Someone's been working in here, haven't they?" Odette says.

"Yeah," I say.

"Where's the field?" she asks, even though I told her before we came. She and Hurst both studied the maps with me.

"Over there." I point. "You stay as far from that part of the cockpit as you can."

"I'm not going any deeper," she says.

But she's looking. So am I.

After a moment, she says, "I think the best place to put the explosive is on the floor."

I glance at her.

"In the exact center of the room," she says. "Then we can be sure to get the maximum effect *inside* the ship."

I had envisioned putting it on the walls I had investigated with Karl. But I think that Odette has made a good point.

"All right," I say.

She has gotten me moving. I would have hovered longer, thinking about the past.

Getting lost in it, like Karl was afraid I would do in the Room.

You'll be looking for your mother. You know you will, he said, *and you won't be focused on the small but necessary details. I will.*

He had been right. I had just looked for Junior.

Part of me can feel Karl here.

Because the cockpit, without its furniture and debris, reminds me of the Room.

That thought makes me move faster. I pick a spot in the exact center of the floor, away from the broken areas. I remove the bomb from the packet and attach it, just like Odette showed me how to do.

It seems ridiculously easy. Just like the bomb seems ridiculously small to cause such extreme damage. It's not much bigger than my laser pistol.

I set it down. "Okay," I say. "Remind me again how to activate this thing."

She does. She's the one who programmed it. She gave us forty-five minutes to clear the area—which is the very minimum we could come up with.

I move slowly, repeating everything she says, touching each part of the device as I activate it.

Which I do.

It snaps into place and seems to sink into the floor.

"Is that normal?" I ask.

"That's what it's supposed to do," she says.

One small blue light appears on the top edge. That's the only indication that the explosive is armed.

"All right," I say. "Let's get the hell out of here."

THIRTY-NINE

We do. We get the hell out of there.

We move faster than we probably should. I don't monitor my heart rate or my breathing. Both are elevated.

I probably have the gids.

I don't care.

We reach the hatch and we climb. Odette stays with me. Halfway up, she removes one of her breathers and adds it to her suit. So clearly she's been breathing too hard too.

We're both nervous, which isn't a good thing.

But we're almost done.

I reach the top first. I ease myself out and down to the tether. I'm about to contact Hurst when something stops me. I turn and look at the skip.

It's dwarfed by a ship I've never seen before. The ship is the size of the *Business*, but it isn't the *Business*. It has Enterran Empire logos and the military's red, square symbol along the side.

Apparently, this is the command ship that Mikk had seen. It has returned.

And it's grappled onto the skip.

It could have taken the skip inside one of its cargo bays, but hasn't, probably because of the tether.

Odette pulls herself out. I hear a crackle in my helmet. She's about to say something.

I extend my hand in front of her in an attempt to silence her. She looks at me questioningly, and again the weird material of her helmet reflects the lights of the ships. I can't see her face.

I hold my gloved index finger up. She looks up, but she doesn't say anything. So I point at the skip.

She lets out a breath of air, which I can hear through our comm system.

If someone is paying attention, they can hear it too.

What I'm hoping is that they've lost track of us, that Hurst is trying to talk with them or deal with them or fight with them.

If he is, and they're not paying attention to us, then we have an advantage.

If they've already captured him and are watching the Dignity Vessel, then they've seen us and are prepared for us.

Either way, we have no choice. We have to get back to the skip and get out of here.

The fact that they're waiting for us is a good sign. I told Hurst to leave if it looked like trouble was coming—unless we were just about to come out of the Dignity Vessel.

If he followed orders—always a big "if" with divers who aren't actually diving—then the command vessel has only been there for a few minutes.

I test the tether. It's holding just fine.

I nod at Odette, and together we pull our way to the skip. We move quicker than we moved going to the Dignity Vessel.

As we travel, I stare at the new ship. It doesn't look like the older models of command ships. I've dived the wrecks of several, and they all seem to be based on the same design.

Up front are weapons, in the back, extra thrusters. Some have life pods scattered throughout. Newer models have replaced many of the life pods with more weapons bays. Along the bottom of the ship are bay doors for smaller ships—about the size of the skip—to exit and also battle.

This command vessel seems small. I don't see all the weapons bays and there are only two bay doors for ships. There's a strange line in the middle of the command vessel and a marking that I've never seen before.

As we get to the skip's airlock, I wait for Odette. She arrives a half second behind me. I hope she follows my lead.

I'm going to release the tether and climb into the airlock in the same movement. She has to get out of the way or the tether will hit her as it comes back to the skip.

I'm doing this so that the skip only shakes once. They might think we're still outside. You should always put the tether back before getting into the airlock. No one will expect me to do both at the same time.

I shove Odette behind me and point to the airlock. She nods. I wish I can see her face more clearly; I get the sense that I've surprised her.

I don't care. We need to move quickly. I reach for the airlock opener. She points to the tether.

It's my turn to nod. I point at the airlock, give her a slight shove, and then turn to the tether. I hit the airlock release and the tether's release at the same time.

Theoretically, two divers can get inside an airlock in the time it takes a tether to release itself and wind back into its holder. I've done it before, but it takes coordination and luck.

Odette makes a slight squeak—one I hope no one heard in the command vessel or the skip's cockpit—and scrambles to get inside the airlock.

I follow.

The airlock's outer door is closing just as the tether bangs into the skip.

Then I turn toward the interior door. I pull my laser pistol. It feels heavy in my hand. The gravity has come on inside the airlock, which means that the environment is almost on full.

Odette has her laser pistol drawn as well.

My heart is pounding all over again, and my breath is coming hard. A warning light goes on in the corner of my helmet: I am consuming oxygen at twice the normal rate.

The interior door opens.

I step in—and am greeted by three people I do not know, holding laser pistols on me. A large woman with dark hair has her arm around Hurst's stomach and another laser pistol pointed at his head.

"Put down your weapons," she says.

I don't even have to think about it. I do. Odette does as well.

"Good," the woman says. "Now step all the way inside."

I do that as well. "Can I get out of my helmet?" I ask. I don't want to tell her that my oxygen is running low.

She shrugs. "It's your skip."

I take off my helmet. My face cools. I realize my hair is wet. I'm covered in sweat.

The woman is not wearing a uniform. Neither are her companions. They're both men. One is thin and wiry, but looks flabby somehow. Had I seen him closely before I got out of the airlock, I might have tried to take him. But all I saw were the weapons.

The other man is beefy and his face is ruddy. Had I met him on Longbow Station, I would have thought him a drinker, someone I didn't have to take too seriously.

Whatever I expected, it was not this.

"What do you want?" I ask, playing dumb.

"What were you doing on the Dignity Vessel?" she asks.

Hurst's eyes are wide. He's trying to signal to me. I'm not sure what he wants me to say, but I know what I'm going to say.

"Let my friend go," I say.

"Answer me first," the woman says.

I shake my head. I have nothing to lose. I'm going to gamble all of their lives, but they don't know that.

"Let him go," I say, "and I'll tell you everything."

"She's stubborn," says a voice from the galley. "Let him go."

The woman pushes Hurst at me. He trips, catches me, and grabs my hand. Something solid hits my glove. It's all I can do not to look at him in surprise.

He has given me something, and I think I know what it is.

"You've hurt him," I say, to cover up my surprise.

"We just held him until you came back," the woman says. "We didn't want to give you warning."

"Warning of what?"

A man steps out of the galley, bending at the waist so that he doesn't hit his head. He doesn't need to stand up for me to know who he is.

It's my father.

"What the hell are you doing here?" I snap.

"I missed you too," he says. "You do realize you were diving my wreck?"

He looks healthier than he did when I saw him at his home. A little thinner, and in better shape. It takes me a minute to realize he's the one who put up all the signs, who left the cockpit door open and cleaned out the debris.

He's the one who has been working inside the Dignity Vessel.

"I haven't been diving your wreck," I say. "I came here to destroy it."

"Well, now you see that you can't. It's military property—"

"We have to get out of here," I say, "because I've already done my damage."

He stops, recognizing something in my tone. "You don't destroy things," he says.

"I do if they're dangerous," I say.

"The wreck isn't dangerous. We keep it guarded, although I was a bit worried when we got back and found our ships were gone."

"You need to be gone, too. We have—" I glance at my watch. We got out in record time. "—fifteen minutes to get clear."

"Clear of what?" he asks, just like I want him to.

"Clear of the explosion," I say.

"You would need something massive to destroy that Dignity Vessel," says one of the men. "Two little things like you can't carry something like that."

"Anyone want to explain gravity to this man?" I ask, still staring at my father.

He knows I'm serious.

"Get your device out of there," he says.

"I would if I could," I say. "But it took us ten minutes to get to the cockpit, and that was after we were fully suited. Neither Odette nor I have enough oxygen to go back. Even if we did, we wouldn't get there in time. And . . ."

I let the word trail before I smile sweetly at him.

". . . I don't know how to disable the bomb."

He curses and turns away from me. Then he looks at the woman. "We have to get out of here."

"She's bluffing," the woman says.

"My daughter doesn't bluff," he says.

"There's no reason to get out of here," she says. "We've got shields. An explosion won't hurt us."

My father glares at her. I had forgotten that look. It is filled with contempt. "We're pretty sure that ancient stealth tech creates a dimensional rift. I have no idea if exploding the ship will close the rift or open it wider. Do you want to be here to find out?"

The woman's cheeks turn bright red. "We can't get out of here with the skip grappled on."

"Then put it in the bay," he says. "But get us out of here."

"It takes two pilots to put a skip in the bay," the woman says. "I've never flown anything this small—"

"I'll do it," Hurst says with a little more panic in his voice than I like. Apparently, he doesn't want to die for this mission.

"We can't trust you," the woman says.

"Then let go of the skip," I say. "Get your people out of here. We'll be just fine."

"We're not doing that," my father says. "Get this skip into the bay. Warn the other ships to stay away from here. If she is bluffing, we'll know within the hour."

The woman doesn't have to be told twice. She goes back through the galley. Apparently the grapple attached to our emergency doors. It also must have an oxygen-filled corridor which allowed them to travel over here.

I've heard of grapplers that sophisticated, but I've never seen one. Apparently, I will see one now.

"Get out of the suit," my father says to me. "We have some business to attend to."

I don't move. Everyone is looking at me. Odette takes off her helmet. Her face is covered in sweat, but she seems fine otherwise.

"I said, get out of the suit," my father says.

"I don't wear anything under my suit," I say. "Either it stays on or you will have to give me some privacy so that I can change clothes."

His eyes narrow. He glances at the others. One of the men is trying not to smile.

My father's look of exasperation grows. "All right then," he says. "Come with me. Your friends can stay here."

"Sorry," I say to Odette and Hurst. Then I follow my father through the galley and to the emergency doors.

They're open. I can see the grappler just beyond—a black corridor, devoid of any decoration at all. It's just a functional space that expands so people can go back and forth between two ships docked together.

My father steps inside. I follow.

"Don't try anything," he says.

I'm tempted. So far, he hasn't noticed the knife. It wouldn't take much to stab him, run ahead, use the emergency controls on the grappler, and set the skip free.

But I can't quite bring myself to kill him. Not here, not like this.

"We have to close the doors," I say, waving my left hand at the open emergency doors between the skip and the grappler. "We can't separate these things otherwise."

I keep my right hand at my side. I'm still holding Squishy's device. My father hasn't noticed that either.

"Well, do it," he says.

I turn slightly. "You don't know how, do you?"

"I usually have people for that." His comment reminds me of my first meeting with Riya Trekov and her tone about her people. That should have warned me away then—I'd even made note of it—and it hadn't.

If I had walked away then, things would be quite different now.

"I can't do it alone," I say. "I need your help."

He gives me an odd look, as if he had expected more of me, then follows me back to the door. I grab one edge with my left hand, bracing my right against the doorframe. I don't lean my right on the frame; I just make it look like I'm using my hand.

He grabs the doors too, and together we tug. The doors slide closed, and I step back.

We're alone in the grappler.

He gives me that measuring look again—I'm not sure why—and heads to the door of his ship.

I follow. We're moving faster now. When we get inside, he hits some kind of release, and those doors close as well.

Then he taps a communicator on his sleeve and says, "We're in."

I hear a squeal as the machinery starts. This ship isn't as high tech as I thought. The grappler begins its procedure to disengage.

I resist the urge the glance at my watch. We don't have much time left.

"Follow me," my father says.

That I do follow him without question says less about his hold over me than it does about my curiosity. I want to know what he's doing here. His presence bothers me a lot. He's not a scientist—or he wasn't when I was a child, but he's lived a lifetime since then. Who knows what he's picked up? Who knows who he has with him, and what they've done?

The grappler slides into place, shaking this ship just a little. I hope the skip is inside the bay now.

I follow my father down a corridor so wide it seems like a room, particularly after that small tunnel through the grappler.

"What are you doing here?" I ask.

"I told you," he says. "I'm diving the wreck."

"You aren't a diver," I say, even though I know I'm wrong. He's not a diver like I am, but he knows how to dive. I have a hunch he's dived the Room. I know he can work in an environmental suit. He rescued me from outside the Room while wearing one.

He doesn't respond to that. Instead he turns and stops in front of large double doors. A green light went on above his head. He taps the edge of one of the doors, and the door becomes clear. Inside sits the skip.

My people have arrived.

"I want to talk to them," I say.

"Later," he says. "Don't you want to see your ship blow up?"

For a moment, I think he means the *Business*. Then I realize he's referring to the Dignity Vessel. I'm not sure if the contempt in his tone comes from the fact that I found the vessel or from the fact that he still might not believe me about the bomb.

I don't answer him. Instead, I follow him to a room across the corridor. He presses the side of the door and it slides open. We step into a platform that seems to jut into space. The walls, floor, and ceiling are clear.

In the distance, I can barely make out the Dignity Vessel. We're moving away from it rapidly.

"By my watch," he says, "it should explode any minute now."

I glance at mine. One minute and forty-nine seconds, to be exact.

"Magnify," he says, and he's clearly not speaking to me. The image in front of us becomes larger. The Dignity Vessel is now the size of my hand.

"Again," he says.

The Dignity Vessel now fills the main window. It looks like it's only a few meters away from us, even though I know it's much farther.

I have turned my arm so I can glance at the time without moving my head. I look down.

One minute exactly.

My father clasps his hands behind his back in a military pose.

"What kind of ship is this?" I ask.

"It's an imperial vehicle," he says.

"Clearly," I say. "But what type?"

"Military science vessel," he says.

Science vessel. Fascinating. It probably doesn't have elaborate weapons systems. If it has weapons at all.

My mouth is dry. I'm still staring at the Dignity Vessel, and I realize I have no idea if that explosive will work.

Then the Dignity Vessel turns white. It freezes for a moment, as if it's suspended in time, and then the whiteness gets so bright that both my father and I have to shield our eyes.

Still I can see the shape of the vessel against my eyelids, this time done in golds. I finally open my eyes again, and it's gone.

There's only a pinpoint of light, tiny and white, where the vessel was.

"You took it off magnify," I say, because I can't think of any other way to respond. I'm lightheaded and nauseous. I wanted to destroy the stealth tech, which meant destroying the vessel, but ruining the damn thing still shocks me.

I've never done anything like this before.

"No," he says. He sounds as shocked as I feel. "No, it's still on magnify."

"Then what's that light?"

"You tell me," he says.

"I'm not the one with a science vessel," I say.

The light fades, slower than I expect.

Finally, it winks out.

We stand in silence for the longest moment. Maybe moments. I don't know. I no longer look at my watch.

I have no need to.

"I can't believe you blew it up," he says. "Why the hell did you blow it up?"

"Stealth tech is dangerous," I say, sounding like Squishy. "It kills people."

"Hell," he says, his voice shaking. "The laser pistol you were carrying kills people."

"At least they know what hit them," I say.

He turns. The view from the window—that point in space where the Dignity Vessel had been—seems black and vast.

"That was working stealth tech," he says. "Such low grade that we could actually make progress with it. It was the best find in a generation, maybe two. You had no right to destroy it."

"You had no right to kill Karl," I snap.

"I didn't," he says. "You did. You were supposed to go in there. You would have survived."

"You only know that because I survived the first time," I say. "Maybe I shouldn't yell at you about Karl. Maybe I should yell at you about Mother. Did you send her in there to see if she had the marker? Or did you know she would die in there?"

He grows pale. "That's not fair."

"Isn't it?" I ask. "You risk dozens of lives for your little experiment and you tell me I'm not being fair?"

He grabs me by the left arm and yanks me forward. "Let me show you something," he says.

If I move to the right and hook my foot around his ankle, I can drop him without much movement at all. Of course, if I let go of Squishy's bomb, I can grab my knife and stab him to death in a matter of seconds.

I do neither.

Instead, I let him drag me out of the room.

I let him control me, one last time.

FORTY

I hear it before I see it: a tiny thrumming, so faint it sets my teeth on edge. Maybe I felt it from the moment I got on this ship.

My heart starts pounding hard again.

"What did you do?" I ask.

"I didn't do anything," he says, "except hire the right people. They're figuring this out."

A headache builds between my eyes. I stumble forward into the corridor. He's still holding my arm tightly. I can feel his fingers pinch my flesh through my suit.

"Why do you want this so badly?" I ask. "Is it the money?"

"If it were the money, I could have quit a long time ago," he says.

We follow an incline, which takes us up a level. I note an elevator to our side, but he doesn't take it, preferring to stay in the corridor instead.

The thrumming becomes a tiny chorus, as if a group of singers were far away, their song just beginning to filter toward us.

"Then what is it?" I ask.

"You were wrong about your mother," he says. "I loved her."

"So you say." I make myself walk fast enough to keep up with him. I don't want to be dragged any farther.

I also stare at the walls, mentally making note of landmarks, as if I were diving this ship instead of walking through it. There's a map of the ship at the beginning of the incline. It has a lot of decks and levels.

I nod toward the image. "How many people are on this ship?"

"It can hold one hundred," he says.

"That's not what I asked," I say.

"I usually run with a crew of fifty," he says.

"But you've been gone. Where were you?"

He doesn't answer for a moment.

"You're running this with a skeleton crew, aren't you? That woman who caught Hurst in the skip, she doesn't know anything about stealth tech, does she?"

The questions she asked made that clear.

"Where's your team?" I ask.

"I don't use the same people all the time," he says. "It's my project."

"You're keeping them in the dark," I say. "You want to be the one to claim this discovery as your own."

"Then you destroyed it," he says, but his words hold no conviction.

"You didn't discover the Dignity Vessel," I say. "You have stealth tech on this ship. Ancient stealth tech. I can hear it."

He stops and turns to me. "Hear it?"

I bite my lower lip. Am I the only person who can hear the thrumming of stealth tech? I thought everyone with a marker could hear that faint singing sound.

"You hear the chorus?" he asks.

I nod, reluctantly, but I do nod.

"Not everyone can hear it," he says. "Not even everyone with the marker. I wonder what that means?"

"I don't really care," I say. "Why don't you understand how dangerous this stuff is?"

"And why don't you understand that if it's dangerous, it's better off with the Empire?"

"Who's trying to re-create it," I snap, "so it can kill again."

"If they understand it," he says, "they can shut off the Room."

"If they understand it," I say, "they can build Rooms of their own."

He doesn't say anything, but he continues to pull me along. We finally get to a flatter part of the corridor. We go past another map. This one has little red symbols scattered in various places on the ship. Five are in the cockpit. Then I remember. This is a science vessel. I'm in the lab.

The front part of the ship can leave us behind if it wants to.

If it deems the lab dangerous.

I see four more red dots some distance from us, and then two in the middle.

Those dots must represent life signs. The two in the middle have to be us.

Eight crew members on a ship that fits one hundred? What are they doing here? Why so few?

My father stops in front of two shielded doors. The chorus has grown. He presses his thumb against the center of the door, then leans forward for the retinal scan. He breathes onto the edge, probably as proof that he's alive. That last precaution is the key. So many of these systems have no indicator for living thumbs or retinas.

The doors open. This room is as closed as the one below was open. There are no portals, no openings to the rest of the ship or to space—just workstations along the side, a long table in the middle, and a giant computer screen on the far wall from where I'm standing. Numbers run along that screen as well as in a three-dimensional graph. It takes me a moment to recognize the graph. It's an energy indicator. It's registering the power of . . . something, although I'm not sure what.

In the very center of the room, on top of the table, surrounded by three different clear shields, is a bottle the size of my forearm.

The bottle appears to be throbbing, but it's not. I know it's not, because it's the source of the sound. And the sound, packed into that little space, makes it seem like it's moving.

Maybe it is. With some kind of vibration.

"There it is," my father says with no small amount of pride. "The first working stealth field in five thousand years. This one was created in our lab."

My mouth is dry. "You didn't," I say.

"I did." He steps toward it.

I stay back.

"How do you know it works?" I ask.

He points to the graph.

"Have you had anyone stick their arm in there?" I ask, and I can hear the maliciousness in my voice. "Have you uncorked that bottle near someone who doesn't have the marker?"

"Of course not." He sounds shocked.

"Then you don't know if it works," I say.

He gives me a withering look. "Of course I do," he says. "And you do too. You can hear it, just like I can."

"How many people know about your little experiment in stealth tech?" I ask.

He smiles at me. "The Empire already has my specs."

"So they can build it?" I hear the panic in my own voice. I've destroyed the Dignity Vessel for nothing.

"Not yet," he says. "But soon. We had to take bits of your Dignity Vessel's technology to build our own."

"You didn't build this from scratch?" I ask.

"No," he says. "Right now, we need a bit of a kick start. You've just made that a lot harder. The Dignity Vessel was perfect because the stealth tech's power had diminished over the years. We could work in it safely."

"Those of you with a marker," I say.

He nods.

"But you can't work in the Room of Lost Souls?" I ask.

"There's no control panel in the Room," he says. "There's no control panel anywhere on that station, at least that we can find."

In spite of myself, I shiver. How hard has he looked?

And, more to the point, how many lives has he sacrificed?

"So," he says with great bitterness, "if you wanted to set us back, you've managed it. If you wanted to destroy the program, you haven't."

I nod. Not yet, I haven't. I try hard not to close my hand too tightly around Squishy's bomb. "Because you have other working stealth tech?"

He grins at me. "Even you should know that Dignity Vessels are hard to come by."

"So you don't."

"Not yet," he says. "We'll find more."

My heart is pounding. I don't want them to find more. I don't want them to have this technology at all.

His words do reassure me a little; they don't have any other functioning stealth tech. It might take generations to find another ship. The setback I've just caused might be as effective as destroying the program.

"What about the rest of your team?" I ask. "Where are they? Shouldn't they be sharing in this glory?"

"I told you," he says, "I don't work with the same people. We weren't here when you arrived because we were dropping off the last group of scientists. The next group is due in a few days."

"But you stay the whole time," I say. "Why is that?"

"My work," he says. "My project."

Then he sighs and looks at the bottle, as if it has all the answers.

"And I thought, somehow, that it was my Dignity Vessel."

"Because I found it?" I ask.

He shrugs and doesn't look at me. Yet I know his answer. His answer is yes. Because of me.

"So," I say in a softer tone. "Explain this thing to me."

He gives me a sideways look, as if he can't believe me.

"Look," I say, "I'm going to lose anyway. The military is farther along on stealth tech than I thought because of you. I may as well know what's going on."

"It's classified," he says.

"Yeah?" I say. "Then you shouldn't have shown me that bottle."

His smile softens. The smile of my father—my childhood father, the one I remember vaguely from the days before Mother died. My heart twists.

His grip on my arm loosens. He doesn't pull me to the containers around the bottle. He guides me there.

"In the bottom of the bottle," he says, pointing toward it, "you see that bit of color? That's from the Dignity Vessel. It carries a charge. . . ."

I stop listening. I don't know enough science to understand this anyway. Instead, I concentrate on the voices rising and falling in my head. The chorus isn't as powerful as it was on the Dignity Vessel, and it certainly is nowhere near as overwhelming as it was in the Room.

It's an accompaniment, something ever so faint, just within hearing range. If the stealth tech on the Dignity Vessel was weak, this is almost nonexistent.

But not quite.

It's there enough that I can hear it, that my father's computer system can measure its output.

I know my team isn't in danger on that skip. They could get one room away from the stealth tech on the Dignity Vessel with no ill effects. They're okay here.

But if my father boosts this somehow, then people will get hurt.

Again.

"It's lovely," I say. I touch the edge of the containment field with my left hand. My father lets me. He releases my arm, leans forward, and continues explaining whatever it is that he's talking about.

I do note that he knows more about stealth tech than a nonscientist should. He has been studying.

I lean forward, just like he is. I keep my left forefinger on the containment field. In my right hand, I run my gloved thumb along the edge of Squishy's device.

She made it very easy. A simple on-off switch that has to be flicked, then squeezed. The timer is built in. There's nothing to set up. Once the device comes in proximity of a stealth field and is turned on, it will weld itself to the stealth field, like a magnet against metal. Only no one will be able to pry it loose.

It then taps the stealth tech's power to fuel its own reaction.

And it will blow within an hour.

Or so she told me. She seemed to believe it would work. But, she kept reminding me (a little bitterly), she never had a chance to test it.

So it's all theory.

A theory that I want badly to work.

I flick the switch, or what feels like the switch through the thickness of my glove. Then I squeeze the damn device, hoping I turn it on.

Another voice joins the chorus.

My father looks at me, alarmed. He hears it too.

I slam the device against the containment screen. The entire screen turns red.

"What the hell is that?" he asks.

"The end to your experiments," I say, and I hope I'm right.

FORTY-ONE

I grab my father's arm.

"And now," I say, "we're getting out of here."

My father yanks his arm away. He reaches for the device.

"What is that thing?" he asks.

"Another bomb," I say. "This one designed by a former stealth tech engineer. Don't try to remove it. It taps into the stealth tech."

"That's not possible," he says. He wraps his fingers around it and tugs. The containment field ripples like water, but it holds. The device does not come off.

"You can't do this," he says.

"I already have," I say. "Now we have to leave. Just like we had to leave when the Dignity Vessel blew."

"No," he says. He's put his face close to the device, trying to figure out how to pull it off.

I don't like seeing his face so close to a bomb. I don't want to kill him—I know that now. No matter what he's done, I can't kill him.

And I can't leave him here.

I pull the knife. It gleams redly in the light from the containment field.

He stands up and looks at me, mouth agape. "You're not serious."

"You have to leave with me," I say.

"Or what?" he asks. "You'll kill me?"

I don't answer that. I figured the knife would be enough of a threat. Obviously it's not.

"Go ahead," he says. "If you're right and this is a bomb, I'm dead anyway. You're just hastening my death by a few minutes."

I don't correct him. He has more than a few minutes, but I don't want him to know that.

"You have to leave with me." My voice doesn't sound like my own. It sounds strangled and young.

And at the same time, it sounds like his outside the Room, when he pulled me toward his ship. Then, it was his voice filled with panic, his voice that sounded strangled.

Because of me? Or because of my marker?

I'll never know.

"Come on," I say. "When this blows, it could open a dimensional rift, just like the stealth field on the Dignity Vessel."

"I'm not going to let that happen," he says.

"You're not going to be able to separate the device from the stealth field."

"It's not attached to the stealth field," he says. "It's attached to the containment field. I can separate your device from that field."

"You don't know that," I say.

"And you don't know that I can't," he says.

"The person who designed this spent decades working on stealth tech," I say.

"And failing," he says. "I'm the only one who has succeeded."

He peers at the device again, his whole face glowing red. Then he looks up at me sideways.

"Put that thing away," he says. "If you believe the bomb will go off, then get the hell out of here and save yourself."

I take his arm again. He shakes me off.

I stare at him.

"You're wasting time," he says. "If you're right and I'm wrong, your friends will die with us."

"What about your friends?" I ask.

"I guess we'd better let them know too," he says. "They'll leave the lab behind and get away. You'll be arrested."

I shake my head. The Empire is the least of my worries.

"If they leave, you really can't get out."

He gives me a withering look. "Have some faith in my abilities," he says. "I know more about stealth tech than anyone, including your little friend."

My stomach twists. In all my time planning my revenge, I never imagined this moment. I had known I couldn't kill him after the Room. I had thought this was better; destroy his research, which would be just like killing him.

Only I imagined him living with the consequences for years, mourning the loss, looking at his failure.

I never imagined him trying to pry a bomb off a containment field, dying because of me.

"Either get out," he says calmly, "or help me with this thing."

I stare at it. I hear the voices swirling in my head. I remember my mother, her face turned upward, light on her skin before it aged and mummified, before it died.

For one brief moment, she had looked beautiful.

He doesn't look beautiful. He looks ghastly, the red lining the bones of his face, accenting the hollows, leaving shadows. That's how I've always seen him—filled with shadows.

I sheathe the knife. Then I back away from him. When I get to the doors, I run.

Fortunately, I know ships. I learn them the first time I go through them, whether I'm diving or I'm traveling in them.

I run back the way we came. My lightheadedness has grown worse, and I know I'm still a bit short on oxygen. I force myself to breathe so that I don't pass out.

I get to the bay doors and slap them open. Then I reach the skip and pause. There should still be two guards inside. I don't want to alert them. But maybe my father already has. Maybe he has let the group in the cockpit know and everyone overheard.

I poke the knife into the controls for the emergency doors. It's not recommended procedure because it opens to the doors too fast. But we're still in the bay, so we're all right.

Then I hoist myself inside.

Hurst hurries into the galley, followed by the two guards. Odette stands just behind them, but it's her face I see first.

"I used Squishy's bomb," I say. "They built a stealth field."

"That's not possible," Odette says. "Our controls would have registered it."

"It's a baby stealth field," I say. "The device is attaching now."

Hurst swears and pushes past the guards. They look stunned.

"Either you come with us," I say, "or you go join your friends in the cockpit."

"Another bomb?" one of the men asks.

"Yes." I'm all the way inside now. No one has helped me up. I grab the sides of the door and sway a little. I am very dizzy. I push the controls, putting in a code that will lock them and maybe repair some of the damage I've just done.

"Like the one on the Dignity Vessel?" he asks.

Odette starts to answer, but I speak over her. "Yes," I say.

"Fuck," the guard says. "That thing destroyed the Dignity Vessel."

"That's right," I say.

Odette closes her mouth. She gives me a little grin. Obviously she was going to tell them that the device was different. She likes my style instead.

The guard heads into the cockpit, knocking Odette aside. His companion joins him. "We have to leave," he says. "Now."

I can't agree more.

"Do you know the codes for the exterior doors?" I ask.

"Don't need them," he says, then taps our communications relay. The cockpit of the science ship answers, and he explains the situation. They sound a little calmer than he does. Apparently my father has already contacted them and told them he can remove the device.

"You can stay if you trust him that much," I say, loud enough for the people in the science ship's cockpit to hear as well as the guard.

The guards look at each other. Then the guard says, "Open the damn doors."

The cockpit says something that sounds like compliance. A warning appears on our screens. The bay's gravity has shut off.

They're going to open the exterior doors.

Hurst pushes into the guard. "You want to fly this thing?" Hurst asks.

The guard moves away.

The doors start to open just as our lower thrusters come on. When the doors are open about halfway, we fly out of there.

We can't go back to the *Business*, not with these guys on board. We have to get away, but we can't go far. The skip isn't made for long-distance travel.

Hurst looks at me, then looks at them. "Don't worry about it," I say. "Let's just find a safe distance from here and see if Squishy's device works."

I don't know what we'll do if it doesn't.

Because then the guards will retake us. We'll all be under arrest for destroying imperial property and attempted murder. We'll face years of prison. My father will still have his stealth tech.

And both Karl and my mother will go unavenged.

FORTY-TWO

The bomb does not obliterate the ship.

At the designated moment, the ship bobbles.

"It's still there," one of the guards says.

Then the ship slowly flips, like a child lounging in zero-g slowly deciding to reveal his belly. Only the ship doesn't stop flipping. It just turns and turns and turns, spinning with its own momentum—or the momentum of the explosion.

We're all watching the images holographically. What we can see through the portholes is only the blackness of space.

We've been watching since we steered clear. About a half an hour after we stopped—ten minutes before the explosion—the front section of the science vessel separated and flew off so fast that it seemed to disappear.

The guards say nothing. They don't even try to attack us. They realize there is no point. We outnumber them. Even if they do overtake us again, where will they go? They would have to kill us, and they don't seem willing to do so.

Or maybe I'm just ascribing motives. Maybe they're just stunned at the destruction of the ship, giving us time to outthink them.

Either way, their status has changed from guard to prisoner in a matter of moments.

We can't take them back to the *Business*. We have to make our own escape before the other ships come back.

Before the front part of the science vessel comes back to see what happened.

Hurst turns on the navigational controls. "Where are we headed, Boss?"

I'm not ready to answer him. I'm still staring at the science vessel. Its spin has already slowed. Eventually, it will stop moving and find its own part of space.

I freeze one of the holoimages and walk around it. There, on the far side, is a hole in the vessel's hull.

A small hole, like the one we had found in the Dignity Vessel.

My breath catches. Had someone blown up the Dignity Vessel's stealth tech, and what we found was all that was left? Or had something else happened?

"Boss?" Hurst asks again.

I make myself breathe out.

Then I turn to the guards. "What's procedure in a case like this?"

"There are no cases like this," says the guard who initially thought there was no explosion.

"In war or in the face of an attack," I say. "When your ship is damaged and it's been abandoned, what's procedure?"

They look at each other. The other guard answers. "The smaller ship will come back. The military vessels should be back anyway. I'm amazed they both left."

I'm not. They had no idea we had scheduled an attack. Not after weeks (months?) in which nothing happened. They'll be back as soon as our ships get the all-clear.

"Is there a timeline?" I ask. "Do they have to return in a designated period of time?"

They look at each other again. I finally realize that they believe I'll attack the other ships. I resist the urge to shake my head. Of course I'll attack them. In my little weaponless skip.

But I don't say that. Instead, I say, "Our escape pods on this skip hold one person each. They support life for sixty-four hours at the longest. Will someone be back for you in that amount of time?"

The first guard starts to nod, but the other catches his arm.

"We're not keeping you on this skip," I say. "I just want to make sure you're not going to die out there."

I don't tell them what the alternative is because I don't know of any alternative. I guess we could try to make it to a base and dump them there, but that seems too risky to me.

"We're going to die," the second guard says. "You'll be responsible for killing us."

But the first guard rolls his eyes. "You can put me in an escape pod," he says. "But I will tell the authorities everything I know when they pick me up."

"That's fine with me," I say.

I turn to Hurst. "Move in as close to the wreck as you can safely get. Make sure there are no new energy signatures."

He nods. He sets the navigation and takes the ship toward what's left of the science vessel.

It's amazing to me how quickly it has become "the wreck" to both of us. No one tries to correct me.

I stare at it on the small two-dimensional screen near the controls. It looks vulnerable there, still slowly turning.

Part of me wants to go and see if my father is still inside. But I know he won't be. He probably ran to the cockpit and urged them to escape. He isn't the kind of man who dies for his own causes.

But if he believed he could unhitch the device, he might have stayed too long. Even then, I wouldn't find him because he would have been right near the stealth tech when Squishy's device went off.

I don't know if it obliterated him, or if it sent him into some kind of limbo, like we sent Junior and Karl.

Like my father sent Mother.

But I also know I won't be able to find out.

"You want them in the escape pods now, right?" Odette asks me in a tone that leads me to believe this isn't the first time she's asked the question.

I turn toward her. She looks as tired as I feel.

"Yeah," I say.

"I'm not getting any unusual readings," Hurst says.

I move him aside, and do some searching on my own. I remember how the initial energy signal for the Dignity Vessel appeared as the kind of blip that most ships never register. I search for that kind of blip now.

Behind me, I can hear Odette talking to the guards, taking their weapons, and giving them some food and water from the galley. I almost tell her that there's no need—the escape pods have rations and water—but I don't. Let her assuage her own conscience her own way.

I keep looking for a blip.

And don't find one.

Maybe my father's little stealth tech experiment was too small to leave any kind of reading out here. Squishy's device was designed for something much larger. Maybe it really and truly destroyed that stealth tech.

Or maybe what remains is so minuscule that nothing we have can measure it.

"Do you have anything you want to say to them, Boss?" Odette asks.

I turn. Both guards are pressed into the hatches of their escape pods. They look reluctant to go in deeper. The fit will be tight for them.

"Good luck," I say, then walk over and close the hatches myself.

The escape pods can be released from the inside or the outside. I hit the release buttons before the guards can even find the interior controls. The first pod slides down its tube. The tube seals off the skip from the pod, then sends the pod into space.

The pod floats away from us. The second pod follows only a minute later.

I stare at them through the nearest portal. I'd rather be out of the ship in my environmental suit, clinging to a tether, than inside one of those things.

But if their companions come back within two days, they'll be fine. Testy, but fine.

And I can't imagine why the military wouldn't be back. After all, they have to catch us.

"Let's get to the *Business*," I say to Hurst.

Then I close the portals and close my eyes.

I did it. I destroyed the stealth tech. And I may have killed my father in the bargain.

I expected success to feel better.

I expected it to make a difference.

FORTY-THREE

We meet the *Business* at the designated coordinates. Squishy, Roderick, and Tamaz are full of questions, which we answer in quick sentences, promising more when everyone returns.

Mikk and Jennifer returned shortly before we did. *The Seeker* is permanently barred from this area of space, and both Mikk and Jennifer are on some kind of governmental watch list.

Jennifer laughs as she sits in the galley. "It worked. They thought I was really drunk and ready to party."

"For a while, I thought they were too," Mikk says. "But at the last minute, they remembered they had a job to do and shooed us away from there."

Neither Mikk nor Jennifer seems too concerned about the watch list. I'm not either. We're all going to have to stay in the far reaches of this Empire's space.

But we knew that going in.

It takes another day before the *Space King* joins us. It actually has some weapons scarring. Turtle, Davida, and Bria look frazzled, but they too managed to escape. However, they're pretty certain that the military vessel got all the specs from their ship.

"They know it's a rental," Turtle says. "They'll be waiting for us to return it."

I hadn't planned for this, but I know what to do. We have to abandon both *The Seeker* and the *Space King*. Then we'll declare them destroyed and send in a fee to the rental agency from the next station we stop at.

I explain all of this before I ever get to the details of our mission.

"What are we going to do now?" Turtle asks.

I sigh. "I guess we find somewhere to hole up."

Davida, who is relieved to be back on the *Business*, offers to cook us a special dinner. She wants us to tell our stories over food.

I figure that's fine.

She cooks—all sorts of things with stored food that I didn't know could be done (but she has just become the designated chef on any trip we're on)—and we all tell our adventures.

Of course, they pay the closest attention to mine. The destruction of both bits of stealth tech, and the possible death of my father.

Squishy is pleased that the bomb worked.

But as we continue to talk, her smile slowly fades.

I'm almost afraid to ask her what's bothering her. I really don't want the mood—which isn't quite victorious and isn't quite sad—to change.

But I do ask her.

"Your father figured out how to make stealth tech," she says. "Ancient stealth tech."

I frown at her. She's sitting to my left. Mikk is across from her. He has a guarded expression on his face.

"And he was gone when you first arrived, dropping off his scientists and getting new ones for something else," she says.

I nod.

"His stealth tech clearly worked."

I shrug. "I could hear it, faintly. But I didn't test it."

"My device worked with it," Squishy says. "My device wouldn't have worked on just anything. It needed the stealth tech to power it."

I have no idea how she built it, and I don't want to know, even now.

"So that's confirmation, then," I say.

"And that's bad news," she says.

Mikk groans. He starts to get up, but I grab his wrist.

"Why?" I ask.

"Because," Squishy says, "you say your father wasn't a scientist."

I nod.

"So someone else put that together."

"It sounded like a group of someone elses put that together," I say.

"Even so," she says. "Enough of the technology has been revived. The military has it."

"Provided," I say, "that they can find some more ancient stealth tech to cannibalize. My father said they can't use the Room."

"And you believe him?" she asks.

"Yes," I say. "They used the control panel from the Dignity Vessel. We've been all over the station around the Room. No one ever found a control panel."

I look at the others for confirmation. They nod. They're interested now.

"The Room, your Dignity Vessel." Squishy sighs. "There's a lot of ancient stealth tech around here. All the Empire needs is another wrecked Dignity Vessel."

"It was a fluke that we found that one," I say.

She shakes her head. "There've been others," she says. "But there's never been any working stealth tech in any of them. That's how the military got the idea to rebuild ancient stealth tech in the first place."

I stare at her, feeling cold. "You're telling me that if they find another Dignity Vessel, they'll be able to re-create my father's work?"

"Most likely," she says. "Now they know about people with markers and they know how to make something that approximates stealth tech. They have the know-how. They just need the right tools."

She sounds like my father. He seemed so certain that destroying the Dignity Vessel and his little bottle wouldn't make that much of a difference. Then he contradicted himself by fighting to save that little experiment.

My stomach twists. I stand up. The Empire cannot get stealth tech. I've set them back, but I haven't destroyed their efforts.

I should have realized how hard it is to obliterate anything. After all, I dive wrecks from the distant past. Wrecks filled with time and history and lost dreams.

I leave the group, distraught. I pace my cabin until exhaustion finally takes me.

I sleep—only to wake up in the middle of the night.

With an idea.

FORTY-FOUR

If we can't destroy stealth tech, we can share it.

We have the know-how. We have the money.

Thanks to Riya Trekov and to Squishy's finder's fee from long ago, we can continue for years without making a dime.

We're pariahs now anyway: Mikk and Jennifer on a watch list; Turtle's, Bria's, and Davida's images broadcast as possible thieves or pirates; and me—I'm a full-fledged criminal who has at the very least destroyed valuable imperial property.

At the most, I've committed murder to do so.

We want to stop the Empire from getting ancient stealth tech, and there's only one surefire way to do it.

We have to find the stealth tech first. We have to find the Dignity Vessels; we have to track down other legends like the Room of Lost Souls. Once we find it, we work with it. We now know we can use bits of ancient stealth tech to create stealth tech of our own.

We also know that some people, with the right markers, can work in a stealth tech field. No one has to die.

Giving the Empire stealth tech will change the balance of power in the sector. But if all of the former rebel governments get stealth tech as well, then the balance remains.

It's a big undertaking, and we wouldn't be able to do it alone. But I have a hunch the Nine Planets Alliance will give us shelter and maybe, just maybe, some funds as well—especially when they hear how quickly the Empire can conquer them if the Empire is the only one in the sector with stealth tech.

I work up a presentation for the group. It takes me two days. By then, they've been wondering what they're going to do with their lives.

I sit them down and give them my ideas. A few—Squishy, of course, and Mikk—modify them. We have a plan.

Then I give them a few more days to think about whether or not they'll join.

Not all of them will. And that doesn't matter, because our base will not be anywhere permanent—at least not at first.

At least, that's what I'm thinking right now.

The only person who has a reason to leave us is Squishy, and it's all right with me if she does. No one likes her (except me and possibly Turtle), and I know where to find her. If I need more explosive devices, I can ask her to build them and get them to me.

The team likes my plan. They understand it, and agree with it.

We have a new mission, a complicated mission. We have to find old Dignity Vessels and other forms of ancient stealth tech. We have to create a new version of that stealth tech in the lab.

And we have to keep our efforts secret from the Empire.

I'll handle the search. Someone else can handle the science.

But I have to stay in charge.

I find it ironic, honestly, that I'll be doing this—the woman who never much paid attention to the Empire. The woman who loves to be alone.

Now I have to put together another team. A bigger team.

One that builds on the smarts, determination, and talent of this crew.

One that will get everything right.

ABOUT THE AUTHOR

Kristine Kathryn Rusch is an award-winning mystery, romance, science fiction, and fantasy writer. She has written many novels under various names, including Kristine Grayson for romance and Kris Nelscott for mystery. Her novels have made the bestseller lists—even in London—and have been published in fourteen countries and thirteen different languages. Her awards range from the Ellery Queen Readers Choice Award to the John W. Campbell Award. She is the only person in the history of the science fiction field to have won a Hugo Award for editing and a Hugo Award for fiction. Her short work has been reprinted in sixteen Year's Best collections. She is the former editor of the prestigious *Magazine of Fantasy and Science Fiction*. Before that, she and Dean Wesley Smith started and ran Pulphouse Publishing, a science fiction and mystery press in Eugene. She lives and works on the Oregon Coast. Visit her online at kriswrites.com.

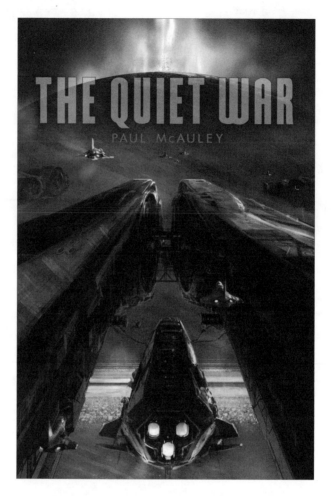